This Love of Mine

This Love of Mine

A MIRROR LAKE NOVEL

MIRANDA LIASSON

Montlake
Romance

Published by Montlake Romance, Seattle

www.apub.com

Amazon, the Amazon logo, and Montlake Romance are trademarks of Amazon.com, Inc., or its affiliates.

ISBN-13: 9781503947092
ISBN-10: 1503947092

Cover design by Shasti O'Leary-Soudant / SOS CREATIVE LLC

Printed in the United States of America

For Debbie, friends forever

CHAPTER 1

Meg Halloran barely managed to squeeze into the ancient elevator at the Grand Victorian Hotel before its heavy metal doors snapped shut. "Sorry!" she called out at the last second to a woman in the lobby whose purse had toppled off her shoulder as Meg had barrelled her way past. She was late for her bridal shop's most important client, the mayor's daughter, whose engagement party was being held tonight amid champagne, prime rib, and carefully arranged twinkly lights in the lush old-fashioned gardens of Mirror Lake's oldest—and only—hotel.

How late, she could only guess. Five minutes? Ten? Maybe it was better that she couldn't get to her watch. She was weighed down with more baggage than Kim Kardashian on a European tour, with her alteration bag, purse, and three dresses. One of which was a ginormous wedding gown that was as foofy as an 1850's hoopskirt and weighed a good twenty pounds. To make things worse, she'd started out the day looking business *chic* but between the balmy August weather and her heavy load, she'd deteriorated into business *sweaty*.

Above the clouds of tulle, she could barely make out the scrolly floor numbers atop the door. One quick glance told her the elevator was going exactly nowhere.

Meg aimed her one free appendage, her elbow, at the fourth floor button while teetering on high heels that were a far cry from her usual comfy flats.

Just . . . out of reach.

She was about to throw her body against the button panel when the doors suddenly shuddered open. A pair of men's fine leather shoes, polished to a spit shine, strode over the purple-toned Oriental rug as a businessman entered and stood near the front. "What floor, miss?" a deep male voice asked.

She startled, her nerves jangling. So much was riding on the Klines' satisfaction. Priscilla's daddy was in thick with the bank and her mother sat on the board. In a small town where loan committees could get away with acting on whims and fancy, their vote of confidence for the bank loan that would change her life meant everything.

"Four, please." Her voice sounded muffled and a bit edgy from behind all her stuff. Okay, she *was* edgy. Maybe because her business partner, Alex, was pregnant with twins and on bed rest, leaving Meg to shoulder more than the usual responsibilities. Ones that had made her uncharacteristically late.

Or because she dreamed of making Bridal Aisle much more than a drafty old warehouse with pink shag carpeting and paltry inventory. Or because her mother's rheumatoid arthritis care cost a big chunk out of her paycheck, even with good medical insurance, forcing her to work longer hours. Her mom couldn't tend to her house like she used to, and Meg longed to have the money to hire out the cleaning and lawn work she currently did herself.

A bigger shop, more customers, more money. A little more time for herself. That was the plan. She wanted that loan. She *needed* that loan.

Footfalls sounded again as her elevator companion backed up a few steps and settled in against the wall.

She caught a whiff of a crisp, woodsy scent—eau de Italian Billionaire.

It accosted her nostrils and channeled exotic places like spice markets in Madagascar that she'd only ever dream of visiting.

Unless she got that loan.

Meg craned her neck to see something besides his feet, which appeared on the large side. Alex, never the bashful wallflower, always said the size of a man's feet reflected the size of another part of male anatomy. If so, then Mr. Hottie Billionaire was very well equipped, indeed.

He was likely some traveling businessman, passing through town, maybe here for a conference. Probably handsome, too, judging by his expensive taste in shoes and the tapered cut of his pants, his deep voice, and his sex-pheromone-inducing cologne. She'd bet her paycheck he wasn't going to be tucked in bed later watching RomComs from the nineties and dreaming of a different life.

The elevator doors finally moved to close, but a well-manicured hand suddenly jutted between them, causing them to seize up and shudder.

"Benji-wenji, there you are!" a woman's excited voice exclaimed. "I thought that was you."

"Ashley." The deep baritone held surprise and relief. Maybe pleasure, too. "You made it."

"Anything for you, baby," the woman crooned. Meg rolled her eyes. Curiosity made her risk losing her footing as she peered around her armload in time to see a woman in a low-cut, clingy red dress race into the elevator, her strappy four-and-a-half-inch sandals clickity-clacking against the old black-and-white tiled floor.

She was tall, polished, and buxom. All traits Meg was deficient in. Meg particularly noticed the woman's sleek blonde hair, shiny and controlled, unlike her own coffee-black hair, which refused to be tamed regardless of how much product Brenda from the Curli-Q salon coated it with.

The loud smack of a lipstick-glossed kiss rent the air. "I haven't seen you in soooo long!"

Great. Now they were smooching. Meanwhile, the Kline women were waiting for her in their undies. Meg tried in vain to shake that visual out of her mind. She cleared her throat, but no one paid any attention.

What was wrong with this elevator? Was it built the same year as the hotel?

"Thanks for coming on such short notice," the man said.

His voice held a soothing, sexy quality that rolled off his lips as smoothly as butter off steaming pancakes, conjuring classic Clint Eastwood or George Clooney.

And it was vaguely familiar. Wait. *More* than vaguely familiar. A sudden spark of panic ignited in her chest and burst into flame like a Fourth of July sparkler.

No, couldn't be. She strained over her load for a glimpse, but no luck. The Benji-wenji she knew—Benjamin, that is—would more likely be wearing scrubs than a suit. An hour away, doing the last year of his Emergency Medicine residency in Hartford. He didn't have time to dress in expensive suits and waste time in fancy hotels. Definitely not his style.

It was probably just her overactive imagination that tended to conjure images of him way too often. But her fantasies had never turned auditory before.

"You know, Benji—" The woman stopped talking, gave a silly giggle, and whispered something Meg couldn't make out.

A flush crept up Meg's neck as she imagined any of a number of soft, sultry words. She shifted a little closer to the wall, her arms aching under the weight of her load.

The man chuckled, a silly, spontaneous sound that was playful and carefree and promised naughty things like hard-driving, all-night-long sex. It made Meg's stomach pitch in a way that filled her half with distaste and half with an unexpected longing that pulled deep down in her gut.

Oh, to have someone want you like that. To banter playfully, to have him nip your neck with soft kisses, gather you up in big strong arms . . .

She had to stop reading those romance novels that were piled all through her apartment and hidden under her bed.

Life wasn't like that. At least, hers wasn't. Ever since her older brother Patrick had died when she was sixteen and her parents had subsequently divorced, she'd been the one in her family to stomp out fires, take care of emergencies, and soothe everyone's frayed nerves. The peacekeeper. It was a good trait except it tended to get her stepped on and taken advantage of. But not anymore. Not since she'd vowed to make some changes.

And the *Love Boat* may not have sailed directly into Mirror Lake Yacht Club so she could board, but it wasn't too late for her to swim out and catch another one.

Someone from the floors above them must have summoned the elevator, because it finally began its ascent, dragging upward like a sleepy teenager.

The scrolly numbers above the door lit up. *Just three more floors.*

"The CEO of the hospital will be at dinner tonight, along with two other candidates for the job." The guy's tone couldn't have been more businesslike, but Meg's heart dropped to her feet, and it wasn't from the lurching of the elevator. It was *him*, as sure as the warm, crusty apple blossom with ice cream at the town diner, Pie in the Sky, or PITS as it was affectionately called, was the most magnificent dessert in the world.

She'd loved Ben Rushford ever since he'd untangled her skinny, scraped, and bleeding body from her ruined pretzel of a bicycle when she was ten. They'd been good friends in high school. But in recent years, he'd barely spoken to her. Oh, she saw him around town and sometimes even at Rushford family events, because her two best friends were married to his brothers. But their conversations rarely passed the *hi, how ya doin'* stage.

Not that she'd sat around waiting for him, but in spite of her other relationships, his big shining personality and hot smoking body still loomed large in her ill-advised imagination.

Too large.

That was why, as of her recent twenty-sixth birthday, she'd kicked the Ben habit. Vowed to take more risks with her business and her personal life. The same day she'd learned her other best friend, Olivia, was pregnant. Two pregnant best friends, exchanging moony glances with their special men. Along with dozens of radiant faces of the brides she dressed smiling at her all day long. Meg was literally surrounded by love fests every day, and she yearned for her own.

Or at least . . . something. She didn't need a man to fulfill her. She had a job she loved, friends, and family. But she wanted the opportunity to find her own life. To at least have the chance to try and find a forever kind of love.

She wasn't ashamed of wanting it. Hadn't her two best friends already found it? She believed—yes, she did—deep inside her doubting soul that it was possible, even in a town the size of a safety pin with a pool of eligible guys too small to make up a Single-A baseball team. But if she had any hope of meeting Mr. Right, she was going to have to find a minute of her week that wasn't booked solid.

"Dinner's at seven." He sounded relieved, like the date was big and important. Not that she could hear very well over the amplified thunk-thunking of her heart.

"Um, yeah, about that," Ashley said. Meg swore she heard gum crack. "I just got a call on the way over that U2 is doing a concert at Times Square tonight and they need hot girls for the front row. This guy I know's got tickets. You know I'd do anything for you, just not tonight."

Silence. *Uh, oh.*

"Tonight?" Ben's voice notched up an octave, which surprised Meg. He rarely showed signs of stress, tending to be lighthearted, carefree, a jokester.

He cleared his throat. "Look, Ashley, I'm a little desperate. The hospital committee is deciding on this job and—"

"You're a shoo-in, baby. But I have to go. This could be my big break."
More silence.

"You don't get it, do you?" Her voice rose way faster than the elevator. "You have no idea how hard it is to break into the modeling business. Every exposure counts."

Well, she was exposing her boobs pretty nicely, Meg thought,
unable to resist another glance. Then, as she rotated her gaze, she saw
him. Her breath hitched and she got that same heart-stopping whoosh
of heat flooding every inch of her body that made her dizzy and weak-
kneed whenever she came within ten feet of him.

And that was only from looking at his *back*.

He was gorgeously elegant, tall and lean, his suit pants caressing his
spectacular ass like a lover's hand. His dark hair waved a little despite its
precisely cut layers, and she noticed as he turned his head that he was
still wearing a beard, close-cropped and dangerous.

Blessed with an overabundance of confidence, Ben had propped
himself up in his usual pose, with one slim hip leaning jauntily against
the nearest wall. But now he stood with feet anchored rigidly to the
floor, his big arms crossed and his jaw set in concrete. "Look, I can get
you to U2 or another concert any time you like. I just really need a date
for this dinner."

Through a gap in the dress bag plastic, Meg saw the woman's eyes
narrow. "Everything's always about *you*, Benjamin Rushford. Well, I
have a career, too, and I need to seize my opportunities. Just because
you're a doctor doesn't make you boss of the universe."

He gripped her arm, maybe to calm her down. "Boss of the *what*?"
Meg bit her lip to keep from smiling at his utter, total frustration. It
was just a little funny. Ben, who'd always had his pick of lovelies, was
having difficulty getting a date.

"That's why we broke up, don't you remember?" Ashley asked. "It
was all about your work."

"I'm doing my residency, Ashley. I'm sorry the hours are long—"

"It was impossible to have a relationship with you. You hardly ever have time for fun and you're always half dead from being on call. Remember that one time you fell asleep when we were in the middle of—"

Oh, God. TMI, TMI. Meg squeezed her eyes shut.

Mercifully, the elevator dinged. Floor Two. But to her horror she saw they were somehow back at Lobby level.

Okay, so the elevator really was as old as the hotel. And she hadn't been paying the least bit of attention to where the hell they were going.

Ashley threw an arm across the door frame and turned to Ben. "I'm getting out. Maybe one day you'll be able to appreciate that other people have needs, too."

"Don't be upset," he said to her retreating back.

She turned one last time. "Good-bye, Ben. Good luck."

Meg's needs were to exit this elevator *right now*. She prayed Ben would exit, too, chase after that woman, beg her, whatever, but no luck. Heels clacked an angry beat and faded into the distance. It took eons for the doors to close. This time, she was aware of the upward *whoosh* that left her stomach in her throat as the elevator's final rise commenced. Just four more floors of staying invisible behind all her stuff and she was home free. *Go, elevator, go.*

The sound of Ben's voice made her jump. "I'm sorry for the delay— um-Miss. Can I help you carry some of that stuff?" She pictured him craning his neck to see her face. Her arms had turned into limp rubber bands from all the weight, but she held them steady. No way was she letting her guard down now.

"It—it's fine and no. No, thanks." She hoped her voice was distorted by all the dress material in front of her face. He was probably too preoccupied by his date's rejection to give her a second thought.

When the ding of hitting the fourth floor finally sounded, she'd never been so relieved. She waited for him to exit. Footsteps sounded as he crossed the threshold. She was seconds away from being in the clear. It was going to be all right.

Meg stepped forward. Only to notice his hand holding the door open for her.

Behavior like that made him so hard to hate. Embarrassed for him as well as herself, she mumbled thanks and buried her face in the yards of white tulle as she crossed over to safety.

Until her heel caught in the tiny groove between the elevator and the fourth floor.

She tugged. Pulled. There was no budging it. Her heartbeat accelerated to NASCAR speed levels. As a last recourse, she tried to wiggle her foot out of her shoe but it was as stuck as gum on your sole.

A warm hand encased her foot. She clenched her teeth and tried not to startle out of her skin. His long, piano-player fingers touched her ankle and the shock of the unexpected contact made her gasp. Capable hands gently twisted her shoe back and forth as her sexy companion focused all his attention on the problem.

The top of his head bent low, and his thick brown locks made her ache to drag her fingers through them and scrape his scalp in wanton delight. *This is how he'd be at work,* a voice whispered inside Meg's head. All competence and complete focus.

That same little devil of a voice wondered if he gave his women the same laser-focused attention when he—well, never mind that. An involuntary shudder wafted over her.

His touch was gentle as it slid carefully over her skin. She could feel the unexpected but very masculine roughness of a callus as he ran his hand over her calf and tugged.

She curled her toes in her shoes and swallowed hard. *Dammit, no.* How could he still affect her after all these years? If only she weren't tied to this horrible town. If only she lived somewhere where everyone hadn't known her from birth, where no one remembered her glasses or her buck teeth or every blushing gaffe she'd ever made.

Like the time when she'd gone with her two best friends to toilet paper Ben's house during soccer season, and his Grandma Effie, who had helped raise the Rushford kids after their parents had died, had caught them. When she asked just what they thought they were doing, Meg had lied and said she'd lost her contact lens. At midnight on a Friday night in the middle of his tree-lined yard. *Right.*

"Oh, is that you, Meg, Olivia, Alexa?" his grandmother had said, staring down at them through wire-rimmed spectacles. "I thought you girls were hoodlums." Then she'd come out, helped them toss a few last rolls, and fed them cookies and hot chocolate afterwards.

Meg swallowed hard at the simple pressure of Ben's hand as it squeezed her poor stuck foot. The claustrophobic air of the elevator dragged into her lungs as slowly as thickly set pudding. Then it happened.

He looked up. Saw her. His eyes went wide with surprise. For the briefest flash, she stared into his gorgeous eyes, soft brown with flecks the color of clover honey that had never once failed to turn her boneless.

One swift tug dislodged the shoe. But his touch, so firm yet gentle, his nearness, his possessive grip on her foot, it was all too much. Instinctively, she jerked back.

Her stuff toppled. Dress bags collapsed. The sewing bag tumbled. Her purse whacked him in the head before it crashed and spilled.

When the avalanche stopped, they were both left on the ground, a little stunned and surrounded by debris.

"Well, I'll be." Ben rubbed the back of his head and cast her a bemused look. "If it isn't Meggie Halloran."

CHAPTER 2

"I'm so sorry," the petite firecracker sprawled on the floor next to Ben said as she shook her head to clear it. Delicate lines of worry and disbelief creased her smooth forehead as she surveyed the fallout strewn across the elevator floor. The lines soon faded, replaced by anger that sparked from green eyes as vivid as the moss that grew on the north side of trees at the lake. "And thanks for trying to help me but *don't call me that.*"

"I've *always* called you Meggie."

"Well, that was fine when I was twelve but not anymore."

He held up his hands in a gesture of surrender. "Fine. Sorry, *Margaret.*" She blushed furiously. He'd always been good at tormenting her and was pleased to see his comment hit the mark.

"And may I please have my shoe back?" One elegant hand extended in determined supplication.

He'd expected her usual sweet smile and thanks. The belligerent attitude surprised him from a woman he'd always known as tame and even tempered. He hadn't expected burrs in his ass.

He kept his hands high, the shoe dangling at a jaunty angle from his fingertips. She snatched it back and surprised him again by pulling off her second one and standing up to gather all her fallen belongings.

"Why didn't you say hi?" he asked as he helped her gather up the wedding dress that seemed to weigh half as much as she did.

She stabbed him with a look that said *Seriously?* "Before or after your girlfriend huffed out?"

"More like she hightailed it out of here faster than if the hotel were on fire." He rubbed his neck, a little embarrassed, and met her cool gaze. "And she's not my girlfriend." As soon as he said that, he felt worse. Why was he trying to justify himself in front of her?

As they talked, the elevator door snapped shut and they began to move. Away from her floor.

Meg looked up to see the numbers blinking in descent. "Oh, no. Now I'm even more late." She ran to the panel and pushed random buttons. The doors clattered open on the second floor. An elderly couple was walking in slow-motion towards the doors. She pushed the Close Door button. "Sorry!" she called and gave a little wave as the doors slid shut.

He couldn't resist whistling. "Must be an important appointment." He gathered a lipstick, a brush, a pack of gum, and a dog-eared paperback with a picture of a tortured-looking, bare-chested, tattooed guy in tight black pants. A woman, also in black, stood behind him, her hands all over him. "Intriguing."

She snatched that, too.

"Priscilla Kline's engagement party starts in an hour. I've got her and her mother's dresses and her bridal gown. And I'm *late.*" She glared at him like it was *all his fault*.

"You shouldn't be carrying this all by yourself, Half Pint." He grinned at the old name he and her brother used to torment her with as teenagers, when it was clear she wasn't going to grow an inch beyond her five-two-in-her-socks height.

She stopped gathering her stuff to shoot him an exasperated look. "Things have been a little hectic with Alex out." She shook out a dress that had crumpled to the floor. Ben knew from his sister Samantha—who was working in the bridal shop over the summer to help plan the upcoming

Labor Day bridal show—that Meg was overextended. Even with Meg's grandmother Gloria, who used to own the shop, temporarily filling in.

"I'll carry that," he offered.

"I don't want your help," she said adamantly. "You should run after your date."

Disdain dripped from every word. But then, over the years, he'd given her no reason to like him. In fact, he'd done his best to elicit exactly this very reaction from her. Yet she'd never been this indifferent—or angry—and somehow it rankled.

Now she was on her knees, scooping junk back into her purse, her gorgeous ass in the air as she reached far and wide to gather her possessions.

And a fine ass it was, curvy and molded into a form-fitting black skirt that rode a little high on her creamy thighs, definitely not her usual hippie-chick look. She must have caught him ogling because she yanked her skirt quickly down into professional zone.

She wore a classic black suit jacket but underneath, a bright pink cami exposed the curve of her breasts as she bent low. Her hair, usually long and thick, was caught up in a businesslike twist, sleek and shiny and rich in color like his grandmother's mahogany dining table.

She stirred him in a primal way. She always had, even though he'd never go there. His gut and his fists clenched in a feeble effort to stave off the potent mixture of sadness and regret that pierced his heart, but there was no escape.

Suddenly, he felt short of breath and stood, sucking in a deep breath of musty elevator air to halt his panic. It was probably the close quarters and that fragrance that drifted around her, airy and light, that reminded him of apples.

A memory nudged him. From that sweet, innocent time before Patrick died and changed their lives forever. She must've been sixteen, and Ben had walked her home from school. They'd taken a shortcut through old man Stedman's property, and she'd reached up and picked an apple from one of the scraggly trees and took a big bite.

It was green and sour and made her pretty lips pucker. On impulse, he'd snatched the apple from her hands, and she gave an indignant "hey!" He stood inches from her and took a long, slow bite, chewing with as much relish as if it were a decadent piece of chocolate.

Her protests subsided, replaced by silence as she stared at his mouth and swallowed hard. He stopped laughing, mesmerized by the bright, intense look in her eyes. Something sparked between them, quick as an electrical short that plunges the world into darkness. He reached for her, their apple-tart lips pressing together. Her lips were warm and soft and delicious, and he didn't even realize he'd dropped the apple and tugged her closer.

He used her soft gasp as an opportunity to slide his tongue gently over hers, loving the way she pushed up on tiptoes, meeting his every stroke with her own as he wrapped his arms around her soft body and pulled their bodies flush. She was heaven, her taste sweet as strawberry lip gloss, her smell like fresh fall air and fruity shampoo.

They broke apart when the old farmer moseyed out onto his porch and yelled at them to scat, to get along and go home.

Even through the old man's tirade, he couldn't bear to break the spell and let her go. "I thought Eve was the one who got them in trouble, not Adam," she whispered.

He would've gotten them in plenty of trouble, if she weren't Patrick's sister. The sister of his best friend. And then the sister of the boy he could not save.

She was a nice, nice girl, and he didn't do nice girls. Ever.

And especially never her.

In the elevator, as Meg bent to collect the rest of her possessions, he caught a glimpse of black lace and creamy flesh from underneath that electric pink cami. His mind went blank, replaced by one thought: Did her panties match the bra?

He'd almost forgotten the urgency of his own dilemma, but he'd take the distraction any day. He gathered a lipstick, a pen stamped with a local politician's slogan, a tampon.

"I'll take those." She used both hands to accept the objects and dumped them in her purse. Her hands were so much smaller than his. Her stature gave the impression of fragility, but her recent edginess had him rethinking that impression for the first time.

"I'm here for a business dinner," he said. "With Dr. Donaldson and his wife." For the job of a lifetime. One he was sure to blow without a date.

She stopped and looked at him, appearing surprised at what he'd just shared. Hell, he was surprised, too. "My mom told me you were thinking of applying for the ER job," she said.

Ben nodded carefully, unable to even begin to explain how critical getting this job was to him. Donaldson, the CEO of the hospital, was a longstanding bastion in Mirror Lake civic society. He'd taken a fledgling hospital and built it into a decent and reputable operation. He was determined to get the right candidate for the job. Someone who understood the community. Who wanted to establish roots.

Unfortunately for Ben, that meant someone married, preferably with a kid or two to fill up the Mirror Lake school system.

But Ben understood this town more than anybody. He would not let the fact that he was a confirmed bachelor stop him from getting the job he was meant for.

"Well, your grandfather would be proud of you," Meg said, "carrying on his legacy and all."

She mystified him with her ability to put her finger on the very heartbeat of what drove him. His paternal grandfather had died a long time ago, shortly after he'd graduated from high school, but he still missed him. A family doctor, beloved by the town, he'd been Ben's mentor, his savior, given him strength and purpose and taught him he was worthy, even though he couldn't stop what had happened to his best friend. This job would be Ben's way to pay him back for everything he'd done for him.

"You're the hometown son. They'll hire you in a heartbeat." She flicked her wrist in an of-course-you'll-get-the-job gesture, for a second forgetting to be angry. Her honest, genuine smile shot straight through to his groin. She was beautiful even when she was mad, but when she smiled, she was all delicate features, a small nose, and full lips that made him want to—

He shook his head, as much to shake off his lusty thoughts as to correct her thinking. "Dr. Donaldson is looking for the one thing I don't have."

She raised a skeptical brow even as her gaze raked him over the coals. "What exactly haven't you got?"

"The other two candidates are married, and the wife of one is expecting twins in September. Donaldson wants to be assured the winning candidate settles well and permanently into town, and having a family is the best guarantee of that."

He expected a sympathetic look. He got a laugh.

"What's so funny?" He frowned. "God, Meggie, you're just as infuriating as you were when you were twelve." She and her two best friends had known no bounds to the constant torment of him and his brothers. Like the time on a Scouts campout when they'd tied Ben's and his brother Tom's shoelaces together and woke them up screaming that a bear was coming. Of course they'd fallen flat on their faces.

But she wasn't twelve any more. She was curvaceous and lovely, with sparkling eyes the color of fresh spring grass. She concealed her mischievous smile apologetically with her hand. "I'm sorry. If you need a potential wife and kid before dinnertime, I just wonder what possessed you to ask a woman who looks ready to perform in a Vegas show, not join the rotary club. What were you thinking?"

He shrugged. Desperation, that's all it was. Until yesterday, when one of the administrative assistants in the ER tipped him off that tonight was a personal test, he hadn't even planned to bring a date.

Meg frowned. "It's discriminatory to pick someone for a job based on their marital status."

"Tell Donaldson that. He's been around for forty years and he can damn well do what he pleases."

All the stuff was gathered. Ben took the dress bags from her arms and her purse and sewing bag from her shoulders as she stepped back into her shoes.

"Are the dresses ruined?" he asked.

"The wedding dress is just a fitting, so a few wrinkles won't matter. I can touch the others up with my iron if I have to."

He led the way down a graceful high-ceilinged hall with elaborate crown moldings and dizzying wallpaper with enough gilt to coat the palace at Versailles.

"Thanks for helping me," she said graciously enough, but her look was wary. As if she were contemplating what kind of man he'd become and found him coming up way short.

For the thousandth time, he wondered if she judged him, like it seemed so many others had, for what had happened to her brother. Not a day went by that he still didn't feel the pain of that loss. He'd gone out of his way to avoid her, unable to accept that she might hate him. *I would never let him go alone to that quarry now,* he wanted to cry out. *I would never have let him drink alone, or swim alone, if I had known. If only I would have known.*

There was no way in hell he could ask her to help him out. He'd worked hard to push her away over the years and for both their sakes, it wasn't a good idea.

Besides, he'd have to be near her for an entire evening, smelling her sweet fresh fragrance that reminded him of those lazy summer afternoons of his youth at the lake, spent fishing and swimming and sunning. He'd be tantalized by watching those luscious lips when she turned them up into a killer smile, imagining what it would be like to kiss her until her hot curves melted into him. His mind would wander, thinking what her body looked like under that conservative suit in that black lacy underwear. And that would be a very, very bad idea.

She tugged down her cami, straightened her jacket, ran her hand over her hair for flyaways. Then she held out her hands to accept the rest of her stuff.

"You look great," he said.

And winced inside. He'd blurted that out like he was fifteen. But she was a knockout and he hadn't stood this close to her for a long, long time. He'd forgotten how creamy her skin was, how striking against the near blackness of her hair. Her eyes sparkled with a no-bullshit candor that was so, so appealing.

With horror, he realized he wanted to kiss her. Right here in the middle of this old hallway with its oriental rugs, the dim-lit sconces for atmosphere, and crazy patterned wallpaper that kind of made his eyes hurt. He stepped back to clear his throat and his thinking.

"Well," she said. "Thanks again, Ben. See you around." She turned to walk away from him forever.

Unable and unwilling to let her go, he grabbed her arm. Her gaze flew from his fingers gripping her suit jacket to his eyes, which may have looked just a touch crazed.

She was just what he needed—for tonight. She was appealing and approachable in that girl-next-door kind of way that drew everyone in. And she was the town do-gooder. She knew every senior citizen and lost cause for miles.

But no, he couldn't. It wouldn't be right, it wouldn't be fair. His conscience struggled. *Just walk away*, it told him.

"What is it?" she asked, looking concerned. "The top of your head is sweating."

He tried to let go of her arm. Willed his feet to work. But nothing in him would obey. His whole body had gone rogue in the desperation to keep his one chance for this job from slipping though his fingers without a fight.

"Would you consider being my date for tonight?" he blurted. He hadn't felt this awkward since a hundred years ago when he'd asked a girl to prom.

Her eyes narrowed, and his stomach pitched worse than when he'd rode the old roller coaster at the now-defunct theme park outside of town. "Sure, right after I grow three more bra sizes and get collagen injected into my lips. I'm nothing like your—friend."

Her words were definitive but for a moment he thought he saw confusion in her eyes. Or at least hesitation.

"I-I wouldn't want you to be. You're perfect just like you are." *Shit*, what could he possibly say to make this worse? That sounded like he was pumping her up with fake compliments just to get her to help him out. "What I mean is, you've got everything they're looking for."

And maybe everything I'm looking for, too, a rebel voice whispered that he immediately shrugged off.

She rolled her eyes. "Benjamin, if I hadn't known you practically from birth, I'd have guessed you were the youngest Rushford brother. You're too used to being a Charming Charlie."

"Meggie, I'm not trying to charm you. You're adorable and effervescent and personable."

She stared at him like he had a fever. And like she didn't believe a word he'd said.

Why should she? For years he'd given her the cold shoulder. He'd never flirted with her after Patrick died and had never, ever, encouraged her in any way.

Because she had no idea that her brother might still be alive if it weren't for him.

There was no way to atone for the foolish mistakes of his youth, and God knew, it wasn't for lack of wishing. The best he could do was to save as many other lives as he could, to build all the skills and gather all the knowledge he could so others would have a chance.

But even that would never bring back his best friend. And he would never be able to face her with his most horrendous shame.

He understood her pain even more than she knew. He'd lost his own brother, Kevin, and his wife Trish, a little over a year ago in a car accident, leaving his oldest brother Brad and his wife Olivia to raise their little daughter, who was now one and a half.

He'd lost his parents in an accident, too, when he was thirteen, and he and his brothers and his baby sister had gone to live with their maternal grandmother. Effie was a widow by then, but she'd stepped forward to take them because his Grandma Rushford had been fighting a battle with cancer, which she'd ultimately lost. Life sometimes hurt. A lot.

But by God, he was not going to let some old administrator fart who had some cockamamie idea that his physicians had to be happily married stop him from getting the job he was born for. He was determined to carry on his grandfather's legacy and help the people who had believed in him when he was a young boy. Give back to his town for what they did for him.

He fisted his hands. "This job is the most important thing I've ever wanted. I belong in that ER, Meggie. I have every qualification and I'm a damn good doctor. It's not fair to disqualify me because I don't have a wife or a steady girlfriend."

She looked straight at him, her gaze unwavering. "I agree, Ben, but I'm a terrible liar. Plus, I know the Donaldsons. I've worked with them on the library levy and on the blanket project for the hospital. They'll *know* we're not really dating."

Conflict flickered over her face as she wrestled with the decision and he did his best to tip the ball to his side of the court. "They'll know you're genuine, that you're always doing charitable stuff around town." He touched her shoulder. "Please," he added. He'd known her a long time, since they were kids, and he knew her character. Meg didn't let people down. Not her sick mother, not her best friends.

When the library levy was up for renewal and not getting much support, she rallied half the town to come to a charity ball that was such a success, the levy passed with rainbow colors. When the assisted-living center threw a bake sale to raise money for new exercise equipment, she baked twelve dozen cupcakes herself. And sold them all at the Mirror Lake July Fourth celebration. And wasn't she staging a lakeside bridal show at the end of August to showcase her business, to get it on the map as a destination shop, despite the fact that her partner was laid up?

Her green eyes softened. He'd never noticed how unusual they were, a pure emerald color that reminded him of photos of the green hills of Ireland. Her full lips held a touch of lipstick that matched her shirt. Bold for her, but tasteful. It had been so long since he'd really looked at her, he'd forgotten how stunning she was.

People had whispered she'd had a crush on him for years but he didn't believe it. She could do a lot better than him, that was for sure.

He wasn't for her. And he couldn't ever be.

But this date was temporary, just for tonight. Not a real date by any means. How much damage could one night do?

"What do you say?" he cajoled. "Just a couple hours. For an old friend."

She smiled sweetly. He knew he could count on her. He released a pent-up breath.

"No."

He thought he heard her wrong. She was still smiling.

Wait a minute . . . she'd said *no*. That had happened exactly never.

"Come on, Meggie." He wasn't beyond begging.

Her shoulders straightened. "I'm sorry, Ben. I'd love to help you but . . . I've got plans."

She glanced at a thickset grandfather clock standing stalwart in the middle of the hall. "You've still got a couple hours to find another willing female in Mirror Lake to help you. Best of luck. I've got to go."

His pleading hadn't budged her. Nor had his natural charm. At a loss as to how to crack this egg, he did what he had to do. Called a retreat. "Well, if you change your mind," he called after her, "I'm in Room 225."

She half turned as she walked away. "Thanks again for your help."

"Anytime." Irritated and strangely disappointed, he watched her walk down the hall and disappear into the Klines' suite.

A strange, unsettling feeling tossed in his stomach that had nothing to do with the damn dinner. He wanted to tell her how nice it had been to see her again. He wanted to ask how she was doing, get her to stop frowning and exchanging comebacks with him, and see what she looked like when she really smiled.

But all that was madness, and she was already gone.

CHAPTER 3

"Stand up and take a deep breath." Meg grasped the fragile zipper tab on the delicately beaded lavender silk dress and prepared to pull, pausing only to say a few prayers. Ancient, rote, time-tested ones, because she needed to summon all the help she could get. Because there was no way in hell Priscilla's dress was going to fit. She knew it with as much certainty and dread as she knew when a guy she never wanted to date again was about to ask her out.

The seam was about to split even worse than her head was about to right now, and when it did, her day, which was circling the bowl as it was, would head even farther south and totally tank.

"I don't understand why it's not fitting." Priscilla flicked back her thick mass of honey-blonde hair. Concern filled her deep blue eyes. She was a pretty woman, but her personality was as venomous as a brown recluse spider.

For as long as Meg had known her, Priscilla had been sure to inject herself into the middle of every conversation and every social gathering. She'd been liked by the cutest guys, worn the trendiest clothes. While Meg and her friends headed off to their jobs after school, Priscilla took trips to the mall with her toxic posse. She lived to insult, and it seemed as if no one in all these years had ever really stood up to her.

Her mother, a reed-thin woman with platinum blonde hair in a poofy hair-sprayed bob, was already wearing an elegant champagne-colored dress and matching high-heeled sandals. She approached for a closer view of the disaster. Meg could feel her alcohol-tainted breath on her back. The mayor, a large, bald man in a tuxedo, sat in a Queen Anne chair by the window of the elegant suite and read the paper, oblivious to the unfolding drama.

"The dress is too small," Irene Kline said, accusation creeping into her voice. "Are you certain you brought the right size?"

Meg met Mrs. Kline's cold silver eyes in the full-length cheval mirror. Sweat broke out on Meg's lip. The room started to spin, and she gulped more air to steady herself. Of course it was the right dress. She had the proof in her pocket, the order slip where Alex had written, *Against advice, customer is ordering a smaller size than recommended.* Hell, Priscilla's signature was on the bottom.

Dammit, why had they allowed her to get away with that? Their policy was always to have customers sign off on against-advice orders, which they had, but how could they ever enforce it with her, the mayor's daughter? Especially when Irene Kline sat on the bank board? They should have ordered a duplicate dress, one size up, specifically to avoid this disaster.

Meg was so screwed, because any answer would be the wrong one. Instead, she tugged and pulled, resisting the comical impulse to brace her foot on Priscilla's back for leverage. A sudden ripping sound made her freeze.

"Oh, my God," Priscilla said in a panicky voice. "You're ripping my dress."

Meg stood up and walked over to open a window. It was that or pass out. She sucked in some late-afternoon August air, still hot and humid but with a just a hint of coolness, a harbinger that something a little different was to come. "If you take it off," she called to Priscilla over her shoulder, "I'll work on letting out the seam." Major work with little time to spare, and Meg was not a seamstress. All their alterations were done off-site. But her Grandma Gloria had taught her enough about sewing that she could stitch herself out of this mess. She hoped.

"I don't think we should have to pay for this if you brought the wrong size," the mayor said from across the room.

"Perhaps you should go back to the shop and bring a larger one," Mrs. Kline said.

Meg shook her head. "It was a special order. There's only one."

Meg stared at Priscilla, who glanced at her quickly then looked away. *She knew.*

Of course she knew. They'd discussed this with her the day she ordered the stupid dress. Told her not to order the smaller size. They'd always advised women not to order down, even when they were dieting. That usually created more stress than it was worth. Yet she'd signed on the dotted line, accepting all the terms and conditions.

But how could Meg call her out? No matter how much she disliked Priscilla, she would never make things worse right now, less than an hour before her party.

Not to mention risk losing her most important clients. Which in turn would make her lose her loan, that precious key that was so critical for her scheme of self-improvement. And her future success as a well-respected entrepreneur in this town.

"This is . . . So. Not. Fair." Priscilla paced back and forth clutching her zipper across the plush, nearly white area rug. Water in a giant vase of white lilies reflected the slanted afternoon sunlight from the window. The wooden floors gleamed. Meg bet there was a giant spa tub in the large adjacent bathroom, nothing like the old claw-foot in her century-old apartment above the bridal shop. It wasn't luxurious but it would do just fine for the six-hour soak she would need after all this stress.

"I can make a minor adjustment." *Minor adjustment my ass.* The entire seam would need to be ripped out and resewn.

Meg looked at Priscilla and for the first time in her life, she felt sorry for her. She had a gorgeous figure, and she would have been stunning in a dress of the proper size. But she had fallen prey to the ridiculous get-thin-as-a-stick pressure brides often felt.

"What if I don't look good?" Priscilla said, pacing nervously. "This is a huge party. Half of Connecticut will be there. And all of Evan's colleagues. I have to look my absolute best."

"I can make this work," Meg said, injecting fake confidence into her voice. "There's still plenty of time. Why don't you both make some tea while I start?" She pointed to the beverage brewer sitting on a chest.

Priscilla seemed frozen, the one colorful thing in the middle of the gorgeous all-white room. In fact, she was becoming more colorful with every passing moment. Bright red blotches appeared on her creamy cheeks, her chest, even her upper arms. Suddenly, she turned to her mother. "Mommy, I can't—I can't breathe." Priscilla flapped her perfectly manicured nails in the air, an expression of real panic on her face.

Meg unzipped the dress, hoping that would solve the lack-of-oxygen problem. Priscilla inhaled a deep breath and turned on her. "The dress is all wrong. One hundred and fifty people are about to show up for my party. I'm going to look completely ratchet and it's all your fault!"

Her mother turned an identically pinched face toward her, but with strangely less expression, probably from a recent Botox fix. Across the room, the mayor harrumphed.

Priscilla turned to her mother. "I should have known not to trust that little country bumpkin. How would she even know what style is when she dresses like a reject from the sixties and the last guy she dated got drunk and crashed his boat into the dock?"

Bumpkin and a reject from the sixties? Those she could take, because Alex had assembled her outfit today and assured her she looked stylish and trendy, but the dating comment was the one that pierced. And it was so untrue. Her date had not been drunk. His glasses had flown off when he'd hit a wave and he'd just so happened to be legally blind without them.

Well, Priscilla should try finding a decent guy in a town the size of a safety pin. She'd found hers through her daddy, as her fiancé, Evan Wallmeyer, was the son of a neighboring mayor.

Anger and hurt welled up inside of Meg despite her trying to fend them off with humor. The reputation of the shop she'd given her heart and soul to over the past five years dangled in front of her like a carrot on a stick, one big, satisfying cussword away from being ruined forever.

She bit her teeth into her lip hard so she wouldn't say it. F. Fffff. Oh, *Firetruck*. "I know I can make this right," she said calmly. "Give me a few minutes."

Meg laid the dress out on the bed, opened her sewing bag, and got to work. As she threaded her needle, she skimmed her hand over her Grandma Gloria's old stuffed sewing tomato, stashed into the corner of her bag. It wasn't just any old red sewing tomato with little green leaves. This one had a bit more personality, and reflected her grandmother's love of all things British. A thick black marker line ran down one of the seams, her crazy grandmother's version of a butt crack. On one side were the letters "FE" and on the other side "AR." And the narrow ribbon sewn at the top stated in blue embroidered letters: "POKE FEAR IN THE ARSE." That's what she had to do now. She could hear her grandmother saying it. And she'd probably say something else, too— *For God's sake, keep sewing!*

Priscilla began to cry loudly. Out of the corner of her eyes, Meg could see her mother holding out a glass of ice water. Tributaries of tears weaved through her once-fresh makeup.

Meg worked fast, opening the seam, knowing the faster she finished, the faster this awful night would end, tub or no tub.

Suddenly, Priscilla began to gasp loudly, holding her throat. A panicked expression flooded her face, reminding Meg of how her mom looked once when she fell on the ice and couldn't get up on her own.

At first, Meg thought Priscilla was simply performing, but that terrified look in her eyes was real.

"Dear, are you all right?" Mrs. Kline asked Priscilla, then called out to the mayor, who dropped the sports section and strode over to assess his daughter.

Meg walked over to stand behind Mrs. Kline. She pulled an empty brown lunch sack from her bag and handed it to Priscilla's mom. "Have her try breathing into this."

Priscilla had enough wits about her to shake her head and smack the bag away. Anger and fright flashed in her eyes. "Call—911." She clutched at her throat. "Can't—breathe."

Meg couldn't believe this was happening. Her gut told her even if there was a good possibility that Priscilla was merely being her usual histrionic drama-queen self, she shouldn't take any chances. She punched the emergency numbers into her cell and gave the appropriate information. "Ben Rushford is staying one floor below," she told the Klines. "I'm going to get him."

The mayor nodded, busy telling his hysterical daughter to calm down and take deep breaths. Meg kicked out of her high heels and threw open the door, rushing down the hall to the stairwell and running two floors down. She pounded on the door of Room 225 with all her strength.

"Ben! Ben, are you there?"

No answer. He was probably in the lobby, reconnoitering another date.

She threw her body against the door. Pounded with both fists. Yelled again.

Maybe she was a bad person. Because the thought at the forefront of her mind was that there was no way in hell she was going to allow Priscilla and her panic attack to be the end of Bridal Aisle.

She raised her hand to pound again but suddenly the door opened, causing her to launch forward like a toy rocket, stopped from disaster only by Ben's rock-hard chest.

Whoa. Make that his *bare* rock-hard chest. And a fine one it was, with a smattering of hair over lean, defined muscle that was currently grazing her cheek. Oh, lordie, she was touching his solid, satiny pecs, by accident, of course, but what a fine way to break a fall.

His hair was a little rumpled in an adorable way. Most disturbing, he wore gray boxer briefs that clung to his thighs like a second skin, accentuating thigh muscles so tight you could bounce a penny off them. And some other parts of his anatomy she quickly averted her eyes from.

"What is it?" he asked, all concern and zero embarrassment. He clutched at her arms, steadying her back onto her feet.

Meg forced her focus on the crisis instead of the heat of his smoldering body. What if it wasn't a panic attack? What if Priscilla had choked on something? Or what if her heart was giving out—if she had one, that is. She couldn't allow herself to be sidetracked by his hotness.

She grabbed his arms and shook. "You've got to come with me right now. Priscilla's having a panic attack. At least I think that's what it is. She got really upset that her dress didn't fit and now she says she can't breathe."

In a split second, Ben turned and ran into his room, grabbed his pants off a chair, and tugged them on. She followed him in, closing the door but still leaning against it, watching, fascinated, as he shoved his bare feet into a pair of loafers.

That elfish voice in her head was still stirring up trouble. *This is what he looks like after he makes love*, it said. A little rumpled, his beard shadowy and shorn close and sexy as all get out.

Meg looked quickly away, but not fast enough to stop the heat from rising up her neck and engulfing her entire face in flames. As if she'd never seen a half-naked man before. Which she had, although not for a while. The last one didn't really count, the night of the assisted-living Christmas party, when old Mr. Thompson got a little drunk and went streaking through the snow-covered courtyard, wearing only his favorite red plaid flannel shirt.

But even compared to the younger male parts she'd seen, Ben Rushford's raw-muscled masculinity set her to quivering from head to toe.

"Let's go." He pocketed his hotel key from the television stand and opened the door.

"Don't you have—tools?" Meg asked as she followed.

He shot her a quizzical look as they ran down the hall. "Honey, I have great tools."

"I mean your *doctor* equipment."

He held up his hands like a surgeon would before donning his gloves. Fine, capable hands with long fingers made for suturing and saving. "These are the only tools I need to handle whatever problem you have." Then he grinned, slow and languid, and the heat that had ebbed rose up again to wash all over her.

"But I also brought this." He pulled something from his back pocket and then held up his left hand. A stethoscope snaked down from it. He'd probably had it from one of his moonlighting shifts in the Mirror Lake hospital ER. *Show off.* His mouth was curved up in the faintest smile, but before she could respond, he'd found his way to the stairwell and began to take the steps two at a time.

"Why aren't you more—afraid?" she asked. "You're so—calm."

"I'm always calm." His voice was low and steady. He moved quickly and fluidly, as if he were born for this very moment. With an athletic grace, as fleet of foot as a greyhound. Not a panicked bone in his lithe, sizzling body. While Meg could barely keep up with his long strides, and every nerve in her body was freaking out completely.

When they reached the room, Priscilla was lying on the couch with a plastic bag of ice on her head, her arm outstretched like a Hollywood diva. She wore one of those fluffy Turkish cotton hotel robes, while her dress lay crumpled where Meg had abandoned it on the bed. Sniffling sounds and pathetic little squeaks emanated from under the ice bag.

She was alive. *Thank God.* Bridal Aisle wasn't dead yet.

Ben had snapped into doctor mode, nodding a quick greeting to the mayor and his wife, and going to kneel beside Priscilla where he immediately caught up her hand and took her pulse.

"Hey there, Priscilla." His doctor voice was smooth and soothing, like a massage. "Are you still having trouble breathing?" Priscilla nodded solemnly, her pretty lashes fluttering. Meg knew her entire body would be fluttering if Ben was holding her hand like that.

"Your pulse is kind of fast." He shot Priscilla a full-out grin. Any human female would have blushed, and Priscilla was no exception. She even managed a little return smile between her god-awful gasps. Meg rolled her eyes while the show continued. "I want you to focus on breathing slowly and deeply while I ask you a few things, okay?"

Ben helped her sit up as he volleyed questions. What happened? You felt fine before? Eat anything strange? Choke on something? Heart or breathing problems? The list went on. Priscilla sat looking pitiful, slowly calming down. Her mascara had run big-time down her cheeks, rimming her eyes with black and making them look huge, like a child's. Even zombified, she looked beautiful.

"You're not wearing that to your party, are you?" Ben asked, pointing at her robe as he placed his stethoscope in his ears.

She glanced down and clutched the lapels of her robe. "What, this silly thing? Of course not."

"Well, whatever you wear tonight, you'll look great."

Gag me. Meg had heard enough. She walked over to the dress, sat on the couch, and continued her task.

"The bridal shop screwed up my dress," Priscilla said, tossing over a glare that Meg caught from the corner of her eye.

At that moment, Meg knew the real Priscilla was *ba—ack. Terrific.*

"That's really strange," Ben said, scratching his head.

"What do you mean?" Priscilla asked.

"Because Margaret here just let it slip that Pippa Middleton heard so much praise about our own little bridal shop right here in Mirror Lake that she's ordering a batch of dresses." Ben paused, stethoscope hovering over Priscilla's back, and winked in Meg's direction.

Winked. She gasped at his audacity. His *nerve.*

Priscilla's eyes widened. Her mother's jaw went slack. They both stared at Meg. "Is that true?" they asked in unison.

What the hell was he doing? How was she going to get out of that lie? He'd just batted her the ball, but left her to catch it with a bare-handed grab. She cleared her throat. "Well, I really can't say. We guard our customers' privacy very thoroughly."

"Kind of like bridal-store HIPAA," Ben added.

Meg shot him a *you-are-completely-deranged* look.

"That's—incredible," Mrs. Kline said. "Why, I had no idea."

"I trust you'll keep it hush-hush," Meg said, lowering her voice. "For Pippa's sake."

Within minutes, Priscilla had calmed down. With his easy-boned manner, Ben had her and her parents chuckling at his bad jokes and drooling over his good looks.

When he stood, the mayor thanked him and shook his hand. Mrs. Kline hugged him.

"Thank you so much for coming." Priscilla smiled a sweet smile, no evidence of her real Tasmanian devil self in sight. "I'm so much better now that you've come, Dr. Rushford. Weddings are just so stressful."

Ben picked up the crumpled lunch bag littered on the floor. "Next time the stress starts getting to you like that, try breathing into a bag," Ben said.

"What an excellent suggestion. We hadn't thought of that," Mrs. Kline said.

Meg really had to stop the eye rolling before her eyes got stuck up there.

"We've ordered some appetizers from room service for Priscilla's lightheadedness," the mayor said. "Will you join us, Dr. Rushford?"

Ben declined graciously and headed to the door. Meg stood up with the dress. "I'm going to need to spread the dress out to finish," she told the Klines as she picked up her alteration bag. She wasn't sure exactly where, but anywhere except this room would do fine. "I'll bring it back in twenty minutes."

"And not a minute later," Mrs. Kline chided with a starched smile.

"Not a *second* later," Meg replied, smiling back sweetly.

"I'll walk out with you and make certain you get the dress back in time," Ben said with a wolfish grin. He guided her out of the room, his hand burning an imprint on the small of her back. Lowering his voice, he said, "We can discuss that favor you owe me."

Halfway down the hall, he cornered her like a snared animal. The confidence of a man who always got what he wanted radiated from his large brown eyes.

"Physical intimidation won't get you anywhere," she said, staring up at his hovering six-foot-four height. And avoiding his gaze, which was giving her goose bumps. Ben responded by leaning against the wall, placing his hand near her head, and lowering his face within inches of hers.

"There. Is that better?"

She swallowed hard and crossed her arms around the dress, not that it was going to protect her from his large spicy-smelling body. Or those dark, dark brown eyes that were so full of male arrogance. "What was that back there, the Ben Rushford show?" she asked, refusing to give in to her hormones. "Geez, I've never seen such performance art. Except at the comedy club. Maybe you could get a gig with Jimmy Fallon."

He grinned, displaying a smile that melted underwear. She'd done so well saying no to him, but now she was so screwed.

"Honey, I do whatever it takes to succeed. And I got the results." He poked her mid-chest with a finger, making tingles spread through her body clear to her toes. "I saved your ass. Now you owe me."

What could she say? He *had* saved her ass, big time. And now she would have to pay.

CHAPTER 4

"Okay. Fine. Tell me what I have to do." Meg rolled her eyes and leaned back against the wall. "But if you're as charming at dinner as you were in front of Priscilla and her parents, you won't even need me." She made the gag-me sign with her finger.

Ben smiled at her sass. Not only was she not intimidated, but she was also not at all impressed. "I'm not taking anything for granted. Preparation is the key to success." He was going to keep this professional. No emotion, no messy feelings.

"Fine. But I need to have this dress ready in twenty minutes so you're going to have to let me use your room if you want to do a pre-game briefing."

He led her back to his room and watched from the sofa while she set the dress on the bed and began to sew. "I have to warn you," she said, "when I lie, my face gets all blotchy, I start stuttering, and I lose eye contact. It's bad. So bad you might want to reconsider taking me to dinner."

"Not a chance." He took the opportunity to study her. Despite her intense focus on her work, she seemed more relaxed, now that Priscilla hadn't died. All her concentration was on the dress as she ripped out stitches, her fingers working with the skill of a concert pianist over the fine fabric.

"I thought you and Alex hired out all your alterations," he said.

Her bright green eyes momentarily flicked up at him. "We do. But my grandma is a great seamstress and she taught me a lot." Meg used her teeth to break a thread.

"You certainly look like you know what you're doing."

"All that matters is what the Klines think. They're our biggest clients. Plus Irene is on the loan committee at the bank. If they don't walk away happy customers, my shop won't survive."

Ben saw the irony. His job depended on him impressing people just as hers did. "Well, you have your work cut out for you, and so have I. And I'm not asking you to lie. Just be super positive and madly in love with me for two hours."

She ripped and tugged, pulled and pinned, her delicate fingers mastering the fabric like a surgeon in the OR. It was the sexiest damn thing he'd ever seen. "Like you don't want me to keep my hands off you?" she asked.

"I don't like showy displays of affection in public."

"Okay. Got it. No tonguing at the table. So what's acceptable? Hand-holding?"

"I don't generally enjoy that but for tonight I'll have to make an exception."

She shot him a *you've-got-to-be-kidding-me* look. "Can I ask why you don't like to be touched in public? A terrible childhood trauma?"

He shrugged. "Women tend to want to be touchy-feely and this is a business dinner. I want to keep it professional." Just as he would keep their relationship. Brief and directed to one purpose only. A professional one-night stand, so to speak.

"Okay, Iceman, any other restrictions?"

She was funny, and snarky, and that surprised him. Maybe because he hadn't seen her like this since—well, since before her brother had died. But then, there weren't many things about her that *hadn't* surprised him—in a good way—in the past few hours. He couldn't wait to see what dinner would reveal. "No, but let's review our goals. We're serious but not engaged. But we're looking to the future. If it comes up, we want to settle down here in Mirror Lake, of course. Find a home, raise a family here."

"What kind of house do you want to live in someday?" Meg asked.

"Something modern and lofty, maybe a high-end condo," Ben answered.

She snorted. "*Hello.* This is Mirror Lake. Shiny, lofty bachelor pads don't exist here. Any home on the market is at least sixty years old. Think plaster moldings, wainscoting, nooks and crannies, restoration and renovation."

"Okay, a money pit with a lot of character that will take years to remodel and accommodate a whole brood of bratty children."

"Much better. Now you're thinking like Brad and Olivia. You like their house, don't you?"

"Yes. Mainly because they have a three-car garage and they let me stow my Mustang there in the winter."

He was talking about his maroon '67 Mustang with a white racing stripe. The real love of his life, which he'd bought in high school for a song. He'd worked on that thing for years and it was his pride and joy.

She sighed heavily. "Well, it's a start. How many kids do we want?"

"A handful." He paused uncertainly. "How's that sound?"

"Stressful. How about half a handful?" She licked her index finger and threaded a needle. "But I'm glad you're conferring with me on it," she added.

"I couldn't make that decision without you, honey buns." He got up and started pacing. "They may ask how we met."

"That's easy." She bent over the dress to put in the stitches, and he nearly died. Because there was that great ass again, in all its fabulous glory as she knelt on the bed, supporting herself by her elbows as she sewed.

He swallowed down his very male reaction. Every stunned brain cell of his was now signaling that this whole date thing was a very bad idea.

"In fifth grade, you and my brother were peeking in the school windows to check out the girls at a Girl Scout meeting, and Alex and I came up behind you and scared you so badly you tumbled backwards into the bushes and got poison ivy."

"And detention for a week, thank you very much, because you two went and tattled to Mrs. Tailor."

She shrugged. "I was protecting my girlfriends from peeping toms."

"Goody-goody."

"Pervert." She held a finger up to her chin in deep thought. "Maybe we need a better story. Something unlikely but amazing and utterly romantic."

He rolled his eyes.

"I've got it!" she said. "We need a meet cute."

She was really getting into this, and he wasn't sure if that was good. "Sounds like a chick thing."

"You know what a meet cute is. Like in a romantic comedy, how the two leads meet."

"Like Richard Gere and Julia Roberts on the street corner?"

"Yes, and like in that new movie where the guy and the girl run into each other trying to be the first ones into Target on Black Friday."

"Does she dump the entire contents of her purse all over him, too?" She looked offended and that made him grin. "Look, forget meeting cute for now. I think I should tell you a little about the other candidates. First, there's a guy I've done my entire residency with. His name is Jackson. He goes by Jax. What are you doing?"

She'd run over to the desk and grabbed the notepad and pen. "Taking notes."

"Anyway, he's pretty competitive."

He didn't know what she just wrote down, but he pictured *competitive*. "What do you mean?" she asked.

"Always comparing numbers. How many admissions, how many procedures, how many awards. Always the first guy there for the really tough cases. The more action, the better. An adrenaline junkie. He was born to be an ER doc. And he's good at what he does."

She mouthed *adrenaline junkie*, deep in concentration as she scrawled it down. "Why does he want the job?"

"He's got family an hour away. Thinks it might be a nice community to raise kids. His wife's pregnant."

"Why are you scowling?"

"Just because he's perfect for the job. He's the main competitor I'm worried about."

"There's another?"

"I've only met her once. Her name is Cynthia Rhodes and she's finishing up her residency at Mass General. Her husband is a Harvard MBA. That's all I know."

She'd gone a little pale. "You all right?" he asked. "Need some water or something?"

"Just that I've lived here my entire life. I commuted to Central State for college. Everyone who's coming tonight seems very . . . worldly."

He reached over and squeezed her hand. "You're the owner of an up-and-coming shop. You know everyone in town and they all love you." Her hand was soft and warm, and it fit perfectly in his bigger one. Her gaze was filled with skepticism, like she wanted to believe him but was struggling. For the first time, he realized that she was fretting about tonight—for him. She was doing this for him, without thought of compensation. How many women could he have called upon to do the same?

Zero. But that was the way he wanted it, wasn't it? He enjoyed being loosey-goosey, happy-go-lucky, leading the life of Riley. No commitments, no clingy, needy women, no hassles.

And no reminders of a past he'd tried hard to leave behind.

He was suddenly relieved when Meg stood and gathered up the dress. "I think we've covered the important points," he said. "I'll see you tonight down at the restaurant entrance, a little before seven thirty, okay?"

She smiled, the forced kind. He gave her a platonic little side hug. *Awkward.* She looked . . . worried. He didn't want her to be worried on his behalf. "Meggie, I just want you to know how much I appreciate this. You're the perfect date."

Their gazes tangled again, and that same hormonal zap passed back and forth between them. Ben tapped her nose. Like she was his five-year-old niece instead of a grown woman. Like he hadn't dated a million beautiful women. What was it about her that had him so . . . discombobulated? "Thanks for helping a guy out." He stepped toward the door. "See you later, Princess." Then mentally smacked himself for saying and doing two of the lamest things ever.

She rolled her eyes. "Hey, Prince Charming, flattery won't get you anywhere. And tweaking someone on the nose is sexist."

She flashed a *what-the-eff* look that made him smile.

"Seven thirty, Meggie," he called, tapping his watch. "On the dot."

"Oh, I'll be there. With bells on." She flashed a wicked smile and waved her fingers as she walked past him into the hall. A crazy picture flooded his brain, of her wearing a string of jingle bells and that smile and nothing else, beckoning him with a come-hither look.

He reached up to pinch his own nose to squeeze the vision from his head. He was surprised to find his forehead covered in sweat. He was so screwed.

CHAPTER 5

Meg stepped off the notorious elevator at seven twenty-five to find Ben pacing and checking his watch next to a giant floral arrangement at the glass double-doored entrance to the restaurant. She was struck by his unusual hyperness, which underscored the high stakes that were involved for this dinner.

But mostly she enjoyed the few stolen moments of being able to unabashedly stare at how well his broad shoulders filled out his dark suit jacket, how his bright white shirt contrasted with his tanned skin, and how the tapered cut of his pants accentuated the lean muscle of his legs. A deep, reverberating thrill resounded through her entire body. How was it possible that she was actually going to spend this entire evening with him? Not a dream, not a fantasy, but flesh-and-blood *real*. Now that she was over the initial shock of it all, she thought of it as an opportunity. One she couldn't screw up. Not for his sake, and not for herself.

Fortunately, Meg's alterations to Priscilla's dress had worked out and she'd looked as lovely as ever as she sailed off to her champagne-laden engagement party, leaving Meg free for the rest of the evening.

She realized that with all her heart, she actually wanted to be here. Despite the stress and strain, she was determined to help him through this dinner. Not that she was getting all hopeful about anything romantic starting between them, but this crazy series of events had given her an opportunity to relate to him one-on-one in a way she hadn't for years.

Her grandmother's infamous words echoed. *Poke fear in the arse.*

Delicious, cool air-conditioning wafted over her almost-bare shoulders, and she was grateful for it because her nerves had her sweating up a storm. But it was time to roll. Forcing her spine into perfect posture, she resisted the urge to scootch down the hem of her borrowed clingy black dress, and stepped forward.

Ben looked up. His neutral expression morphed into one of pleasure, surprise, and something far darker that sent a total-body shiver trailing down to her toes. He cleared his throat. "Um . . . wow. You look . . . nice." She watched him take in Alex's slinky dress with lacy black off-the-shoulder sleeves that was stylish and pretty, but, according to Alex, conservative enough for a business dinner. Too bad that when Alex wasn't pregnant, she was a size smaller than Meg. As long as Meg didn't eat much, she'd be fine.

Olivia had had the emergency mission of running the dress over to Meg's apartment, and even managed to dig out a pair of black heels from Meg's closet that she'd never worn before.

"Why do you have fifty pairs of shoes in your closet and all you ever wear are flats?" Olivia had asked.

"Fun, nice, colorful flats," Meg had said.

"Not even in the same league." Olivia had held up the four-and-a-half-inch Louboutins with bows at the toe and a Mary Jane strap that Meg had bought on eBay.

Forced out of her comfort zone, Meg had to admit the shoes made her feel more confident. Plus they got a reaction her flats never got. And judging by Ben's dropped jaw, quite a positive one.

"Are the other people here yet?" Meg asked in a low voice.

"Actually, they're just sitting down. They're at the table next to the windows."

She tipped her head subtly. "You mean that group over there looking at us?" Gawking was more like it. Three couples were checking them out, until an older man in a business suit stood and waved them over.

Meg seized Ben's arm. "Oh. Well, should we—show affection? You know, like a couple?"

"I don't do PDA." There went that pacing again, accompanied by tugging on his collar as if it were choking him, and curling and uncurling his fists. She pulled his sleeve to get his attention. "You have to show them this is real. Even if it's just holding hands and a simple kiss on the cheek. You know, gentlemanly stuff. Because real couples show PDA, and if you want my help, you're going to have to act like a real couple, dammit." And maybe he would discover he really enjoyed kissing her. And wanted to be a real couple.

No, no. She'd given up that kind of thinking. She was not still employing that fantasy. At least, she was trying really hard not to.

His gait stilled. His mouth edged up in a wicked grin as he slowly raked over her body from head to toe. "I can be a gentleman."

Meg managed to frown despite the blush that must have lit her up from chest to roots like a Christmas tree. At least she'd gotten his attention off his nerves. "Then stop focusing on my cleavage."

His gaze snapped back to her face. A devilish twinkle sparked in the depths of his mahogany eyes as he took up her hand and slowly touched it to his lips.

She gave a little gasp as her fingers tingled and every erogenous spot in her body hummed from that simple graze. "Oh, you're good." Her voice came out a little breathless as she struggled not to dissolve into a boneless puddle at his feet.

He flashed his usual grin that must have bedazzled a million women. "Thanks for doing this," he said. "It'll be fun. Are you ready?"

"Sure. Plus, I'm starving," she said with a fake smile. Of course she wasn't—ready *or* starving. Because every part of her that wasn't shaking from his nearness and his clean masculine scent and the light touch of his sinfully full lips was trembling from nerves. She was not a risk taker. And this *was* a risk. She wanted to help Ben get the job, but did not want to be caught in an embarrassing lie in front of the hospital administrator. On a personal level, this evening was an opportunity for Ben to see the real Meg, not the tongue-tied head-up-her-ass version she seemed to display so often in front of him. Not because she was trying to recapture some chemistry she thought they'd had so long ago, but because she was an adult now, and it was time to leave childish fantasies behind.

She had to hold it together for the next few hours. No matter what her personal feelings, she truly believed Ben was a good man and a good doctor and deserved this shot at the job he so passionately wanted.

They walked to the restaurant entrance together, Ben's hand resting lightly on her back, his touch sending ripples of heat coursing through her body faster than the deluxe chair massager she'd once demo'd at the mall. One simple touch generated enough warmth to pay her gas bill through February.

"Don't forget to pretend you love me, sweetheart," Ben reminded her as they crossed the threshold.

"Of course, precious," she retorted.

He swung her around and kissed her. Probably just to be perverse. Their lips collided on the momentum of his swing and sort of smacked together in full-on contact.

And oh, my, they were soft lips, full-bodied and strong like fine wine and just as intoxicating. She laughed self-consciously as they separated, but he surprised her by cupping his hand around her neck and demanding more. Softer this time, exploring her lips, feeling every contour of her mouth, tasting her and stealing her breath and leaving her with an unrelenting ache that shot straight to her abdomen.

Wow.

As he broke the kiss, she blinked, stunned and off balance. His expression was tranquil, confident, and utterly unfazed. With acting skills like that, she had no doubt he'd land this job with or without her. She adjusted his tie, an automatic gesture when you were used to dressing people for a living, but that didn't break the current of electricity that flowed full force between them. His gaze was filled with some unfathomable emotion as he searched her face for something she didn't understand. Just as quickly, it was gone, and his usual lighthearted, carefree mask stood up and in place.

"Who says I can't do PDA?" he said in a low voice.

"Um, right," she managed, trying to catch her breath, and praying the scarlet bloom making her resemble a dyed carnation would abate before they reached the table.

Dr. Donaldson's face held a stoic expression. Meg hoped he wouldn't be too judgmental of such a shameless display. He was almost as tall as Ben, with a strong build that made him look more like the head of a Texas dynasty than the CEO of a hospital. He smiled when he saw Meg, hugged her, and asked, "How's your mother doing?"

"Better on the new medicine. Thanks for asking." If Dr. Donaldson resembled a genteel but astute silver fox, his wife projected an unquestionable sense of entitlement honed from years of sitting on every charitable board in town with the authority of someone who felt just a notch superior to everyone else.

"Hello, dear," Lillian Donaldson said. "What a surprise. Your dress is so . . . nice. So unlike your usual flower child attire."

"You look nice, too." She'd expected Lillian to poke her with a sharp edge or two, but for Ben's sake, she'd endure it with a smile. And after today, she was definitely pitching all her long flowered skirts and cork-bottomed sandals.

"She's a beauty, no matter what she's wearing," Ben said, to her utter amazement. There was his hand on her back again, steadying her nerves—or rather, rattling them.

"Why, Benjamin," Lillian said, "I had no idea you two were seriously—"

"We are indeed, Mrs. Donaldson," Ben said, coming forward to greet her with a kiss on her cheek, which seemed to startle her. Then he turned to Meg. "I'd like you to meet my colleague at U Conn, Jackson Marshall—Jax—and his wife, Stacy. And this is Dr. Cynthia Rhodes, from Boston, and her husband, Paul. Everyone, this is my girlfriend, Meg Halloran."

My girlfriend. In so many ways, Meg felt she had died and gone to an alternate universe. She fought the overwhelming impact of those two little words. How many times in all these long years would she have given her right arm to hear them?

Well, that was then and this is fake, she chided herself. And she couldn't ever forget that.

Jax was tall and good-looking in a mercenary, Navy SEAL sort of way, tanned and rugged with a buzz haircut and handsomely intimidating in his tailored suit. His wife Stacy looked about ten months pregnant. She sat flapping the menu in front of her face for relief even though the restaurant was on the cool side. From her genuine smile to the way her pure blue eyes lit up when she shook hands, Meg liked her instantly and was happy to take the chair next to her while Ben held it out and then sat down himself. "When are you due?" Meg asked.

"Not soon enough. The twins are due in six weeks."

"My business partner is expecting twins, too," Meg said. "I'll have to introduce you."

Ben nudged her knee under the table, which she took to mean she wasn't supposed to make nice with the competition. She decided to ignore him.

"What business are you in?" Cynthia Rhodes asked. Her handshake was strong and no-nonsense, her clothes and makeup polished and perfect.

"I own the bridal shop on Main Street. Next to Mona's Bakery."

"Best cinnamon rolls in town," Paul said. "Or so I've heard."

"You'll have to try them while you're here," Meg said. "The owner brings us leftovers in the afternoons. They are melt-in-your-mouth with the fresh-baked dough and all that warm, gooey icing."

Smiling rapturously, Stacy said, "Wow," as if Meg's description had been X-rated.

So far the conversation wasn't so bad, considering Meg's lungs felt caged in by the narrow sheath of Alex's dress. Dr. Donaldson ordered wine and the waiter poured. A few liquid calories wouldn't expand her stomach too much, would they?

Ben and Dr. Donaldson conferred about ordering appetizers, but Meg didn't pay much attention. She'd be lucky if the dress could take her dinner.

"Your girlfriend is charming, Benjamin. Are you two engaged?" Jax asked.

Ben pulled Meg close and massaged her shoulder. For a man vowing not to show affection in public, he was doing pretty damn well. His thumb made small circles through the lace of her dress. Warm, sure strokes made her wish they could forgo this awful dinner and put his big fluffy bed upstairs to good use.

"No, but we've known each other since childhood," Meg said, smiling her most radiant smile at Ben, who beamed right back, displaying magnificent white teeth.

That smile should be illegal. It was like getting blinded by someone's brights on a country road at night. Brazen. Disconcerting. *Lethal.*

"How did you two meet?" Stacy asked.

"We met as kids in school but reconnected recently when Ben was doing health screenings at the assisted-living facility I volunteer at." There. No mention of Girl Scouts or tattling to Mrs. Tailor, and she'd even managed to throw in his civic-minded qualities. It was even mostly true. He'd done health screenings about a month ago for the assisted-living facility where his grandma lived, and Meg had helped him. They'd had the best time, both of them joking with the seniors and each other.

Ben took up her hand on the table and played mindlessly with it. Being next to him was like having too much wine, constantly fighting against the fuzzy feeling of intoxication.

"I used her as the demo for the blood pressure machine," he said, "but when I took her heart rate, it was way off the charts. She couldn't resist me."

Meg knocked against his shoulder in a playful way. "Oh, c'mon now, honey, let's tell them what really happened." Because she would play the doting girlfriend, but she was not going to let him present her as meek, unassuming, and a pushover. "Truth is, my heart was racing because one of the seniors chose that exact moment to have a pacemaker malfunction."

"Oh, dear." Lillian grasped her long string of pearls in alarm.

"Yep, *oh dear* is right," Meg said solemnly. "Ben went from taking blood pressures to almost doing CPR. Fortunately it all turned out well." Ben had insisted on riding in the ambulance with Mr. Lambert, while she'd stayed for a couple rounds of bingo to help lift everyone's mood. If there hadn't been a crisis, she'd envisioned a very different ending, but like so much about their history, the timing was just off.

Except *she* was going to need CPR if he didn't stop stroking her hand like that.

"Since you two are both from Mirror Lake, why don't you tell the others what a great community it is?" Dr. Donaldson asked.

"I'd like to know something," Paul asked. "New York is over two hours away. What do you do about the arts? Theater, specifically?"

"We have an excellent community theater," Mrs. Donaldson said proudly. "In fact, we even have a famous actress."

"We do?" Ben looked perplexed.

"Ida Mae Spencer, who works at the hardware store, did a splendid Evita. Except we had to close down the show when the store flooded so she could do damage cleanup. Of course, the entire crew helped."

Cynthia rolled her eyes and Paul stifled a laugh. Stacy and Jax were too polite to react, but Meg could feel them thinking that Mirror Lake was Podunkville Reincarnate. So she tried to do a save. "Mirror Lake has a fabulous old atmospheric theater from the 1920s."

"Atmospheric theater?" Stacy crinkled up her nose. "What in the world is that?"

"It's one of only five remaining in the country," Meg said. "It used to be a movie palace, where above the screen, there's a realistic, beautiful sky full of twinkling stars and drifting clouds. Around the stage, it looks like a Moorish castle, with alabaster sculptures and medieval-style carvings."

"The Ladies' Guild saved that theater from being razed back in the seventies," Mrs. Donaldson said. "I was their president then."

"Yes you were, darling," Dr. Donaldson proudly gave his wife an affectionate little squeeze.

Meg nodded. "We have a big ball every year right in the theater to raise funds so we can attract great live entertainment. The programs are almost always sold out through tourist season."

Dr. Donaldson smiled, clearly pleased with her representation of the town. The tension in Meg's neck abated a little. All she had to do was keep emphasizing how great Mirror Lake was and how connected Ben was to his town and her job would be done. She'd just taken a breath and felt herself starting to relax when the appetizers arrived.

"I ordered your favorite, sweetie," Ben said with a pleased-as-pudding look.

Meg looked at the plates that were being passed. Fat chilled shrimps hung over the sides of a giant martini glass. The glass was filled with some kind of seafood concoction mixed with fresh salsa and avocado and surrounded by chips.

Great. Except she wouldn't be having any of that since eating any kind of shellfish made her body try to die.

"It's the Inn's specialty," Ben said. "Seafood martini. Shrimp, crab, avocado, and homemade salsa. Meg loves it. Here, sweetheart, have some." He dipped a tortilla chip into the glass and held it up to her mouth.

"How cute," Stacy said.

Meg tried to wipe the horrified expression from her face. With a shaky smile, she swallowed hard. Her eyes darted back and forth around the table. Yep, everyone was watching.

"Here you go, honey." Ben's expression was expectant as he pushed the chip closer to her mouth.

She looked death in the eye. There was no way she was going to allow that food to touch her lips. So she did what any mature person would do. Dropped her napkin. "Oops," she said, bending down to get it and tugging on Ben's pants leg. Hard. No response.

She tugged again until finally his concerned face appeared next to hers. "Stop trying to get me to eat, you doofus," she hissed.

"I thought you were starving. And I'm trying to show I know you."

"Well, you clearly don't know the important fact that I'm allergic to shellfish."

"Oh, shit." His face twisted up in a panic. He looked genuinely appalled. To see his Cool Hand Luke demeanor crumble was indecently satisfying.

"I'm pretty sure four ER docs could save me," Meg said, "but do we really want to end the evening that way?"

"Let me order you something else."

"No. Just—just eat it so I don't have to."

He grabbed her napkin and her elbow and yanked her up, smiling a bit too broadly. Then he picked up the chip and put it in his own mouth. "I forgot you're on that diet, Blossom, even though you're perfect just the way you are."

Meg blinked. He looked pretty sincere, except for the *this is completely effed up* expression in his eyes. The absurdity of the evening made her want to laugh crazily out loud, but she didn't dare.

Dr. Donaldson cleared his throat. "While we're waiting for our entrees, I thought we could go around the table and discuss the reasons each of you wants to live and work in Mirror Lake. And of course,

Lillian and I can answer any questions you might have about our town. Cynthia, would you like to begin?"

"I'd like to raise our children in a town with history and culture and access to big cities. Boston and New York are both in drivable distance."

Jax went next. "Stacy's family is from Hartford, an hour's drive, so we'd be close to family. And I'd like the opportunity to have a big impact in a small community."

Then it was Ben's turn. He draped an arm casually around the back of Meg's chair and took up Meg's hand again in his free one. "I was born and raised here. I understand the people who live here, and I know most of them, too. For years I dreamed about coming back here to practice."

Cynthia tipped her glass of wine in salute. "Looks like you've got the hometown advantage, Ben."

"You talk the big talk, buddy," Jax said. "But we all know you haven't been in a relationship. Just two weeks ago, you showed up with a different woman at that residents' barbecue."

The few bites of buttered bread Meg had managed to swallow churned fitfully in her stomach. *Dammit, that's what he gets for being such a showoff.* That cocky confidence was nothing but trouble, but he certainly looked like he needed a save now. "Who, Ashley?" she asked Ben, who confirmed with a small nod. "Oh, she's just an old family friend." She had no idea how to play this out, so she took a swig of wine.

Stacy fisted her husband in the arm. "Mind your business." At least she seemed nonjudgmental, but who knew? These doctors were a tough crowd, aggressive and competitive. It made her wonder how compassionate they'd be to sick people.

"Meg and I reconnected recently," Ben said, his gaze cool under pressure as he stared Jax straight in the eyes.

Recently, yes. Like, two hours ago. Meg forced a smile. This was not looking good.

"When you know it's right, it's right," Ben said matter-of-factly.

"You mean to tell us, Ben," Dr. Donaldson asked, "you've been dating this lovely woman for less than a month?"

"Look, Dr. Donaldson," Ben said. "Whether it's a week, a year, or a lifetime, I would hope that whichever of us gets this job, it's because we're dedicated to the community and have the leadership skills to do it right."

"True, Ben," Dr. Donaldson said, "but we're a small hospital and a tight-knit community. We want to do our best to find someone who fits in well with our town, who will establish themselves here and stay here for a long time. Anyone who's single is at high risk for leaving, in our opinion."

A muscle in Ben's jaw twitched. "Finding someone who's committed to the community and to the job shouldn't depend on marital status."

Mrs. Donaldson chimed in. "We've always known that an unhappy wife means an unhappy life." She looked at Paul. "Or husband, as the case may be. "

Meg cringed at the sexist comment, but if the others were bothered, no one showed it. She was proud of Ben for speaking his mind.

Dr. Donaldson nodded. "The last doctor we hired left after less than a year. His wife wasn't cut out for small-town life. We're trying to be smarter this time."

"Besides," Mrs. Donaldson added, "we want someone with outstanding moral character. Someone mature and God-fearing."

Mercifully, the dinner was served. Ben kept an amicable expression on his face but the tension was evident in the stiffness of his posture and the set of his jaw. He was an honest, driven man who detested playing games but these people were all nuts. She wished she could say something to lighten the mood.

"Oh, look. There's a band," Meg said, eager for distraction. A man sat behind a shiny black piano, and a bass player and drummer took their places next to the parquet dance floor and began to play. A female vocalist in a long red dress held a microphone.

Stacy sighed. "I love to dance. Too bad I have no balance now."

Jax massaged her back. "Soon, baby."

"We've been taking dancing lessons, haven't we, Meg?" Ben asked out of absolutely nowhere.

Dancing. The one thing she never, ever did in public. She wasn't going there. She would take this topic off the table right now.

"You must show us," Mrs. Donaldson said.

"I-I really don't have the proper shoes on," Meg said, taking another big gulp of wine. She would have to hold her ground, just as she'd done with the seafood. Flat-out refuse if necessary. Anything to save the embarrassment—for her and Ben's sakes—of other people seeing how abominably she danced.

Ben stood and pulled out her chair just as she was setting down her wine. "C'mon. Let's dance."

"But I feel—" She never got to finish the sentence, because he'd whisked her out of her chair before she could concoct a decent ailment like a headache, dizziness, or nausea that would cause him to leave her the hell alone.

As soon as they were out of earshot of the table, he spoke. "I just wanted to get away from that table for a few minutes."

He had no idea what he'd just done. "Ben," she said quietly.

"Can you believe all that nonsense? *Happy wife, happy life.* It's like marriage is the number one quality they care about and to hell with being a good doctor."

"Ben," she said a little louder.

"Oh, and I appreciate what you said about town. You're so involved with everything, that will be one thing in my favor." He finally looked at her. "What is it?"

She stopped walking and grabbed him by both arms.

"You look a little pale," he said. "Are you all right?"

"I can't dance," she blurted. It was a trauma from her teenage years, when her prom date had gone so far as to mock her, saying dancing was an indication of how sexual a person was and she was clearly frigid. After that slap down, she'd never set a toe out on any dance floor ever again.

"Everyone can dance." Ben said it as easily as if he'd said *everyone eats* or *everyone farts*. "It's terrific stress relief. Just fake it." How far did she have to go to spell this out? She planted her feet and stood her ground. "You don't understand. I was a wallflower in high school. I never danced. I only dance at home under the most private of circumstances." And even then her cats tended to hide under the bed. "I'm completely missing the dancing gene. I suck. A klutz. I'll totally embarrass—"

He laughed.

She almost stomped a foot, for lack of any other way to get him to listen. "Did you hear what I just said?"

Before she could finish her sentence, he grabbed her by the hand and strode out to the dance floor with her in tow.

"I don't expect this night could get any worse than it is now. Just follow me."

Before she could protest, he wrapped his arms around her waist and held her securely. Under any other circumstance, she would have thought she'd died and gone to heaven. But as it was, her hell was only just beginning.

"What possessed you to tell them we're taking ballroom dance lessons?"

He spun her around and caught her expertly. As if she weren't dizzy enough from his nearness, his hot body, and dammit, his amazing dance moves. She managed to calm down enough to look him in the eye.

He was still smiling. Not just any old smile, either. One that was big and wide and reached all the way to his eyes. It was a tragedy. Because it said, with every bit of its radiance, that beyond a doubt, Ben Rushford loved to dance. Little crinkles surrounded the corners of his eyes, giving him a mature, sexy look that made Meg want to settle her hands on his cheeks and pull him closer and kiss those lines and every other blessed part of his too-handsome face.

"Stop worrying so much," he said, boogying down to the beat. "Do you realize what you've done?"

"No, but I know what I'm about to do. Embarrass us both on this dance floor."

He shook her gently. She loved the feel of his hands on her, firm and sure. Hands that knew exactly what they were doing. And she wanted them roaming over every other part of her body right now.

"Meggie, you saved my ass. You reassured Donaldson. You showed you love our town. In other words, you made *me* look good and I'm so grateful to you for that."

She scanned his eyes. They held honesty and sincerity in their chocolate-colored depths. And something more. A desire to make her feel better, to take away her discomfort. That unabashedly touched her more than any compliment he could give her. Before she could process all that, the music tempo changed to a hot Havana beat.

"Okay, baby, here we go. Hold on tight!" Ben's face lit up with clear glee as he spun and twirled, tipped and swayed, keeping a hard and fast grip on her at all times.

He put his hands on her hips and had her mimic his own movements.

Terror threatened to freeze her limbs but she couldn't not do . . . something. Maybe it was the fact that she felt responsible for doing whatever she could to help him get this job. But maybe it was the look of pure joy on Ben's face that mesmerized her, made her feel giddy and . . . happy. Yes, happy in a way that made her throw herself into the dancing with reckless abandon for the first time in her life. She shook, she shimmied, she did wild and crazy things like swung and swayed and twisted. The disastrous evening seemed far away, and she was enveloped in Ben's smile, his confident touch, and his cocky swagger as he clearly loved every move.

He drew her near and said into her ear, "Hang on for the finale, sweetheart." Before she could respond, he pushed her until she flew away from him, then when their arms were fully outstretched and they were holding on only by their fingertips, he reeled her slowly back in until their bodies were touching, hips swaying together in a rhythm fueled by the erotic beat of the music.

As he flung her out one final time, she lost balance a little and cast out an arm to compensate. She stumbled, clutching at him to avoid falling. That was when she heard the rip.

The first sensation was relief—she could finally breathe. But that was followed quickly by terror as she realized the entire seam along the backside of her dress had ripped wide open, and the entire restaurant was about to catch a full and unobstructed view of her ass.

She spun and backed up against Ben's body, plastering herself flat against him.

"Wow, Meggie," Ben said as she ground into his crotch. "I never realized dancing got you so hot."

She twisted her neck around far enough to send him the stink eye. Then she clutched at him for dear life.

"Do *not* move away from me," she managed.

"Sure, no problem. Are you . . . flirting with me? Because if you are, I'm all in." As she pushed against him, he wrapped his hands around her upper arms, a move which normally would have caused goose bumps to course up and down their lengths.

She scooched up against his chest and put her mouth near his ear. "Listen to me carefully. I'm only going to say this once. I am *not* flirting with you. My dress tore and . . ."

He stilled suddenly. "And what?" he asked.

"And I always wear undies. I never go anywhere without them. Except maybe for today."

He tried pushing her away, no doubt to see the spectacle for himself, but she clung to him with the suction of an octopus.

"I didn't think you were that kind of gal, Meggie." His voice sounded choked.

"Panty lines are embarrassing. I had no choice."

"Nice."

"Just help me!"

"How do you propose I do that?"

"You're used to dealing with crises, aren't you? Think of something!"

"Keep smiling," he said calmly. "And wave to all the nice people who are staring at us."

Somehow, she managed to hold it together while he slowly backed them both off the dance floor, steering them to an opening to the kitchen.

"Hey, can we have a napkin?" he asked one of the kitchen staff. "My girlfriend just split her dress. Ouch!" He glared at Meg while holding his ribs, which she'd just elbowed. "What'd you do that for?"

"I'm flattered if you think a napkin is going to cover my ass but I need something bigger!"

"Can I change that to a tablecloth, please?" he asked as he fended off another poke. Then he turned to her. "Your ass isn't that big, honey," he said, biting the inside of his cheek to keep from laughing. A move which accentuated his damn dimples. Then he shrugged off his suit coat and handed it to her. "Try this."

Eyes narrowed in her most practiced Darth Vader glare, she took the coat and tied it around her waist. "Thanks," she managed.

"I can say you don't feel well and take you to your room," he offered.

And leave him surrounded by piranhas? She suddenly felt like they were comrades in this fight, and she wanted to see it through to the end. "I can make it through dessert." She wasn't a quitter. Head up, she walked back to the table, making sure the arms of his jacket were tied in a snug knot.

"Those were some moves, Ms. Halloran," Dr. Donaldson remarked.

"Yes, you two have quite the raw sexual chemistry," Cynthia said, a glint of evil in her eyes.

"I think they have amazing dance chemistry," Stacy said, giving Meg another reason to like her. For the first time that night, Meg rejoiced in one positive thought. Unrestrained from the confines of the dress, she could finally eat her dinner in peace. As her hungry eyes roved about the table, she realized all the plates had been cleared.

At least there would be dessert, and after all she'd been through, she was totally ordering some.

"Anyone for dessert and coffee?" Dr. Donaldson offered.

"I'm stuffed," Jax said, patting his stomach.

"Me, too," Stacy chimed in.

"I never eat dessert," Paul said.

"I'm vegan and I'd rather keep my arteries clean," Cynthia said.

Ben looked at Meg strangely. She'd tried to hide her disappointment, or rather her ravenous hunger, but maybe she hadn't been as successful as she thought. "Would you like dessert?" he asked her.

"No, thanks." She smiled, wanting him to know she was grateful for his concern. At least skipping dessert would get them out of here quicker, which couldn't happen fast enough.

"Well, it was a pleasure getting to know you all better," Dr. Donaldson said. "Don't forget we have our little weekend with the diabetic children coming up at Camp Mohican."

"Diabetes camp?" Meg asked with a false lilt to her voice. She reminded herself that tonight was a one-time thing. She hadn't signed on for anything else. Besides, they probably just needed doctors at the camp, right? Not non-outdoorsy, hate-all-bugs types of people like her.

"The ER physicians staff the camp every summer," Mrs. Donaldson said. "It's jam-packed full of activities and friendly competitions for the staff and kids. A perfect time for bonding and confidence building."

"We'll be there," Ben said, reaching over and squeezing Meg's hand. *Right. And I'd gladly sign on for another night of hell like this one.*

As they said their good-byes, Meg watched Ben thank the Donaldsons graciously and bid farewell to his colleagues, his hand lightly on her back. It was so, so easy to pretend his smile was real, that his touch was a prelude to real touches and caresses that real couples shared. But even as Meg smiled and nodded and pretended, she reminded herself that nothing about tonight was real. She'd stood up for Ben when his buddy Jax had just called him out on that other woman from a few weeks ago, but in real life, that was who Ben was. He didn't want to settle down, didn't want to date only one woman, and he certainly didn't want to date *her*—Nice Meg who helped everyone and said yes to everything whether she liked it or not.

In the past several hours, she'd survived Priscilla's panic attack, a near-poisoning, dancing in public, and a split skirt. And the most perilous thing of all, the proximity of Ben Rushford's company. She'd done her part. She knew her limits. There was no way in hell she was spending an entire weekend in his company, diabetic kids or no.

CHAPTER 6

Ben stared at the half-naked woman in front of him and swallowed hard. Meg's hair was dripping wet, her creamy skin flushed pink, and miles of toned legs peeked out from underneath a fluffy white robe ending in a grand finale of toenails the color of pink Laffy Taffy.

They'd parted ways after dinner, but he'd been restless. So he'd walked the few blocks from the hotel to Mirror Lake's downtown, past the rows of quaint shops to her apartment, one of a handful located in the same hundred-year-old warehouse building that housed her bridal shop. Yet the shock of seeing her looking so . . . spontaneously unguarded, so not-put-together . . . made him forget why he was standing in the hall with his jaw dropped open, his hand suspended in air from knocking on her door.

"You look hot," he blurted. *Shit.* Why had he said that? Meg turned red as a strawberry, pulled her robe tighter around her neck, and tugged the belt tight.

"Warm," he rushed to say. "You know, flushed—like, from your bath." For someone who was usually Mr. Rico Suave, he was really bumbling everything.

He swept his gaze up and down her magnificent body. "I'm just sad your ass is covered." *Fuck, what was he doing?* He tripped over his words to cover. "I mean, *glad*. Really glad. After the rip and everything." Sweat rolled down his back. Maybe he needed to take his own temp. Because he really wasn't acting like himself.

His stupid comment put her on the offense, her eyes narrowing down like a crocodile's ready to snap its prey in half. "Why are you here, anyway? Please don't tell me you've come to bring me more bad news." She paused. "No, wait. Don't tell me. We'll be competing in a survival contest at camp, and the candidate who comes out alive wins the job."

He threw back his head and laughed. Couldn't help himself. The fact that her sense of humor was still intact put him more at ease. "I would never throw you to the wolves, Katniss." Impulsively, he reached out and tugged on a wet lock of her hair. "Dinner wasn't *that* bad, was it?"

Another wrong move, because she immediately swatted his hand away. "Have you no boundaries?" He grinned in response. Most women would melt into his arms after that, but not her.

"I wanted to thank you for what you did for me at dinner," he said. "You were terrific." More than terrific. Bringing her tonight was brilliant. A stroke of genius.

Not that he was getting all sappy as far as she was concerned. No, siree. Because he was here on business. He had to secure her for next weekend. That was his primary objective, and he'd better not lose his focus.

Meg adjusted her hot librarian glasses, the ones she always wore when she wasn't wearing her contacts, and eyed him suspiciously. Her eyes looked bigger and greener than usual behind the dark-framed lenses. She was this tantalizing mix of sexy and sweet that drove him wild.

She sniffed the air. "I smell something. Something delicious and greasy, like a double cheeseburger from PITS." She craned her neck to see behind him, but he stepped away, still holding the bags behind his back.

"I don't smell anything." Actually, he smelled her. And she smelled like grapefruit and lemons and it was seriously turning him on.

Her eyes went wide as she placed her hands on his chest and craned her neck to see behind his back. Her touch was feather light, but he felt it down to his bones. "Whatever you have behind your back is bribery, isn't it?" she asked. "How dare you think you can sway me with food."

He leaned against the doorjamb and assessed her, as she stood with her arms crossed. Stubborn. Resolute. Beautiful.

Get in and get out, Rushford. Keep your head in the game and stay focused.

"Relax, I'm not here to bribe you." Well, he was, sort of, but he found himself wanting to do other, way more inappropriate things. Like drop the bags of food he was carrying, pull her toward him, and kiss those lovely pink lips, slipping his hands under that robe and exploring that soft flushed skin still radiating warmth from her bath.

Instead, he held out the take-out bags he'd gotten from the town diner, Pie in the Sky.

Meg clapped her hands together, as thrilled as a kid at Christmas. She rummaged through the bags, pulling out cheeseburgers and fries and shakes. Then she grabbed him by the elbow and steered him into the room to a bright green couch scattered with pink and maroon crocheted pillows. A bright floral area rug lay over old wide-plank floors, and a gaggle of plants sat in front of the windows that overlooked Main Street. Everything around him was rife with color, a sharp contrast to his mostly beige apartment back in Hartford.

Meg sat opposite him in a matching green armchair. She poked a straw in one of the shakes and took a long pull, closing her eyes and giving a little sigh of pleasure.

Sweat beaded on his forehead. Since when was drinking a chocolate milkshake from the local diner cause for a cold shower? Another reason he should play delivery boy and take off. But he couldn't seem to move.

He watched her attack a burger and fries like she hadn't eaten since breakfast. She possessed a kind of *joie de vivre* that attracted him like a ray of sunshine after weeks of rain. Probably because it had been so many years since he had allowed himself to feel happiness at such a simple pleasure, that the feeling was foreign to him. Surrendering to it, he snagged a fry, dipped it in ketchup, and popped it into his mouth.

"I'm starving," she said, passing him the other burger. "Don't make me inhale this alone."

Ben was just about to take a bite of his dinner when an animal hopped up on the arm of his chair. A small black and white cat missing an ear. He scratched behind the cat's one good ear. "Sorry, buddy, the cheese-burger's mine." The cat rubbed up against his hand and stretched out.

Ben preferred dogs. The bigger the better, but cats didn't bother him.

Until a lean black cat with white paws crawled out from under the couch, quietly swishing its tail and staring at him.

With its one eyeball. Only God knew what had happened to the other one. It looked wary and maybe frightened, but didn't shy away when he reached down to pet it.

That was when a third cat, an all-white longhair, walked out with delicate steps from what he assumed was the bedroom. The animal rubbed itself against his legs, mewing loudly.

"Oh, so you want attention, too." Ben leaned over and checked it over carefully as he patted its head. All appendages and sensory organs appeared to be intact. The animal sat and swished its tail, poised to hop into his lap. "This one's got to be a girl."

"Why do you think that?" Meg asked.

"She knows she's cute. She's flirting with me. Plus she won't stop meowing."

Meg rolled her eyes. "Actually, she is a girl. Her name is Kate. Her hubby is William and the little guy is George."

"You're kidding."

"Gran's idea."

Everyone in town knew of Grandma Gloria's predilection for anything royal. "I never would have guessed."

"Kate and William decided to start a family underneath the Dumpster in the alley behind my shop. Teddy from Mona's discovered them, and the rest is history."

"No explanation for the missing body parts?"

"It belongs to a sordid past they'd rather not talk about."

Ben chuckled. Maybe he had more in common with these scrappy old cats than he'd thought. "So, what crucial body part is this one missing?" He looked under all the hair to be certain he could count four paws.

"Actually, she's had nearly all her teeth pulled."

One glance at Meg told him she was serious.

"She has an autoimmune disease that inflamed her gums. But she gets along fine now. Just takes her a little longer to chew, is all." She imitated a chewing motion with her own mouth that was so ridiculous it made him laugh out loud.

He diverted his eyes to the food and tried to retain what composure he still had. "You made a great impression tonight. I wanted to thank you." He meant it more than she'd ever know.

She rolled her eyes. "Considering I didn't have to break out my EpiPen and I survived embarrassing myself to death on the dance floor, one of my biggest phobias, yeah. It was quite an impression."

"You showed your true personality. You're kindhearted, civic-minded, and funny." And pretty.

Meg set down her burger and cast him a calculating glance, one that said she knew his game. It was all over her face—she thought he was a blowhard. "I knew there was more to this than kindness." She wagged her finger at him. "Don't deny it. I'm not going to diabetes camp, Ben."

It was so much more than bribery, but he would never admit that. "Just one more weekend." He considered dropping to all fours and groveling.

"Remember my business? Saturdays are insane. Alex is out and my grandmother is great for a cover but she doesn't know the ropes like we do. And I have to do some things for my mom. I have responsibilities."

She couldn't leave for even a weekend? Ben knew a life that was full of constraints—long, exhausting hours of work, followed by more hours of studying, when other friends his same age had much more time and freedom, not to mention a far better salary. But he could always travel wherever he pleased, and he considered playtime essential for blowing off steam. Opportunities she, apparently, did not have.

He backed down. "You're right. I've already asked too much. But I'm really grateful for what you did for me."

She looked surprised, like she'd expected him to push it. "Honestly," she said, "you've got more commitment and energy than either of the other candidates. And you're not afraid to speak your mind. I hope you get the job."

Ben shrugged. "My grandfather was the definition of what a real doctor should be. He knew everyone in town, and he really cared about more than their physical aches and pains. If I could be a tenth of what he was . . ."

She looked at him oddly. Of course she did, because he was blathering like an idiot. "He'd be proud of you, Ben," she said softly, lightly touching his hand.

For a second, their gazes locked. The compassion and understanding he saw in her eyes struck a raw nerve. He needed to get out of here before he did something even more stupid. He kept the talk light while they finished eating. "So, I think you have the potential to be a fabulous salsa dancer. You really let loose out there."

She put her hand up to stop him from saying more. It was clearly a sensitive topic. "I'd rather not discuss my hang-ups."

He leaned forward and stabbed a finger in the air. "Before your dress ripped, you were liking it. Admit it."

She shook her head vehemently. "I've never been more mortified."

"Aw, c'mon. You weren't enjoying it just a teensy bit?"

"I was enjoying watching you. You're a crazy man out there."

"I love to dance."

"Why is that?"

"It gives me a freedom I don't get anywhere else. With a couple lessons, you'd like it, too. You have the innate rhythm, I can tell."

"Right. Like a Buckingham Palace guard." To illustrate, she made her posture rigid and saluted, another thing that cracked him up.

Just this tiny glimpse into her life told him a lot. She was hardworking—overworked, for sure. She'd never say so, but he knew she spent most of her free time helping her mother. And while in some ways she was confident and charming, and certainly won over everyone's hearts, in other ways she wasn't confident at all.

She'd been a shy girl. He had vague recollections from long ago of her looking gangly and awkward with braces and skinny little chicken legs. But she'd grown into her looks in high school. At one time he'd seen her trying out for the school play, singing and dancing. She'd gotten the part of Dorothy in the *Wizard of Oz*. It wasn't until Patrick died and her world fell apart that she'd gotten so cautious. He wanted to hunt down whoever had capitalized on her insecurities and humiliated her into never dancing in public again.

He wondered what she would be like if someone released her from the confines of her life and let her fly. But that someone sure as hell wasn't going to be him. He didn't do relationships. Ever. He rode the fun and good times train until it pulled into the station. As long as he was clear about that up front, he had no problem with that.

Ben tapped on the corner of his mouth. "You've got a little speck of ketchup right here."

A frown creased her brow. Her tongue darted out to lick the corners of her mouth. "Did I get it?"

No, but lordie, *he* wanted to. "Not quite." He leaned over the table to point at the spot.

She ran the back of her hand over her mouth. "Now?"

He leaned over further and picked up a napkin. "Let me see it."

He'd meant to use the napkin to wipe it off, honest he did. But as he leaned in closer, some crazy electrical jolt zapped him and took his sense away. He froze in midair, mere inches from her face.

Her lush lips beckoned. He bet they'd be just as soft and pliant as he'd imagined. Up close, her skin was smooth and scrubbed clean of makeup—so different from the women he usually went for—making her look fresh and even more beautiful. His gaze locked with her tentative one. He watched as, incredulously, apprehension lifted. Her eyes grew soft with desire. And he knew—just *knew*, judging from what he knew about women, which was a lot—that she was feeling that same intense rush, too.

Something tickled his shins. The one-eyeballed cat had wrapped itself around his legs, and was weaving its lithe body in and around. He swooped it up and held it to his chest, stroking down its back.

The diversion was just as well. In his heart, he knew Meg was not the kind of woman who would go for fun and fooling around without commitments, which was all he could offer. And out of respect for her brother, he would never ask it of her.

He'd come here to thank her and yes, to sweet-talk her into coming to camp, but he was the one who had ended up getting reeled in by *her.* She was an intriguing mix—savvy businesswoman, kindhearted animal rescuer, unpretentious beauty—all of which spelled trouble with a capital T.

"Thanks again for helping me out tonight," he said, lowering the cat and forcing what he hoped was a pleasant, platonic smile. Then he gathered the take-out trash and headed to the door before he got himself into real trouble.

CHAPTER 7

"Did something terrible happen?" Ben's sister Samantha asked him from behind the bridal shop cash register. "Because I never thought I'd see the day *you'd* walk into a bridal shop." She opened her mouth and lifted a hand to cover it in feigned shock. "And are those flowers? Wow, you really have gone off the deep end."

"Relax, Sam, I'm here on business."

"Carrying a bunch of daisies?"

"Just tell me where Meg is."

"Upstairs with the last client. Want me to take a message? Or perhaps I could put those flowers in water while you wait?" Samantha scrunched up her cute nose, as she'd done hundreds of times before when she was giving him grief.

Ben crossed his arms. "You're not treating me very nicely considering I'm your favorite big brother."

"All my big brothers are pains in the asses, thank you very much. But come to think of it, let me get you some coffee from the back. I may need your help this weekend. I'm bringing Harris home."

"Harris, the cute guy who just got into Princeton Law?"

"Yep. Cute, funny, nice. Graduated from Brown. And his family's been in the Boston area since the *Mayflower*. Everyone's going to love him."

Well, that was a relief. Because everybody hated the boyfriend from last summer. He hoped this guy was more mature and treated her better. She'd spouted off his credentials a little too quickly, which worried him. The fact that he had an Ivy League pedigree didn't mean squat if he was an a-hole. But he didn't dare say any of that out loud. "Well, I'm looking forward to it."

"And I don't want you three to give him a hard time. Okay? Promise?"

Ben raised his hands in a *who me?* gesture. "You know I'm not the one you have to worry about. I'm always charming."

Sam rolled her eyes. "Talk to Brad. For me. Please." Brad, their oldest brother, considered himself their father figure after having navigated them all through their teen years when their parents died and their Grandma Effie struggled with health issues. He was also the brother Sam butted heads with the most.

Ben tousled his baby sister's dark curly hair like he'd been doing since she was three. "Okay, Squirt, no problem."

"I think there's a little vase on Meg's desk. Can you check while I finish this last order?" she turned back to the computer screen on the counter. "What are you doing here, anyway? Did you just finish a shift at Mirror Lake Community?"

"Nope. Just drove in from Hartford for a night shift." Ben walked over to an old desk that was painted a bright pinkish-purple color, heavy as a horse and twice as wide, positioned near the window. He knew it was Meg's not only because of the crazy color, but also because only she would have photos of herself not only with her nieces and nephews, mother and sister, but also with a group of seniors from assisted living, the library committee, and the theater preservation society.

Amid the paperwork, which was arranged neatly in stacks, there was a round canister full of pens, painted by a child, and a candy bar.

Snickers. He snagged an antique white vase with a rose painted on it, and took it through the door behind the glass counter to the giant storeroom that had a little kitchenette in the corner where he filled it up with water. When he came back, Meg was escorting a very pregnant woman to the front of the store.

"Please send me a photo, okay?" Meg asked.

"I will. Thank you for helping me find a dress that doesn't make me look like a beached whale and also fits even though I'm seven months pregnant."

"You're going to look radiant, Hailey. Just like you look now. I'm so happy for you."

"I can't wait to wear this dress. It makes me feel beautiful. And that's saying a lot when you can't even see your feet anymore."

"Let me help you get this to your car."

The woman took the dress instead. "I can manage fine. Wish me luck."

"I will, but I know you're going to have an amazing day. And an amazing life."

Ben watched the woman hug her tightly and even wipe a tear from her eye. When Meg returned, he was sitting behind her desk pretending to be very interested in her tin of breath mints.

"What are you doing here?" she asked, a telltale blush creeping up her neck. It was strangely pleasing to find her so affected by him.

"He brought you flowers," Sam said, being her bratty little-sister self. "And I'm done for the day. Okay if I leave? I've got a hundred things to do to get ready for the weekend."

"It's only Tuesday," Ben said

"Saturday will be here before you know it," Sam replied, making a face at her brother.

"See you tomorrow," Meg said. "Have a good one." As Sam walked out the door, with the bell tinkling overhead, Meg said to Ben, "I see that you bring out quite a bit of maturity in her."

He laughed. "What's an older brother good for except to torment?"

Meg lowered herself into one of the pair of cushioned chairs across from her desk. "She's a hard worker. You should be proud of her."

"I am. She's grown up a lot in the past year. Had to after Kevin died."

Her gaze flicked briefly to his, showing the slightest acknowledgement of the pain that came with the loss of a brother. She knew it like he knew it. In that one thing, they would be bonded forever.

Meg absently rotated the daisies toward her and fingered their petals gently. "First cheeseburgers and now flowers. Where'd you get these?"

"Picked them."

Her eyes widened in surprise. "Since when do you have time to pick wildflowers?"

He shrugged. Actually, he didn't have time but he'd made time. Scrambled around some field while getting bug bitten and muddy. "I remembered that open meadow over on the east side of the lake where they grow like crazy." He remembered that long ago, she used to pick them by the armfuls. Make daisy necklaces and crowns and carry them back in big batches for her mother.

"Well, I do love daisies, and thanks for going through the trouble. But I'm sorry, I'm still not going to that camp with you."

She looked calm and resolute. He smiled. "Can't blame a guy for trying." Truth was, he'd done the daisies on impulse. He didn't really know why. Frankly, he was enjoying just sitting here talking with her. "The shop looks good. It suits you, this job." He turned to look at a large white-painted wooden post covered with photos of happy brides in their gowns.

It was her turn to shrug. "We have big plans for this place."

"Such as . . . ?"

"For starters, ripping up this old rug and refinishing the floor in a glossy dark hardwood. Putting some dramatic color on the walls and using a new system of displaying the dresses. We've stopped using the old runway in the back and replaced it with an entire room upstairs where the brides can see themselves in their gowns. Unless, of course, a bride isn't able to climb the stairs."

"That's great about the shop but I was talking about how you interacted with that woman. She was really appreciative."

"It's fun helping people look and feel amazing on one of the most important days of their lives."

"I'm sure that's not easy, pleasing everyone."

Meg leaned over and unwrapped the Snickers, broke it in half, and offered the other half to him. He took it with a nod of thanks and immediately bit off a large chunk. "No, especially when everyone has a certain picture in their head of how they want to look on their wedding day."

All he knew was how she looked now. *Hot.* She wore a narrow skirt and a flowing blouse, and she'd kicked off her shoes when she'd gotten up to turn the sign on the door to Closed and bolt the lock. "Guys aren't like that," he said. "They don't spend a lot of time thinking about their wedding days."

"Don't you ever envision yourself getting married?"

"I'm not cut out for marriage." *Ne-ver. With a capital N.*

"How do you know that?"

He shrugged. "Too much trouble."

"I'm the one with divorced parents, with the father who's moved to Brazil with his new wife and kids, and you're the one with the big happy family. I'm surprised you feel that way."

"I love my family. Love my little nieces and nephews. But all my energy's channeled into my career right now." Truth was, he'd lost his parents, his best friend, and more recently, a brother. He never wanted to risk putting his heart on the line for another loss, which would surely kill him. It was better to channel his energy into being the best doctor he could be.

Meg perused a paper on the desk in front of her. "Would you mind reaching into my top left drawer and handing me my stapler?" she asked.

Ben took another bite of chocolate, opened the drawer, and handed her the stapler. But something else caught his eye. A large red sewing tomato stuck full of pins, but the pins were arranged in a very unusual way. He couldn't resist pulling it out.

Meg stopped stapling, stood up, and tried to snatch it away from him. "Hey, put that back."

He held it just out of her reach. "Why do you own a sewing tomato with the word 'FEAR' on it? Stuck full of pins around a—what is this?" He examined the thick black line drawn in marker down one of the seams, between the "FE" and the "AR."

She followed him and tried to grab it back. "It's—private."

"Oh, come on." His gaze held hers, which he read as part embarrassment, part reluctance. "You tell me your secrets, I'll tell you mine." He waggled his eyebrows to bring home the point.

"It's not a secret. Just a personal story. When Alex and I first took over the business from my Grandma Gloria, she knew how frightened I was. I was fresh out of college, it took a ton of money, and I wasn't sure if staying here in Mirror Lake was the right thing. So one day she gave me her sewing tomato, but she put a little twist on it."

"And what was that?"

"Read the ribbon."

Ben picked up a thin ribbon attached to a tiny stem. "POKE FEAR IN THE ARSE." He laughed. "I always did like that woman."

"So when I feel especially worried about something, I try to remember that."

"It's your voodoo tomato." He tossed it lightly into the air.

"Exactly. So what's your story?"

"My Grandpa Rushford gave me a kid's kaleidoscope before I left for college."

"Interesting gift," she said, waiting until the tomato was airborne, grabbing it, and shutting it back in the drawer.

"I was having a tough time after my parents died." And after her brother died, but he didn't mention that. "He wanted me to keep moving forward, keep looking to the future. He said to look in it and each day would be exciting and different."

"That's actually a great gift."

"My grandfather really understood me. My grandmother got cancer around the time my parents died, so we went to live with Effie instead of with them. But he kept an eye on all of us. Even loaned me five hundred dollars to buy my Mustang."

"You mean when you had it towed out of that farmer's field?"

He couldn't help smiling at the memories. "It had been in a flood and every single part needed to be rehauled."

"And now it's a beauty."

Their gazes caught across the desk. "Sure is," he said with a little smile, but he wasn't talking about the car. "Their house on Forest Glen is about to be torn down."

"Over by the funeral home?"

Ben nodded. "It's been rezoned for business and for the past fifteen years or so, there've been about three or four local companies in there."

"Oh, I'm sorry to hear that," Meg said.

"My grandfather's office was built into a wing of the house and I want to see it one last time."

"Aren't you afraid it'll be . . . different?"

"Yeah. But part of me still wants to go."

"Sometimes you have to revisit the past to put it to rest," she said pointedly.

"Yet sometimes it's better to leave well enough alone."

"*Touché*. So how'll you decide what to do?"

"I'm going to try and look at it from the perspective of what my grandfather would want me to do. I'm not sure yet what I'll decide. But maybe seeing it one last time would be a good bridge as I move forward into my own career."

Meg snatched up the last bite of candy, popped it into her mouth, and tossed the wrapper into the trash. "Speaking of moving forward, I've got to get going," she said.

"Now that we've told each other our secrets, I feel so close to you," Ben said with a wink. "You're sure you won't consider being my date for next weekend?"

As she shook her head, her dark silky hair fell over her shoulders. He could imagine its smooth waterfall texture between his fingers. "Too complicated."

"No, not complicated. Easy. I'm easy. You'd have fun."

"Is everything always about fun with you?"

"In a nutshell, yes. I don't do relationships."

"Maybe you should say that again, this time with more conviction." She laughed. "You're twenty-eight years old. You've never tried one?"

"Not my thing. But at least I'm up-front and honest about it."

She snorted. "You know, Ben, that's the typical playboy excuse. You say, 'I don't do relationships,' and because you're young and single, I bet that gets everyone off your case, doesn't it?"

"I *am* in the prime of my life." He flashed a grin at her. Better for her to think he was on the asshole side of the scale than to know the real reason he would never risk starting a relationship with her.

"Well, good luck with that, Mr. Prime. Nice chatting with you, but I'm still not coming to camp." He felt a little surprised. It was unusual for him to get rejected, and he thought for sure she'd cave. He'd said it sarcastically, but he wasn't really kidding when he said he'd felt close to her. He'd never told anyone about that kaleidoscope for fear they'd laugh. "Lock the door on your way out, okay?" she said, flicking off the lights, closing the door, and leaving him alone in the dimly lit room.

CHAPTER 8

Meg rang Alex's doorbell three times before her husband Tom answered the door. It was the last Tuesday evening of the month, time for book club, and Meg was ready to get her mind off the recent turmoil Ben was causing and just kick back with her friends. "Come in," Tom said. The big burly guy was out of breath, his Mirror Lake P.D. T-shirt sopping wet, and he held a naked two-year-old under one arm.

"Hey, Jacob," Meg said, ruffling the toddler's wet hair. He held a toy airplane in one hand and was whizzing it around while making puttering noises. She bent down to his eye level and smiled. "Who had the bath, Jacob, you or your daddy?"

The toddler grinned and ran his airplane up her arm.

"I'd love to chat but I've got two more kids waiting for baths upstairs," Tom said.

Over his shoulders, Meg surveyed the usually picked-up house. Chinese take-out cartons littered the table, along with plates and primary-colored sippy cups. Toys lay scattered along the carpet.

"I can help you get them ready for bed," she offered as Tom headed back up the staircase.

He turned around, a pang of concern furrowing his brow. "I'm all right. Alex needs you more."

"That sounds ominous."

Tom set Jacob down at the top of the stairs and watched him streak back into the bathroom, letting out a bevy of giggles. "She's going stir-crazy lying around all day."

"I heard that," Alex said from the family room couch. Their friend Olivia was there, picking up toys and throwing them into a straw basket in the corner.

"What happened in here? Did you fire Rosa?" Meg asked, giving Alex a peck on the cheek and placing a paper bag full of romance novels from the library book sale at her side.

"Ha, ha, very funny," Alex said "Her sister just had a baby and she took two weeks off to help. She arranged to have a friend of hers come starting tomorrow. I'm sorry for the mess."

"Don't worry about it. That's why we came early to clean up before book club." Meg sat next to her on the couch and asked, "How are our babies doing?"

"They are fine but their mother is bored to tears, and I'm dying for adult company," Alex rubbed her large belly. "Thanks for the books, by the way. Now tell me what's been happening with Ben since the dinner."

"Oh, not much," Meg hedged. "I'd rather talk about you." Any mention of Ben was bound to wield a bunch of head shaking and piteous looks, and she didn't want to set herself up for either.

"Honey, I can't drink or have sex," Alex said. "So spill."

Meg sighed. Better to get it over with because they would just find out anyway. Small town, no secrets. "Ben asked me to be his pretend date again this weekend. At Camp Mohican. For kids with diabetes."

Olivia handed Alex a glass of water and pretended to choke. "Wow, a guy who only asks for pretend dates. Sounds like a winner to me."

"Can't you be a little more charitable? He is your brother-in-law," Meg said.

"And I love him," Olivia said. "He's a smart man. Except where women are concerned."

"Excuse me," Alex said to Meg. "I thought you resolved to end this after the one time. You went out with the new vet last week and you said it was fun. I thought the plan was to kick the Ben habit for good."

At the sound of a lawn mower, all three women looked out the window. Ben Rushford was pushing one through the grass. *With his shirt off.*

Meg swallowed at the sight of healthy, bare-chested male striding though the big yard. Especially *that* particular male. "I told him no."

"Wait. I missed something. Why'd you do that?" Olivia asked.

Alex didn't hesitate to answer. "Because she's being wise. Ben's a heartbreaker."

Olivia shook her head in protest. "Everyone told me that about Brad, too, and I took a chance. Maybe Meg should, too."

"She needs to move on," Alex said firmly. "This crush has been going on for years."

"What better way to move on than to let herself explore the possibilities?" Olivia asked.

"She's not a fling-haver," Alex said. "And Ben is. I see disaster on the horizon."

Meg sat up straighter on the couch and finally got a word in. "Stop talking about me like I'm not here. Even if I wanted to go to the camp, I can't. My mom needs taking care of, plus I have to be at the shop on Saturday. It's our busiest day and it's not fair to leave Gran and Samantha there by themselves."

"If you have the opportunity to spend time with Ben, you should," Olivia said. "Then you'll know for sure whether you actually *like* him or if you've just built him up to be larger than life. Maybe your sister could help your mom for a day or two. And I can pitch in at the shop this Saturday."

"Thanks," Meg said, "but it's crazy enough with Alex gone. I should be there to take care of stuff." She debated mentioning the most important reason. "And, to be honest, there's something else."

"What is it?" Olivia and Alex asked together.

"My mother still harbors ill feelings about Ben, even after all these years. She'd be upset if she knew I was going somewhere with him. Especially overnight." Even though she was an adult who made her own decisions regardless of whom they pleased or didn't please. It was just that this was . . . Ben. And Ben was a hot-button topic in her family, to be avoided at all costs.

Except maybe it was time to change that.

Alex grabbed Meg's hand. "Oh, honey. She still blames him after all this time? He was just a kid."

Meg shrugged. "I suppose she feels like he was a bad influence. He used to get beer, and he and Patrick and their friends used to go drink it at the quarry all the time."

"But Ben didn't go that night," Olivia said. "Patrick went by himself and Ben found him later."

"She's never bought that story," Meg said. "She thinks Ben said that to get himself off the hook." But Meg knew in her heart—not because she had objective evidence—that Ben didn't go out with her brother that night. She'd never doubted him. No matter what her mother and sister chose to believe.

"Ben may come across as not having a care in the world, but it's an act," Olivia said. "Brad's told me he went through a lot after your brother's death. Pulling him out of the water was traumatizing."

Meg flinched a little. Olivia saw and put an arm around her. "Oh, honey, I'm sorry to bring this up."

"I'm all right," Meg said. "It's just that when I think of what Ben must have gone through that night—" She shook off the memory. "At least you both can talk about it. My family pretends it never happened."

"I just thought of something a little scary." Alex sat up on the couch. "Do you think Ben's stayed away from you all this time *because* of what happened to Patrick?"

Meg shook her head, even as a traitorous flush exposed the mayhem beneath. Ben didn't need reasons to stay away from her. It was obvious she wasn't his kind of woman, regardless of what had happened in the past. "That's—crazy." The words sounded raspy and weak. Thinking of her brother made her emotional, and she'd learned over the years to hold the feeling in until it gradually dissipated. There was really no one she could talk to about him, share fond memories, or her pain. Her family had sealed off the topic for discussion long ago. Even now, her mother could barely tolerate hearing his name. In some ways it was as if he'd never existed.

"Not so crazy," Olivia said.

"You've got to talk to Ben," Alex said slowly.

Panic and horror made Meg's voice raise an octave. "Impossible. How can you ever talk about something like that?" Until last week, she'd barely been able to carry on a conversation with him. The circumstances of their disastrous dinner had changed that, but this was a whole other level of openness she couldn't even fathom.

"When you love someone you can," Olivia said. "Love makes it possible."

Alex patted Meg's hand. "It might seem impossible. But it just might be necessary. For both of you."

"Especially for him," Olivia said. She glanced at her watch. "Sorry to tell you this, ladies, but we have five minutes to do something else that's necessary."

"What would that be?" Alex asked.

"Help you change," Olivia said. "You are not wearing those awful sweats to book club."

"Nothing fits me. Everything looks terrible."

"Get me a pretty blouse," Olivia commanded Meg, who rose and headed to the back bedroom. "And something with a forgiving waistband."

As Meg dug through Alex's closet, she tried to digest their conversation. *What ifs* rankled her. What if all this time, the remorse Ben might feel over her brother's death *had* kept him away? How could such a thing ever be made right? There was no bringing back the past.

Only dealing with it.

Meg found a striped pink and white tailored blouse. On closer inspection, it was one of Tom's shirts, but it might be just the thing. "I found something!" she called out to Alex. "This is going to make you feel like a new woman."

Confrontation and talking honestly was work for people with far more courage than Meg could muster in three lifetimes. She could tell by the way her gut seized up and her hands went cold with terror just by thinking about it that her nervous system wholeheartedly agreed.

Yet unanswered questions swirled around her head, long ago brushed into the corners of her mind and covered with cobwebs. Letting them out now would only lead to disaster. If only she could clear up the past as easily as they could freshen Alex's sour mood with a brand new shirt. She'd vowed to be braver and take more risks, but this seemed out of her league. Because sometimes what you wanted the most was the one thing you were most afraid to get.

⋅•◦•⋅

"Goodness," Grandma Gloria said, walking into Alex's house holding a covered cake pan in one hand and fanning herself with the other. "Benjamin Rushford is out there with no shirt on. Reminds me of a photo of Prince Harry a tabloid ran a while back. But he was in Vegas, not cutting the grass."

"I don't think Harry ever has to cut the grass at Buckingham Palace," Ted Lawrence, the owner of Mona's Bakery said as he followed Gran in.

Meg greeted Ted and Gran and her grandmother's best friend, Effie, the Rushford siblings' maternal grandmother. Meg tried not to look out the door but she couldn't resist sneaking a peek at Ben's tanned body and amazing pecs that were perfect—not too pumped up, but definitely not the muscles of a bookish man who was on call all the time and never worked out. If only shutting the door could shut him out of her thoughts.

"Gran," she said, "you're all dressed up."

"Why, of course I am," she said, handing Meg a heavy box. "It's a special occasion. Little Prince George's birthday was just a few weeks ago. I brought the Royal Doulton to celebrate!"

Effie, who sported a hot pink running suit and white tennies, winked. "We heard Alex was a little blue, so we wanted an excuse to have a little party with book club tonight."

"I can hear you," Alex said darkly.

Meg helped her grandmother take off her bright blue suit jacket and matching hat with a blue chrysanthemum that covered her red hair. When Meg took them to the closet, Ted was still looking out the window. He nudged her and whispered, "Mmm-hmm, those Rushford brothers are fine. Too bad they don't ever cross the street to play on the other side."

"Sorry, Teddy," Meg said, giving him a sympathetic squeeze. As a gay man who dressed like Usher and sounded like Chris Rock, Ted sympathized more than anyone with her love life. He once told her it was harder to find eligible gay guys in a small town than it was for people to believe he owned the bakery and was not a kindly middle-aged woman with flour all over her apron named Mona.

"Hey, girls," Ted said, moving into the family room to hug Olivia and Alex. "How're the preggies doing? Oh my God, Alex, baby, you've expanded exponentially since you've stopped working."

Alex made a face as she lifted her cheek for his kiss, then playfully smacked his well-muscled arm. "You say another word about my size and I'll start nasty rumors about your cinnamon buns."

"My buns are just as fine as ever, thank you. Right, Grannies?"

"Everyone knows your buns are sweet, Theodore, just like you," Effie said.

Grandma Gloria approached. "You do look very handsome tonight, Ted. I especially like your diamond earrings. I think Princess Kate has a pair like that." She pulled her glasses down to peer better through her bifocals. "I read that if a man has his right earlobe pierced, it means he's gay. If he has both, does that mean he's bi?"

"Gran!" Meg said.

Ted chuckled. "Granny, the one-earring thing was from the nineties. Now guys can do whatever they want. I wear two because I'm double special. And just for the books, I only like guys."

"This dessert I brought is guaranteed to work on your love life regardless of who you like," Grandma Gloria said, taking the lid off a rectangular Pyrex container. "It was the only thing I could stomach during those first few months when I was pregnant."

"What's in it, Gran?" Meg asked.

"Well, there's a crust. Then there's a cream cheese layer, a layer of chocolate pudding, and Cool Whip. It's divine."

"Oh, I love that dessert!" Meg exclaimed.

"Is that the dessert with the weird name?" Olivia asked.

"Better Than Sex Cake," Gloria said proudly. "I'll let you all be the judge."

"I prefer to call it *pudding dessert,* Gloria," Effie said.

"Let's have some right now," Teddy said, then whispered to Meg, "Is it an aphrodisiac?"

Meg suppressed a giggle. "I heard that, young man," Gloria said. "And the answer is yes. People who partake of it have seen that particular effect."

"Gran, you are so full of it." Meg helped pass out the pieces of dessert her grandmother cut.

"Sometimes the unexpected does happen, dear," Gloria said, waving a knife. "If you let loose a little, life might just surprise you."

She wished she could let loose a little, but at her age, what could surprise her? So far she'd learned that sex was good but not great, men were mostly immature, and she wasn't getting any younger. At least the cake could take her mind off her man problems. "Gran, what are you doing?" Meg asked.

"I'm cutting a piece for Ben."

"Ben who?" Meg asked, her eyes narrowing.

"Why, Rushford, of course," Gran said. "I invited him in for dessert just now."

As if on cue, the door opened. Ben stood there all lean and tanned and—wait, was his chest *glistening?*

Meg did a double take. Normally she wasn't into sweaty sheens but his was—spectacular. Oh, holy hills and valleys! And hard muscles with just the right amount of hair and six-pack lines so deep a woman could trace them. With her tongue.

"Oh, sorry," he said. "I was looking for Tom and I thought book club was meeting out back on the deck."

Gran strode over to Ben with singular purpose and snagged him by the elbow. There would be no quiet sneaking away with her in charge. "We were just serving dessert. You must join us. In fact, you're welcome to stay for our book discussion, too."

"Thanks, Gloria, but I was just helping Tom with his lawn and I've got to—"

"Why, dear, is that lemonade you're drinking?"

Ben looked at the tall glass in his hand. "Some nice neighbor handed it to me because she thought I was hot."

"I'm sure she did," Meg said, giving him the eyeball.

"Before Alex and Tom moved in, I lived here for thirty years and no one ever brought *me* lemonade," Effie said.

"That must be from our neighbor, Helene," Alex said. "She hits on any Rushford brother in sight."

Gloria pushed a piece of dessert into Meg's hands. "Will you hand this to Ben, dear?"

Ben took the plate Meg offered, flashing her a wide smile that shot straight down south of the equator. "It's delicious, thank you," he said, taking a bite.

"It's called Better Than Sex Cake," Gloria said.

Meg suppressed a choke, but Ben just grinned. "Well, they sure named this right."

Meg rolled her eyes. She couldn't believe what a kiss-up he was.

"Well, Benjamin," Gloria said, "I don't know what kind of girls you've been dating, but maybe you should try a girl from Mirror Lake."

"Grandma!" Meg said.

"Well, it is, after all, only dessert," Gloria said. "But it can help move things along, if you know what I mean." Gran winked at Ben. Meg fought the urge to hand her grandmother back her Queen Elizabeth hat and send her royal behind back on her way.

"Gosh, I hope not," said Alex. "I just ate a whole piece. Don't tell Tom." She set her plate down on the coffee table. "By the way, Ben, Meg tells us you need someone to go with you to diabetes camp this weekend."

Meg tossed her friend a look that shot daggers. The members of this book club, composed of her closest family and friends, were throwing her to the wolves.

"I think she'd be great with the kids," Ben said. "It would be fun."

"Oh, Meg would never go," Gran said. "She hates getting all mucky and mosquito-bitten."

"That's not true, Gran." Meg had to stand up for herself if no one else was going to. "I love the outdoors." *Not*, but there was no way she was going to sound like a wuss.

"Why, remember that time your parents took you camping when you were ten? You went potty in the woods and accidentally sat on a wasps' nest."

"That was a freak accident," Meg said. "Hardly enough for me to say I hate camping."

"So that's why every time we'd go for a hike in Girl Scouts you brought a can of Raid," Olivia said.

"And Amazon-jungle-strength bug spray," Olivia said.

"Fine, you all have a good laugh," Meg said. "So I'm not a risk taker."

"I don't know about that," Ben said, displaying that mega-watt grin again. "She dances a mean cha-cha."

"What did you say?" Olivia asked.

"Meg does *not* dance," Alex said.

"Oh, yes, she does," Ben said. "She's recently taken it up. And she has great potential, I'd say, to be a *rip*-roaring good dancer."

Meg frowned and tried to summon outrage, but when she looked at Ben, he was chuckling at his own joke, and his eyes were dancing with laughter. Her heart gave a little involuntary squeeze because when he smiled, he was hands-down the most handsome man she'd ever met. And the fact that he'd stood up for her in front of her friends made her tingle all over.

"So why don't you want to go to camp?" Ted asked.

"Because—" Why *didn't* she want to go to camp? Ben's questioning look accosted her. *Because you'll be there,* she thought to herself. *Because it's an entire weekend in your presence.*

Wait a minute. Weren't those reasons to *go*?

"I—um—the shop is super busy. We've got appointments booked all day Saturday." When she glanced at Ben again, he was innocently drinking his lemonade. She noticed something stuck on the bottom of the glass—a sticky note—and plucked it off. "It's a phone number."

"Let me see that." Ben grabbed for it but she held it out of his reach.

"That little hussy stuck her number on the bottom of your lemonade," Meg said.

"Got to admire a woman with skills," Ben said.

"Oh, she's skillful, all right," Meg said. "At getting her hooks in gullible men who go for her type."

"Maybe she just needs a handyman," Ben said, holding back laughter.

"The only handyman she's looking for is a *randy* handyman," Gran said.

"Gran!" Meg said. It was a full-time job policing her grandmother, who of course ignored her, especially since everyone else was laughing at her joke.

"You haven't had a piece of dessert, dear. Here's an extra-big one." Gran made the huge mistake of passing it to Ben to give to her.

"Here you go, Meggie." He dropped his voice low. "Extra big. Just what you need, being as you're a little on edge."

"I am *not* on edge," Meg said with a glower.

"Do we have to talk about the book?" Ted asked as Gloria took a seat on the couch and Ben and Meg sat on dining room chairs that were pulled up for extra seating. "It was depressing as hell."

"It was very acclaimed," Olivia said with just a tad of poorly disguised outrage. She'd spent years as a self-help editor in New York and had just recently hit the bestseller lists with her book for people who unexpectedly found themselves in charge of raising a child. "You didn't like it?"

"Did you?" Meg asked.

"The writing was crisp and sharp. The insights were deep." Olivia's editor brain ticked off the good points.

"And the story sucked," Alex said. "There was no hope, no chance for happiness."

"It made me want to gouge my eyes out with a pencil, but I refrained," Ted said. "Damned dismal, though."

"What was the book about?" Ben asked, digging into his dessert.

Olivia was happy to recap. "The heroine, Fannie, went through a lot before finding love. But her lover Alfonso deceived her. Then they both died, Alfonso because Fannie killed him and Fannie of a broken heart. On death row."

"Optimistic," Ben said.

"You're missing the point," Olivia said. "Fannie drove Alfonso away. She let herself imagine the worst before they even got started. She was suspicious and untrusting."

That got Meg's wheels churning. Or maybe it was the fact that Ben had casually draped his tanned arm around her chair and all of her insides were tumbling from his nearness, from his summer-grass-and-sun smell to the tiny smile he still wore and hey, was that damn dimple peeking out again? Okay, the book wasn't ideal, and the weekend ahead wasn't either. It involved dirt and mosquitoes and other dangers, and Ben certainly wasn't inviting her for herself, but this was an opportunity—probably the last she'd ever have—to be with him for an entire weekend. That was the kind of fantasy she'd only imagined in her wildest dreams.

Before the elevator, she'd decided to give him up, but now she felt on the verge of something too tantalizing to pass up, likely the last chance she'd ever have to really get to know him again. She was coming to realize that the attractive, fun Ben with the great sense of humor he wielded so easily for a crowd might just be a front for a deeper, more complicated person. Meg might be considered sweet but she wasn't naïve, and she knew the looks he gave her were the kind a man gave a woman he desired. She wasn't the type he usually went for but she wasn't without her charms. Maybe it was time she turned them on *him*.

She had to stop watching her life unfold from the sidelines. She had to get in the game and muck it up, or she'd be alone and crazy like the heroine of this dumb book.

Poke fear in the arse, Grandma Gloria would say.

"While we have you here, dear," Gloria asked Ben, "what do you think of books that end badly?"

Everyone waited for his answer, but no one so intently as Meg.

"I'm all for a well-written novel," Ben said. "If it ends badly, it ends badly. As long as the protagonists tried their hardest." He paused a minute and let a crooked grin settle on his face. "And if there're some kick-ass FBI agents, some gratuitous violence and sex, and a couple of explosions, all the better."

Meg rolled her eyes. "And guys complain about chick flicks." Suddenly a giant lump, like one of her cats' hairballs, formed in her throat. Everyone told her she was insane to have liked him for so long. For years, she'd craved his attention, and she'd waited for him to notice her. Well, now he had. So what was she going to do about it?

"Thanks for the cake, Gloria. It's amazing." Ben set down his plate. "Now, if you all will excuse me, I'll get out of your way."

His gaze settled over Meg for an extra beat before he left the room to seek out Tom.

Was there the tiniest chance he felt what she did—a slow burn of desire spreading through her faster than a storm surge that had absolutely nothing to do with that godforsaken cake?

She must've been pretty flustered, because she suddenly felt Teddy shaking her arm and Effie saying, "What did you think about what Benjamin said, dear?"

"I—we all have to do our best, and where the cards fall, they fall. But I still always hope for a happy ending." She stood, still a little dazed. "I-I'll be right back."

Meg walked straight to the back of the house and out to the large deck, where Ben and Tom were sitting in the shade drinking beers. Ben had covered his spectacular pecs with a white shirt that said U Conn in blue letters.

"Hey, Meg," Tom said. "Any chance I could go snag a piece of that dessert?"

"Sure, but be careful. Gloria told everyone it was an aphrodisiac. So whatever you do, don't let Alex see you take a piece."

Tom headed for the house and Meg sat down on one of the cushioned deck chairs. "Listen, Ben, I—"

He held up a hand. "I know what you're going to say. You don't have to apologize for not going to camp. Look, if those administrators can't pick the best candidate based on skills, then maybe this job isn't the one for me. I was wrong to get you involved."

That was unexpected. "I was going to say thank you for sticking up for me back there. And . . . I want to come."

His dark brows shot up in genuine surprise. He set his beer down carefully on the deck as if he were buying time to digest her statement. "What changed your mind?"

Some depressing book club book. A damp sticky note on the bottom of a glass of lemonade. "My sister's coming into town and I can get her to stay with my mom. I'm free to go." At least, she was ninety-nine percent sure she would be.

He looked relieved. And something else, too, that made her heart skip again.

"Great," he said. "I'll pick you up at five on Friday." He held out his hand. "Can I have your cell? I want to give you my number, just so you have it."

Wow. He was giving her his number. And she didn't even have to make him lemonade to get it.

She handed him her phone, and he took it, his long, masculine fingers gliding over hers and lingering just a few seconds longer than necessary. He glanced up and she suddenly got lost in the warm chocolate color of his beautiful eyes.

"Did you finish your lemonade?" she asked as he punched in her number.

"It was a little too sweet for my taste. Did you finish your dessert?"

Weird question. "Yes, considering my gran is force-feeding it to everyone in the house."

"It was delicious," he said. "But definitely *not* a substitute for the real thing."

"Well, I guess you never know if you're going to like something unless you try."

His gaze wandered over her so slowly she felt a rush of heat flood full force into her face. She tried to look somewhere, *anywhere* else but in those dark, full-of-mischief eyes, but she was as inexorably drawn to them as the tide was to the beach. She was melting under the heat and fire of his intense perusal that made her feel stripped down to the bone.

Was he flirting with her? Warning her? Or just telling her there might be something better in her future if only she would dare to break free and look for it?

She was done waiting, pining, hoping. She was going to plunge into this headfirst, give it her all, and hang on for the wild, crazy ride.

CHAPTER 9

Ben pulled back the yellow ER curtain, the rings scraping on the metal rod with their familiar tinny sound, and assessed the woman sitting on the gurney. He looked up from his electronic tablet with a frown.

"You're not Mrs. Anderson. What are you doing here?"

"Surprise," his sister Samantha said tentatively, giving him a little wave. She pulled an oxygen sensor she'd obviously been playing with off her index finger, jumped off the gurney and into her big brother's arms. "I wanted to tell you in person." She gave him an expectant look that reminded him of when she was three and wanted him to play Barbies with her. Of course he couldn't refuse his baby sister then or even now that she'd just turned twenty.

"Tell me what in person?" Ben asked, frowning.

"Aren't you happy to see me?"

Ben set down his tablet on the gurney and wrapped his sister in a bear hug. "I'm always happy to see you. I'm just a little tense. We've got an accident on the way."

"I won't stay. But I have exciting news. Harris is coming in tonight—a day early. And Olivia told me to bring him over for dinner. Everybody's coming to meet him. Can you make it?"

A nurse walked up to them. "Dr. Rushford, Dr. Livingston wants you to check the sutures she just put in and that trauma will be here in five. We're setting up Room One now."

"Do we know how bad yet?" Ben asked.

"Twenty-three-year-old motorcycle victim, unconscious but with stable vital signs. Right arm pretty messed up, looks like it might need surgery."

"Call CT and the surgeon on call." He steered his sister toward the door.

"Effie told me you want to work here for good, not just moonlight," Samantha said as Ben walked her out.

"Hoping to. Look, I've got to drive out to the camp tonight for a special weekend we're running out there. What time is he coming into town?"

"Four or five-ish."

"I get off at five, but maybe I can leave a little early and stop by." He gave her a kiss on the cheek and was about to say good-bye when two paramedics wheeled a gurney through the glass doors. He caught a quick glance of a young guy strapped to a backboard with dark, matted hair and a big gash under his eye.

"He wasn't wearing a helmet and he was going way too fast over the inlet bridge," a paramedic said. "Nearly ran into a chicken truck. He swerved and rammed the guardrail and got thrown. Only thing that saved him was he landed headfirst in the lake. A fisherman waded in and pulled him out, lucky SOB."

A sharp gasp sounded beside him. Dammit, his sister had no business being here, witnessing stuff like this. She was clutching her stomach with one hand, her other hand covering her mouth.

"Gina." Ben flagged the nearest nurse. "Show my sister out, will you?"

A hand clamped his arm, forcing him to turn. Sam's eyes were filled with tears and she'd gone pale as the white fluorescent lights. "I-I know him. That's Spike."

Shit. Her dickbrain ex-boyfriend. Damn irresponsible biker dude really effed himself up but good. "Go with Gina," he barked, guiding his sister firmly to the nurse. Then he followed the gurney into the trauma room with the flock of carts, machines, and staff to do his best to save the idiot's life.

>—•—◦—•—<

"Dr. Manning, please come out of the rain." Meg opened the door and beckoned for the white-haired gentleman who was standing under the old brick building's overhang to enter her shop.

Let's just say it wasn't the first day he'd stood there, and she knew exactly what the retired surgeon was doing. Waiting for her grandmother to show up for work.

He was carrying a rolled-up newspaper, a cup of coffee, and something in a brown bag that had to be from the bakery next door. "Wasn't expecting the downpour. Forgot my umbrella today," he said with a touch of Irish lilt.

"I've got an appointment upstairs. Make yourself at home. There's more coffee in the back room." With that, she headed up the old wooden stairs to the second level where brides tried on gowns.

"Which dress do you like?" the soon-to-be-bride asked Meg. She looked at herself in a strapless dress in the massive mirror that covered the space of an entire wall between two large windows in the empty wood-floored try-on room. For the tenth time that day, Meg wished Alex were here. Alex, who was so tell-it-like-it-is, was ironically the master at subtly conveying to brides which dress was truly the most flattering. Meg was a little too afraid of hurting people's feelings. She tended to be more wishy-washy and sometimes that was a problem.

The bride's mother clearly preferred the last one her daughter had tried on. It featured a satin sleeveless top that was buttoned high on the neck, which completely covered the prominent eagle tattoo on the bride's right shoulder blade. But the dress, in Meg's opinion, was unflattering and conservative. And she could tell from the uptight body language vibes the bride was giving off that she wasn't thrilled with it either. Meg struggled with the best way to convey her thoughts without interfering.

"I have an idea," Meg said. She walked down the rack until she came to a dress. Her favorite one in the shop. Her dream dress, actually. It had a slim A-line shape, with a gown made of satin-faced silk georgette and a permanent bustle. But the best part of all, the entire top was made of delicate alencon lace with cap sleeves. Breathtaking.

She hesitated just one second, needing to remind herself, *This is not your special dress. It's here to be sold. So sell it!*

With that she pulled it down. "The upper back of this dress is lace," she said. "So it would cover the tattoo without completely blocking it."

The bride looked at her mother, then at Meg, then at the dress "It's gorgeous," she said.

"Feel free to try it on." Meg's business phone rang and she excused herself to answer it. "Hello, Bridal Aisle. May I help you?"

"Meg? This is Gina Stevens from the ER. Ben Rushford asked me to call you with a favor."

Her mind went amok, thinking of what could be wrong. Because there was no way he would call asking for help unless someone in their families were critically ill. The possibilities flipped through her mind like a slideshow. Her mother, the grannies, wait . . . the twins. Oh, God, was it the twins? "Is—something wrong?" she managed, her voice struggling to move past a clotted tangle of emotion.

"He needs someone to sit with his sister for a bit. I guess a young guy that was brought in by squad is her ex-boyfriend and she's pretty upset. We've tried to reach both of Ben's brothers and Olivia but everyone's tied up. Any chance you could come?"

Her first thought was *thank God that it wasn't family*, not that she wished any tragedy on anyone else, including the darkly sexy, brooding auto mechanic who unceremoniously dumped Sam last spring in the midst of a lot of family turmoil. He was the only ex-boyfriend of Sam's that Meg knew about from Mirror Lake.

Her second thought was she'd been on Ben's call list. But before she actually got excited about that, she realized he was just being logical, since Samantha had worked in her shop all summer, and of course Meg would do anything to help her. She couldn't read more into it than that. "What happened to the guy?"

"Motorcycle accident. He got thrown. I can't divulge details, except we're trying to locate family and apparently there isn't any."

The word *motorcycle* definitely identified him as Lukas Spikonos, who worked at Clinkers' Auto Repair and had fixed her beat-up old Chevy Malibu a few times. He'd been polite but dangerous looking, with black hair that flopped casually down his forehead, big dark bedroom eyes, and swarthy olive-colored skin, characteristics that together created an uncivilized impression, making him irresistible to ninety-nine percent of the females he came in contact with.

Basically, he was every parent's nightmare. And Sam's brothers had gone ballistic, especially Brad.

"I'm finishing up my last appointment before lunch," Meg said. "I'll be right over."

She hung up and turned to her bride, who was wearing the dress and looking at it from all angles in the mirror. "I love it," the bride said brightly. "What do you think, Mom?"

Her mother blinked back tears. "Tattoo or no, I've never seen you look so beautiful. That dress is the one. Get it and be happy."

"Thanks, Mom." The bride stepped off the dais to hug her mother.

"You look stunning," Meg said. She loved when her hunches worked out and had that result. She did a fist pump to herself in the stairwell as she ran downstairs to do the paperwork and at last ushered them out.

She was about to run out the back door when she noticed Dr. Manning sitting in one of the plush chairs near the front of the shop, propping up his feet on a low table full of bridal magazines. He looked settled in for the day.

One glance outside told her the rain was still coming down. She didn't have the heart to kick the old guy out. "I've got to run over to the hospital to sit with a friend for a little while. My gran will be here within the half hour. How would you feel about keeping an eye on the shop until she comes? That way I don't have to lock up and Gran will be able to get in."

"I'd be delighted to," he said as he sipped his coffee.

Somehow she knew he'd be fine with that, but she wasn't sure her gran would be. "Please tell her I'll call her from the hospital."

He held out the bag. "Better take some sustenance with you."

She peeked into the bag at a pumpkin muffin. That would do for lunch. "Thanks," she said.

"Tell me, young lady," he said. "Did your grandmother like the chocolates I sent her?"

Oh, the notorious chocolates. "Yes, she did. She shared them with our book club, and they were delicious." Actually, she'd refused to try them, saying she was beyond such shenanigans from old men, especially ones she'd never encouraged in any way.

"Perhaps sometime you could tell me what types of flowers she likes? Roses, perhaps? Carnations? Wildflowers?"

Meg wanted to tell him that if they weren't grown at Buckingham Palace or Balmoral he probably shouldn't bother, but she knew that wasn't the real issue. And that wasn't hers to divulge. "My grandmother isn't impressed by gifts, Dr. Manning, but by the things a person does. You know, character things. So maybe just be yourself?" She had no idea why she was pretending to be qualified enough to give this man dating advice about her grandmother, who hadn't gone on a date since her husband died forty years ago, and as far as she knew, never intended to. And judging by her own man troubles, she probably shouldn't be giving advice to anyone.

So she muttered a quick good-bye, grabbed her car keys, and ran out the back door.

⊱─━⊙━─⊰

Meg found Samantha in a corner of the half-empty ER waiting room clutching Kleenex and blowing her swollen nose. "Hi, Sweetie," Meg said, taking a seat beside her.

"H-how did you know I was here?"

"Your brother didn't want you to be alone." Meg rested a hand on her arm.

Samantha tensed beneath her touch so Meg didn't let her hand linger. "I-I'm all right by myself," Samantha said. "Please don't tell my family about this."

"I don't have much to tell. Your friend is hurt and you're upset. I'd like to help if you'd let me."

Sam shook her head, tears running through mascara. "You'll go running to Olivia and Alex and they'll tell my brothers. I told you I'm fine. You can leave now."

"First off, my friends and I have kept plenty of secrets darker than waiting in an ER for a guy some family members don't approve of. And second, I'm not here to judge you. I need your help with the bridal show too much. Okay?"

She shrugged. Meg would take that as a yes.

"Have they told you what's going on?"

"They can't—I'm not related. I even tried telling them I'm his girl-friend."

"Have they gotten a hold of his family?"

"He's got no family," Sam said. "His foster parents were elderly and they've been dead awhile. I had to tell the nurse he's allergic to penicillin. And I was just lucky I remembered him saying that. Spike's got no one."

"That's not true," Meg said. "He's got you."

She shook her head. "Spike was bad news. I've moved on. I'm only here because it's the right thing to do."

Still, she was shedding plenty of tears for a guy she purported not to care for. "Just a minute." Meg walked up to the information desk clerk, an elderly woman who was wearing a pink jacket with a badge that said *Hospital Volunteer*. "Excuse me, can we have an update on the condition of the young man who was in the motorcycle accident?"

"Are you family?" The steely-haired woman asked, tapping her pen impatiently against her hand.

"No."

"No family, no info. It's the rules." She glanced anxiously at her phone, which had lit up like a string of Christmas lights.

"But—she's his girlfriend." Okay, so it was just a little lie. "She gave valuable health information that could save his life—that he's allergic to penicillin. Doesn't that count for anything?"

Meg could tell from the unforgiving expression on the woman's face that it did not. "When he's out of surgery, I'll tell his post-op nurse the situation. It's the best I can do."

Not willing to accept defeat, Meg looked at her watch. Ben worked twelve-hour shifts. He was probably crazy busy, which was why he'd wanted someone to sit with his sister. But he had to have some clout. "Can I ask you to please page Dr. Rushford?"

"He's not the patient's doctor. You'll have to go through the main hospital operator and ask them to page him." Then she picked up her phone.

On the way back to her seat, Meg pulled out her cell, remembering she had Ben's number, but there was no answer. Then she called the hospital operator and had him paged. And just to be sure, she called the ER, too, and left a message.

"Any luck?" Sam asked.

"Not yet, but I haven't given up. Have you had anything to eat?"

"I don't want to leave in case Spike gets out of surgery."

"How about I go to the caf and pick us up a couple sandwiches and some coffee?"

"That sounds good. Thanks."

Meg rose, glad to be able to do something useful. But Sam's quiet voice drew her back. "He broke up with me because I wasn't ready to have sex with him."

"That sounds mature." *Oops*, that snuck out before she could rein it in. "Sorry. Couldn't help that."

"No, it's okay. But part of me thinks there's more to it. Almost like, he broke up with me to protect me—from himself."

Meg sat down again and held the girl's hand, and this time she didn't pull away. *Oh, to be twenty again*, Meg thought, *to be able in your angst to grasp at every straw.* But then, how many times over the years had she thought Ben might share her feelings, only to try to get close to him and be cruelly pushed away? It was a roller coaster ride she wouldn't wish on anybody. Hopefully Samantha would be smarter. And maybe she could help her see that. "What makes you think that?"

"Spike knows my brothers think he's not good enough for me. He hasn't gone to college, he's got a big reputation with women, and he has a lot of body art." She smiled an ironic smile. "But his nose ring was what really set Brad off."

Meg couldn't help but smile.

"I think he backed away because he knew we were from different worlds. Kind of like *West Side Story.*"

Meg did a mental eye roll. *And don't tell me, you're the one who understands him, truly understands, if only he'd realize it.* That thought had certainly crawled under the covers and kept her company through a lot of misguided years.

"Sam, there's a difference between protecting you from himself and being hurtful and uncaring." Like when he broke up with her right after her brother Kevin died last spring.

Sam shrugged. "It doesn't matter. I've met someone else. Oh, I forgot to tell him not to come!"

As she called her new boyfriend, who had the intimidating name of Harris Buckhorn, III, Meg tried Ben's cell again. And had him repaged.

"I heard you're going to camp with my brother," Sam said out of the blue.

Meg played it casual. "How'd you hear about that?"

She shrugged. "You've had a thing for him for a long time, haven't you?"

"Who? Me? *Never.*" Oh, shit. Was she that transparent? Sam leveled her a look that told her there was no use lying. "Maybe a little. Who else knows?"

"Everybody. Except maybe not him."

Meg winced. "Everybody?"

Samantha smiled sympathetically. "Sorry."

"Look, I'd never recommend liking someone who doesn't like you back. I think sometimes we're in love with an idea of someone, you know?" Which was exactly what she was going to find out this weekend, for better or worse. Her own sanity depended on it.

"For what it's worth," Sam said, "I am moving on. I cried my tears, wrote a whole lot of bad poetry, and now I want to be a person my family is proud of, who *I'm* proud of. I can't afford being dragged down by troubled, needy guys. Besides, Harris is the exact opposite of Spike. You'll have to meet him."

"That sounds very mature, Sam. A lot more mature than I was at your age."

As Meg went off in search of food and coffee, she wondered how coming to keep Sam company had turned into a confessional examination of her own love life.

Ben found Meg pounding on the vending machine in the corridor, fighting to get it to release her bad cup of coffee. She wore the same form-hugging black skirt she'd had on that day in the elevator, and simple wedges with cork bottoms that showed off her slim calves. He was struck by her simple beauty, and wished he had more than five minutes to talk with her. Actually he had less, because this was his bathroom break, too.

Placing his fist over the clear plastic shield near the cup, he gave it a good bang. The shield instantly rose up.

"It's about time you showed up," she said darkly, reaching for the coffee.

"It's a little hard not to, when seven people are paging me at once. I thought you'd keep my sister company, not raise a bunch of hell."

"No one will tell her anything because of those damn HIPAA rules. She's been waiting over two hours."

"Well, I fixed that. The kid's out of surgery and they got him to agree to let Sam visit him. He's going to be okay."

"Did you tell your sister that?"

"She's already gone to post-op to sit with him. And don't tell anyone I told you this, but he broke his left arm in two places and he's got a concussion. Maybe it'll knock some sense into him."

Meg released a heavy breath. "Thank God."

"Thanks for sitting with her." Before he knew what he was doing, he gave her an awkward hug. All his smooth moves seemed to go to hell in front of her.

"What was that for?" she asked, looking startled.

"I never thought a rabid pit bull would come disguised in such a pretty package." He paused. "And I wanted to tell you thanks."

"For what?"

"For dropping everything. Sam's my baby sister. We're pretty tight."

Meg smiled and took a sip of the gross-looking stuff. "Is that like saying you're her favorite brother?"

He shrugged. "Draw your own conclusions."

"Well then, you should know she doesn't want the family to know she's here. Can you respect that?"

His turn to let out a breath. "It'll be better for Brad's digestion if he doesn't know. But I don't like keeping secrets. Plus, that kid's bad news."

"Probably. But he's also alone."

"What other dirt did you dig up?"

Meg took a sip of coffee and tried not to make a face. "Well, I learned Sam's stubborn, like all Rushfords. Independent minded. And super concerned about doing the right thing for her family."

"She still feels bad about the bit of drama she caused last summer after Kevin died," Ben said. He looked down at a plastic bag Meg was carrying. "Is there food in there?"

"Sandwiches." She held out the bag while he dug in and grabbed a paper-wrapped sub. "By drama, do you mean changing her major, breaking up with this guy?" Meg asked.

"All teenage stuff. She's doing better this year."

"Forgive me for prying, but she worries me a little."

"You? Pry? What a shocker." He unwrapped the sandwich and took a bite. Turkey. His favorite.

"After Patrick died, in some ways I felt like I had to be the perfect kid. I didn't want to create any more tension in the family or cause any more pain. So I made my behavior . . . safe. Less risky. I'm not sure that's a great idea."

"Well, it'll be interesting to meet this Harris kid. But from all she's told us about his background and education, maybe less risky is good, you know?"

Ben's pager beeped. He unclipped it from his scrubs and read the display. "Break's over. Another trauma's coming in."

She shook her head in disbelief. "I don't know how you do it, being on the line between life and death all day."

"It does have its stresses. But when you help someone, it's the best feeling ever. I guess that's what keeps me going." He looked down at her coffee. "Speaking of keeping me going, that's just what I need for another couple of hours."

She held out the thick, sharp-smelling liquid. "It's dark and strong and stale. Help yourself."

He thanked her for the sandwich and said he had to go. As he took the cup, their hands touched, setting off a flurry of feelings—a heady mix of excitement, desire, and the much more scary feeling of wanting to stay and continue talking, to get to know her better. Things that tended to scare the shit out of him as far as women were concerned.

He took a swig of the concoction and made a face. Surely the bitter liquid would knock any of those unwanted feelings right out of his system. "Perfect," he said, fighting the urge to choke.

But he really wasn't talking about the coffee. Which made him worry that being with her at camp for an entire weekend wasn't such a great idea after all.

CHAPTER 10

"I just don't understand why you've got to help out at the camp this weekend. You'll miss visiting with your sister," Meg's mother said from the chair she'd pulled up to the kitchen table where she was clipping coupons.

"I'm sorry, Mom, but I promised." Meg sipped at the French vanilla tea her mom had handed her, trying to make small talk and not glance at the wall clock while she waited for her sister to come down from upstairs. It was nearly five o'clock, and she was lucky to have left the shop when she did, despite all the loose ends she'd left behind. Especially since she'd spent half the afternoon at the hospital with Sam. She'd have to race through telling Sheri about her mom's routine so she would have time to run back to her apartment, where she'd told Ben to meet her.

She punched a text to Ben into her phone: *At my mom's. Running late. Be there by 5:15 latest. Okay?*

Because it would be mortifying to have him pick her up here.

"Sheri! I've got to get going!" Meg yelled in the direction of the stairs. Like she had two other times already.

"You do too much charity work and I worry about you," her mom said, "especially with Alex gone. Why can't you just stay here and relax?"

"I think camp will be relaxing." Actually, *stressful* and *tense* were the first adjectives that came to mind. Her pulse kicked up and her stomach started doing acrobatics just thinking about it. In truth, she knew very little about what she'd be called on to do. *Survival training* came to mind but that sounded nonthreatening compared to dancing, eating seafood, and worse, being near Ben all weekend.

But just in case, she made sure that this time she brought stretchy clothes with lots of give.

Her mother put down the scissors to rest her hands and sighed. "Besides, I thought we girls could spend some quality time together. Go shopping, have lunch. You know, like the old days."

Meg's stomach felt hollow, and it was from more than lack of food. Shopping with her sister was painful because she was constantly trying to update Meg's clothing. Her sister was what Meg privately called a noisy vegan, constantly questioning ingredients in dishes—someone who couldn't even order a glass of wine without an inquisition about whether or not the clarifier was made from animal protein.

"Mom, she only lives in Greenwich. We should plan a weekend. Maybe we can stay overnight somewhere fun and shop."

A strange expression passed over her mother's face. Maybe disappointment that her daughters didn't gel like they did when Meg was two and Sheri was four. Or during those years when Meg admired everything her older sister did. When Sheri always had her back.

That was a long time ago, and lots had changed since then.

Her sister walked into the butter-yellow kitchen holding a gray tabby cat at arm's length. "Sparkles here, or is this Fred"—she lifted the cat in the air and stole a quick glance at its underbelly—"just coughed up a hairball right near my bed. Honestly, Meg, I don't think these animals are good for mom's health." She said it as if their mother were not sitting three feet away listening to every word. Sheri let the cat down and opened the fridge. Her eyes flicked around critically for a minute before she held up the coffee creamer. "And you shouldn't be drinking this junk, Mom, it's all fake. The only stuff that's marginally fit to eat in here is leftover pizza and that's a sodium nightmare."

"Don't you dare touch my hazelnut coffee creamer and I love cold pizza," Meg's mother said, sending Meg a wink. "And the kitties are great for my health. They soothe my nerves."

"Well, they grate on mine," Sheri said. "They even slept on my feet all night, and when I woke up, the fat one was curled around my head."

"Some people would think that's positively adorable." Meg bit down hard on the inside of her cheek to keep from laughing. She took her teacup to the sink and rinsed it. Under her breath she muttered, "*Normal* people, that is." To her sister, she said. "Would you help me load my car?"

"What, do you have, like, a heavy suitcase or something? I thought you were just going for the weekend."

Meg tipped her head toward the door. *Hello, Earth to Sheri.* She had to tell her a couple things that she didn't want her mom to hear. But her sister wasn't getting it.

Sheri sneezed. "Those damn cats. I need more allergy medicine from the pharmacy."

"Maybe you can pick up mom's prescription while you're there?" Meg smiled sweetly. Suddenly, an entire weekend away was looking better than a tropical vacation. Like a very rare kind of freedom.

Sparkles jumped into her mother's lap. Her mom started crooning to it and it began purring loudly. The second cat, an orange striped male, parked himself at her mother's feet and began crying loudly for attention.

"Just like those two sisters, aren't you?" her mom said, making sure to pet both at the same time.

As her mother tended the cats, Sheri pulled Meg into the small living room. "I want to discuss Mom's care with you. I don't think she's eating well and the yard's a wreck."

The familiar tension she always felt with her sister lay as thick around them as a blanket of fog. Meg tried not to roll her eyes. "She's eating fine. I've just had a busy week and we ordered out last night. When I get back on Sunday, I'll cook a great dinner, I promise. And the lawn is cut, it's just the back garden that's a mess. But you're welcome to pull a few weeds while you're here."

"I just hate seeing it like that. Remember when her garden was the street's pride and joy?"

Yeah. And remember when we were a whole family with a father and a brother who still had an entire life full of potential ahead of him?

Truth be told, Meg hated seeing the garden like that, too. Maybe she should be spending time working on that instead of living out a ridiculous Cinderella fantasy that was going to end all too soon.

"And the bathroom showerhead is leaking."

"Plumber's coming next week," Meg said. Maybe she didn't have the time to haul wheelbarrows full of dirt but she could pick up a phone. Ha. Score one for her.

"Why did you say you're going to camp, again?"

A rope of guilt snaked its way through her stomach and pulled tight. "I told you, it's for charity. I appreciate your staying with Mom this weekend." She cast an anxious glance out the window. She had to say her good-byes and get the sam-hell out before real disaster struck.

"You look a little dressed up for camp work."

She was not that dressed up. She had on khaki shorts and new hiking boots, with socks peeking out of the tops just for fun. And a white blouse and a scarf that looped loosely around her neck, and she'd pulled her hair back in a messy bun. The ensemble had Alex's stamp of approval for being casual but not over-the-top-trying-too-hard.

"I just wanted to tell you a few things and then I've got to get going." Meg pulled a piece of notebook paper folded in four out of her purse.

Her sister's brow shot up. "Wow, that's quite a list there, chickie."

"I just didn't want to forget anything," she said defensively. "Help Mom off with her clothes in the morning before she gets her shower.

She's too proud to ask for help but she's really super stiff in the mornings. I also try to at least start the coffee until her joints loosen up, but she generally fixes breakfast herself.

"Unhook her bra for her at night. And she's been wanting to walk the new trail around the lake, so if the weather's nice, you might consider doing that for fun. There's just that one prescription that I didn't have time to get, and the pharmacy closes at six tonight."

"Fine. I'll run out and get it. Anything else?"

Meg usually cleaned the house on Saturday mornings but she didn't want to ask Sheri to do that. She'd just take care of it on Monday. "I'll be back midafternoon on Sunday. Will you still be here? Maybe we could all have dinner together."

"I've got to get back. Pete will be exhausted from the kids by then. But maybe another time."

"Okay. Well, I've got to run back to my apartment. See you soon? Maybe you can come next weekend for the bridal show? It's outdoors, on the dock, and there'll be great food and music. It's going to be really fun."

"I'll see what I can d—" Her sister broke off to stare out the window. "What the hell is *he* doing parking in front of our house?"

Meg spun around to see a maroon convertible Mustang with a snazzy white racing stripe—with the top down—roll to a stop in front of the tiny yard. Ben opened the door and got out, wearing Aviator sunglasses, a polo shirt, and jeans that showed off his tall lean form. Altogether, he displayed the jaw-dropping good looks of a model in a Ralph Lauren ad.

"Well, got to go," she said, hugging her sister and running into the kitchen to peck her mom on the cheek. *Too late.* Her mom was halfway to the foyer, alerted by her sister's exclamation. "Bye, Mom, see you Sunday."

"Him of all people? Oh, Meg." Her sister used her best I'm-so-disappointed-in-you voice.

"It's not what you think." She sent a pleading glance in her sister's direction. *Not now, please not now.*

"Mom," Sheri said with the cruel expression of a tattletale imprinted all over her pretty face, "Ben Rushford is walking up our driveway."

Meg cursed under her breath. Her mom's face went as pale as one of Teddy's powdered sugar donuts. She hadn't gotten down and dirty with her sister since they were preteens but rolling around on the floor and yanking on her hair suddenly seemed necessary and appropriate.

"He—he's giving me a ride. Talk to you later!"

She hadn't taken more than two strides to the door when the doorbell rang.

Her mom leaned on her cane. "What on earth is going on here?"

Meg tossed up her arms in a gesture of supplication. "Fine. I'm driving with Ben to camp. We're doing charity work. End of story."

Her sister bolted for the door, but Meg grabbed her arm and pulled her back. "I want you—both of you—to be civil. Is that clear?"

"There's no reason for us to be civil," Sheri said. "He's got a lot of gall coming up to the house like that."

"Sheri, I swear. He's not a wild teenager any more. He's a doctor for God's sake. And a damn good one."

Her sister held up both hands in defense. "Hit a nerve there, I see."

Meg stared at Sheri, her pretty frosted blonde hair, her petite figure, her cute little nose surrounded by freckles. Meg remembered a time when she was the only girl in the world to beg and pray for freckles solely because her sister had them.

But her sister was probably the biggest pain in the ass she'd ever met. "Move away from the door," Meg said. She grabbed her tie-dye overnight bag from the floor, a remnant of more fashion-challenged days, and stepped forward.

"You're not *dating* him, are you?" Sheri paused to let that sink in. "Because he doesn't strike me as the type who'd be into you."

Ouch, that hurt. Although it shouldn't have, because Meg had been telling herself that for years. Only recently had she dared to think otherwise.

Except now she felt like a fool. Poor Meg, with the sad, sad crush. Who just couldn't get a clue.

"Why don't you invite him in for a chat?" Sheri was in full mean-tease mode, every comment more obnoxious than the last.

"Stop it," she whispered. "You'll upset Mom."

Meg glanced at her mother, who stood there with a blank look on her face. Sheri took advantage of Meg's diverted attention by reaching the doorknob first and yanking it open.

"Why, Ben Rushford," Sheri said with a crocodile smile. "Long time no see."

Much to Meg's relief, Ben looked as unbothered as the sunbathing cat on the window seat. He pulled off his sunglasses and nodded politely, his gaze grazing over Sheri and coming to settle on her.

"Hi, Meg." That silky smooth sound of her name on his lips made her breath hitch. A blatant blush crept uncontrollably up her neck. His look seemed to say that that even though the situation was awkward, it was going to be okay. She felt his subtle reassurance as a corner of his mouth tipped up in a barely detectable smile that made her forget her unease for just a moment. And while she regretted having put him in this predicament, it spoke volumes that he had bothered to come to the door—for her.

"Please come in," Meg said, stepping forward to greet him. She wanted desperately to grab him and run before irreparable damage was done, but there was nothing she could do.

Ben stepped forward out of the small foyer to stand before Meg's mom, who eyed him suspiciously. Meg saw him briefly scan the staircase wall covered with photos and alight on a framed portrait of a dark haired, blue-eyed boy, smiling innocently at the camera with absolutely no thought of the fate that lay ahead of him. Patrick's graduation photo.

Ben's face blanched. But if there was pain in his eyes, it was gone in a blink. He started to extend his hand, but when it was clear Meg's mother wouldn't reciprocate the handshake, he backed off. "Sheri. Mrs. Halloran. Good to see you both."

Awkward silence pressed down like a dead weight on Meg's chest. Her mother's behavior horrified her. But maybe it was just the shock of seeing Ben after all these years. Perhaps Meg could say something to make them both see what a great man he'd turned into, how he'd left his other life behind. Because ten years was more than long enough for the silent treatment and holding grudges.

"Ben's applying for the Emergency Medicine job at the hospital," Meg said.

"How nice," Sheri said dryly. Even worse, her mother said nothing at all.

"Well," Meg said. "We've got to hit the road." She grabbed Ben's arm and headed to the door.

Sheri pulled Meg back enough for Meg to catch her tersely whispered warning. "Be careful."

"Hope I see you Sunday," Meg said cheerily. She looked over at her mother. "Bye, Mom. Have a nice weekend, you two!"

A minute later, Ben held open the passenger door of his car, allowing Meg to sink onto the soft white leather seats. The outside was as slick and shiny as a water slide and the interior smelled like car wax and dashboard cleaner. The scents and textures were strangely soothing. She hadn't ridden in this car since high school, but it looked exactly the same. Sharp, edgy, classy. Like its owner.

Ben slid behind the wheel and started the car, proceeding as if nothing had happened, but Meg stopped him from putting the car in gear by placing a hand on his arm. The fact that it was firmly muscled but warm and soft all at once made her fumble her words a little. "I'm so sorry about that. I was running late at the shop and had to make sure my sister knew about my mom—"

"Don't apologize. It's not your fault." He didn't look at her, simply put on his sunglasses and began to drive.

There was a definite undercurrent of strain under his usually happy-go-lucky demeanor. "I knew it was going to be uncomfortable if you had to come to the house for me," she continued. "I was trying to get out of there . . ." She had to stop blabbering, but she felt desperate to put them both at ease.

He pulled the car over and took off his sunglasses. "Did you expect me to sit out there and honk?"

His sharp tone threw her. "No, it was just that I put you in a bad situation." Suddenly, an image of her brother appeared in front of her. Laughing, joking around. What on earth would he have to say about how his death had created such a senseless rift between two families? That same pang of sad, desperate yearning she felt from his loss at least once every day walloped her in the stomach. "I'm sorry," she said in a low voice, staring unseeingly out the passenger window. As always, she wished she could mention Patrick's name, tell Ben what she was feeling. Her brother's death seemed like a giant boulder between them blocking their way.

Ben reached over and touched her right cheek, applying steady, gentle pressure with his fingers until she was forced to turn and look at him. "I came over because I wanted to save you the trouble of running all the way back to your place just to spare my feelings. The situation wasn't your fault. It was mine, from a long time ago. But I'm not a tactless teenage boy without the guts to knock on a door."

"I never thought you were," she said slowly, scanning his face, desperate to make him understand she'd never thought badly of him, never blamed him like her mother and sister did.

A flicker of anguish dented his brow. A dogged, determined look appeared in his eyes, making them appear darker and more dangerous than usual. Before she could say more, he spoke again. "Besides, you're giving up your weekend for me, and I don't want you to feel it's going to be work. I'm excited to have you see this place, experience the fun."

Meg released a pent-up breath, relieved at the change in subject. Wishing she could say something funny to lighten the mood. And more than a little touched that he was worried about *her*. As Ben pulled away from the curb, she frowned, and it wasn't from heading west into the afternoon sun. "What exactly is your idea of fun? Canoeing? Archery? Crafts?" She strained to think of things kids did at camp but came up lacking.

That made him laugh. "Tough Mudder competition with *lots* of mud."

She stared at him in horror.

He grinned and eased the car onto the country road that led to the highway. "I'm teasing. There's no mud involved—not today, anyway. So you can stay all pretty looking."

As they left town behind, Meg felt the tension between her shoulders start to ease, and thoughts of her embarrassing family faded mercifully into the background. Ben wanted her to have fun. He'd called her pretty. All the worries that plagued her about being klutzy and awful at outdoor activities fled and were replaced by a much more dangerous thought. The more time she spent with him, the more she liked him as a person. Not the perfect fantasy guy she'd imagined in her dreams. Or the irresistible older boy she'd known from a long time ago. But the man that he was here and now. And that was the scariest thought of all.

CHAPTER 11

"What do you mean, you didn't book a second room?" Meg stood in the middle of the rustic room at the Looking Glass Lodge. Judging by the way her face was changing colors, Ben figured her anger was notching up the scale from slightly peeved to very livid. It was a shame, because after the disastrous beginning to the weekend, the car ride had been . . . pleasant. He'd been filled with that same sense of hopeful expectancy that never failed to surprise him, but that he was actually coming to accept as normal in her presence.

Ben dropped their bags and perused the room, which came complete with a big sleigh bed plumped up with a cushy green plaid comforter and about a dozen foofy pillows he never would understand the use of. Fragrant cedar paneling lined the walls, and across from the bed stood a giant stone fireplace that turned on at the flick of a switch. All they needed was a bottle of bubbly to complete the ambience of Honeymoon Suite Central.

He gave her the eyeball, prepared to go head-to-head if necessary. "You didn't tell me you were coming until Tuesday. When I called for another reservation, they were booked." He focused on her, not the bed. Because some very unprofessional thoughts were invading his mind.

Involving turning that fireplace on and tumbling those sheets and scattering all those ridiculous pillows to the floor.

Meg stood in front of the bed, arms akimbo, looking pissed. And extremely hot in loopy earrings and cute little camp shorts that showed off her shapely legs. "So you just happened not to mention the fact that we'd be sharing a room together all weekend?" She walked forward and got in his face.

He couldn't think with her in his grill like that, all big, angry eyes and a whopping dose of sass. She was right about his reluctance to tell her. He heaved a sigh and put his hands in the air. "I could've told you when I found out. But I was afraid you'd stress about it and ask one of the other women to room with you and then everyone would know we're not really together. So I'm sorry." There, he'd said it.

Anger simmered in the depths of her emerald eyes, but she fidgeted, shifting her weight from one foot to the other, fisting and unfisting her slender hands. "Fine. We'll make do." Did he detect an edge of nerves? He'd bet there was a good chance she was feeling the same trepidation he was. Which stemmed from this crazy attraction that seemed to bounce and reflect off both of them like sunshine on chrome. Because being horny and stuck for two nights in close quarters with her was a recipe for disaster and anyone with an ounce of brain would know it.

"You can get that look off your face," he said.

"What look?"

"That look like you're worried I can't keep my hands off you."

She shrugged. "You're a guy, and it's an opportunity."

"Maybe I'm more worried *you're* going to take advantage of *me*."

She snorted. "Like I said. An opportunity is an opportunity. Unless you're gay?"

"I'm not gay," he said definitively. But he almost wished he was. Because everything about her was turning him on, from the way her gorgeous ass looked in those shorts to those intent little frown lines on her forehead. And that vanilla scent she was wearing wasn't helping.

He pointed to the couch. "Look, I'll sleep over there. It's not a problem." His legs and feet would dangle off like a fishing pole from a dock, but that was the price he'd pay.

She sat down cautiously on the very edge of the bed, as if she hated to crease the perfectly done-up comforter.

Tense. Everything between them was so damn tense. When he'd picked her up, he could sense her thinking about Patrick, but of course neither of them mentioned him. His memory was the elephant between them. How could it not be?

He'd learned a long time ago not to shirk away from what was uncomfortable. Maybe he could never fully atone for his past but he sure as hell wasn't going to run away from it. Even if her mother would never give him the time of day again.

Who could blame her after what had happened to her eighteen-year-old son? His gut clenched at the wish he'd wished at least once every day of his life since that night, that if he could go back and redo his actions, he would. Yes, he would. But life didn't give anybody do-overs.

"It's okay to sit on the bed," he said, looking at her rigid, uncomfortable posture as she balanced on the edge.

She shot him a puzzled look. "I *am* sitting on the bed."

"If you call that sitting. With one butt cheek."

She threw up her hands and made an irritated sound. "I just walked into this romantic room with a bed made for a honeymoon couple and was wondering how the hell I got myself into this mess with you. I couldn't possibly be reliving that nightmare of a dinner last weekend. Maybe just for a moment I want to keep things perfect and undisturbed instead of messy and ridiculous."

He looked at her then. Really looked. Her eyes sparked. There wasn't a cell in her body not passionately on fire, and he loved it. In his mind, he conceded the fact that she was absolutely right. They were in a bizarre situation.

"Life is messy, Meggie," he said quietly. "Sometimes you've just got to wade in with both feet."

Her mouth opened and then snapped shut as she chewed on that. She got up and started to turn away but he caught her elbow.

"Do you know what you need?" he asked in a wicked tone.

She turned fifty shades of scarlet.

"I could help you with that," he said. "But I was actually referring to someone maybe removing that giant stick up your ass."

Meg rolled her eyes. "And do you know what *you* need?" She picked up a pillow and tossed it at his head. "Someone to control that overconfident, giant ego of yours."

Before she could grab another one, he pushed her down atop the bed and let himself fall with her. The down comforter billowed around them like a sail. For a flash, he looked down at her, and his breath stole away. She lay there, her dark hair swirled around her like a mermaid's, lips full and pink and open in surprise and shock. She was so beautiful it hurt him in the chest.

Meg started to rise up on her elbows, but before she could recover her senses, he picked up a pillow with a moose head on it and let it loose. It hit her in the side of the head.

For one second, her eyes registered a *what-the-hell-just-happened* look. A beat later, her brows knit down with purpose. Next thing he knew, the pillow whirled back at him, then another and another. Being the youngest boy in a family of mostly brothers meant he'd learned to defend himself early. So he launched them right back.

Her ponytail loosened and fell out. Moose and reindeer and elk flew through the air, and when those ran out, white bed pillows followed.

Meg got up and ran to the other side of the bed, a giant down pillow in her hand, and he pursued. When he got close, she hauled off and smacked him across the ribs. The pillow burst open and a cloud of goose feathers filled the air like snowflakes.

She blew at the feathers, waved her hands in the air to clear it. A gallant effort, to be sure, but this was war.

He picked up the discarded pillow and turned it upside down so the rest of the feathers rained down over her head. She stood there like she was stuck in a blizzard, arms outstretched to catch the flakes that were drifting everywhere.

"This reminds me of when we were kids and tilted our heads back and stuck out our tongues to catch the snowflakes." As he demonstrated, a feather landed on his tongue and he reached up to brush it off. "Gross," he said.

She stared at him, the flakes settling like a snow globe that had lost momentum. Then she laughed. Not a delicate gale of giggles but a raucous, snorty laugh. The incongruousness of the sound coming out of her petite body started him laughing, too. She collapsed onto the bed, struggling for breath, and he landed next to her.

When she giggled and snickered, she was luminous. Her eyes lit up like sunlight on the ocean. The planes of her face softened and relaxed and it made him wonder what she would look like fully unguarded, when all control had fled and every tense angle was subdued and softened.

He had no idea if she'd had a boyfriend in the past who'd made her look like that when they'd made love. But if she was his, he certainly would have. Every night. He imagined being the one to scatter kisses on her neck, nuzzle under her jaw, then capture those soft full lips with his. She wouldn't be laughing then.

"Guess we mussed up the bed," he said.

"Guess so," she whispered. Their gazes locked. He pushed back a strand of hair from her face. Her cheek was flushed and hot, and the softness of her skin felt like pure silk under his fingers.

"I'm sorry I got you into this mess," he said.

"Don't be sorry," she whispered, reaching up and grabbing his arm, which sent a sudden zing all through him. "We can make the best of it."

For a minute he froze. Looked into her sea-green eyes, so honest and sincere. One little tug was all it would take to get her in his arms. Then he was sure they'd find a million ways to make the best of it.

Except she wasn't one of his fly-by-night girls. He didn't know exactly *what* she was, but he knew she was worth way more to him than just a good tumble in the sheets.

Ben scootched back, breaking contact. "We better get these feathers cleaned up before we head down to the bonfire."

So *making the best of it* was likely to mean not being able to sleep a wink because of a permanent erection, and fantasizing about her sweet curves and all the things he wanted to do to her in that bed.

>--+-+>--0--<+-+-<

Meg held her plate out to Stacy, gesturing for her to take one of two s'mores as they gathered around a makeshift picnic area with Jax and Cynthia, watching fifty or so kids eat hot dogs, corn, and tater tots as they got excited for tonight's big bonfire.

"Oh, how did you know I really needed one of those?" Stacy asked from her seat in a canvas camp chair.

"You just had that look," Meg said.

"That's her usual look when food passes by," Jax said, nudging her with his elbow. Stacy punched him in the arm.

"Want a hot dog?" Meg asked, passing a platter to Cynthia, who had come without Paul.

"I'm vegan," she said with a drip of disdain.

"Um, okay. How about a bun, then?" Oops, that was a bit snarky. It had slipped out before she could catch it, and she'd better watch it. She didn't want to anger Cynthia and have her go after Ben to retaliate.

Fortunately, Cynthia ignored the comment. "Why do we have to do a Light Ceremony, anyway? I spent an hour hiking around the woods for those stupid pinecones. I'm going to tell Dr. Donaldson it's dangerous for these kids to toss pinecones into the fire. This has nothing to do with practicing medicine."

"Um—maybe you shouldn't," Meg said, restraining her with her hand.

"Why not?" Cynthia looked down her long aquiline nose at her as if she'd just eaten a chipmunk.

"Well, because this is a huge end-of-summer tradition for the kids. Maybe you should see it all the way through and then decide. You know, catch more bees with honey and all that."

A voice whispered in her ear. "There you go, aiding the enemy again."

Meg spun around to see Ben dressed in a Camp Mohican T-shirt and shorts. Several campers were clinging onto his arms and one little boy was on his back, his chubby little hands around Ben's neck. Seeing him interact and laugh with the kids was almost as fun as seeing him without his shirt on, its own crazy kind of crack.

Ben's hungry gaze swept slowly over her, from her sneakers to her jean shorts to the bulky sweatshirt she'd tied around her waist, to her simple gray T-shirt. A mischievous twinkle alit in the depths of his cocoa-brown eyes. How could she be wearing the most modest of clothing yet feel naked under his perusal? How could her limbs feel heavy and weighted down, clumsy and awkward as if she were sixteen again? Getting out of the confines of that damn room and into the fresh air was not helping the situation as she'd prayed it would.

Cynthia rolled her eyes at Ben. "Please tell me you aren't going to lead those stupid songs we had to practice."

Ben stood with his legs apart, arms folded. Then he made an upside-down M with his fingers, the Camp Mohican special hand symbol, and then flipped it over into a peace sign. "I come in peace, Cynthia," he said in a deep baritone. "No worries. The songs go along with the pinecone ceremony and the lantern lighting for the canoes. You'll love it."

Cynthia scowled and headed over to the carrots.

"I think she's hungry," Meg said. "The food here isn't really accommodating for people with special dietary needs."

Ben shook his head. "They have two dieticians on staff for the kids. And it is if you ask. We could tell her that. Or we could just let her forage in the woods for nuts and berries." His mouth tipped up in the slightest smile, and she couldn't help smiling back.

"Want to share my s'more?" she finally asked after she'd caught him eyeing it. "I'd offer the whole thing, but I'm chocolate deprived." She took a bite and then offered him one from the other end, which he surprisingly took. He bent his head low, all the well-cut layers in his thick head of hair catching light from the low sun. Meg had the urge to run her hands through those rich dark locks but she was frozen in place. Because as he took a bite, his eyes drilled into her the entire time. Her toes curled in her sneakers. Her breath came in little fits. Damn it all, the man was setting her on fire with one sultry look.

"Exactly how chocolate deprived are you?" Ben asked, his beautiful face close, his eyes searching hers. He smelled a little smoky from the fire and soapy from a shower, too, an irresistible combination. She took in the warmth of his eyes, his definitive brows, the strong, set jawline, the mischievous tilt of his mouth. She fought the urge to cup her hand over his cheek, prove that the bristle of his beard was as rough as she thought it might be.

"*Dangerously* deprived."

"That right? Chocolate's good for you. How come you haven't had any lately?"

She took one more bite and handed him the rest. "I'm a very discerning chocolate eater."

"I see. No chocolate for the sake of chocolate, then?"

She shook her head. "Not for me."

"So it has to be special chocolate."

"Yep. Chocolate I love. How about you?"

His mouth turned up in a smirk, but his eyes looked wary. "Some chocolate's too forbidden to touch."

"Maybe it's not as forbidden as you think." Wow, had she just said that? Well, why not? She'd sworn she was going to put herself out there. Be bold and daring. Take risks.

His eyes searched hers, but walls had already come up, shutters had slammed closed. She opened her mouth to speak, but words failed, and she deflected to the mundane. "You've got some marshmallow right there." She pointed to the corner of his mouth.

He tried to reach it with his tongue.

"Nope." She wiped it off with her thumb, and as she did so, her hand grazed his bearded cheek. It was surprisingly soft and his lips were soft and moist and oh, so kissable. Maybe she lingered just a bit too long after she wiped off the bit of marshmallow, because Jax cleared his throat.

"Hate to interrupt, but it's time to get the Light Ceremony started."

"See you later," Meg said as he left to lead the traditional songs and help the kids toss their cones. The tossing was supposed to symbolize letting go of something—a problem, a crutch—and using the weekend to help to overcome it. Like maybe she could think of just letting go and having fun with him. Let things go where they may.

"If you're nice to me, later I just might bring you some chocolate." He winked at her, back to his usual joking self.

A simple, quiet wink, followed by the slightest upturn of his beautiful mouth that nearly brought her to her knees.

"Get going." She gave him a little shove in the back. *Oops*, she shouldn't have touched that back, all hard ridges and planes under the soft cotton of his shirt.

He walked off with Jax, but turned around long enough to give her a sinful half smile.

Suddenly she became aware of Stacy standing beside her, watching her intently. She struggled to act normal, as if every hormone in her body wasn't firing off like a Fourth of July fireworks display.

Meg decided to speak, if anything to deflect Stacy's questions. "I can't wait to see all the lanterns lit up in the canoes."

"I wish I could fit into a canoe. I think I'll just stay on shore and put my feet up. My back is killing me."

"Maybe I'll join you. I think seeing it from shore is the best way to enjoy it."

"What I'm enjoying is the smoking hot chemistry between you two." Stacy fanned herself with her paper plate.

Meg could testify to that. Because she was pretty sure her panties had just caught on fire and turned to ash.

"How long have you two been dating, anyway?" Stacy asked.

"Not very long." *Like, did fake-dating a week count?*

"But you grew up together, didn't you?"

"I've had a massive crush on him for years." *True, completely true.*

"You only reconnected recently?"

"Um—Ben was my brother's best friend." She didn't say that Patrick had died, and that Ben had hardly spoken to her for years after that, but she wished she could. She liked Stacy. In any other circumstance, Meg felt confident they would be friends.

"Well, he's certainly crazy about you. In fact, he's staring at you."

Ben was standing in front of the kids, leading them in camp songs she vaguely remembered hearing as a child. He waved at her, and she waved back and smiled. But it felt like someone had tossed a wrench into her chest and was cranking her lungs tighter. It surprised her to realize she'd give anything for this thing between them to be real.

Was some of it real? She was pretty sure she hadn't imagined the way he'd looked at her. Or his flirting. Judging from the sultry glint in the depths of his eyes, he wanted her, too.

Maybe he could never love her. Patrick's ghost would always be wedged between them. Ben had clearly been traumatized by what had happened and her mother could not seem to forgive him for—for what—surviving?

Maybe the best Ben was capable of was wanting her. He didn't do relationships. But if wiping a stray crumb off his face could make every nerve ending buzz, what would happen with anything more?

Complete nuclear annihilation, that was what.

Except she would be the one who was destroyed, while he walked away unscathed. But oh, she did want him. If she could never have his love, should she accept what he could give her instead? And would that be enough to flush him out of her system for good?

"Are you all right?" Stacy asked.

Meg shook herself out of her trance. "Just worried about the obstacle course tomorrow." She smiled at Stacy, who was finally eating her s'more. "I want you to know that I like you a lot, Stacy. I hope that whatever happens with this job, maybe someday we can become real friends."

"You know, Jax and Ben have been through some crazy stuff together since intern year, and they've always had each other's backs. Jax is an intense competitor but he's also a loyal friend. I hope this doesn't ruin their friendship."

"We'll just have to make sure that doesn't happen," Meg said, giving her a side hug and walking over to where everyone was gathered by the fire waiting for the powwow to begin.

Maybe she could let go enough to have him just for now. But she knew one thing as well as she knew her own address, that a brief affair with him would never, ever be enough. She wanted it all, and that was the one thing she could never, ever have.

CHAPTER 12

Nothing like a good obstacle course to get Ben's adrenaline going and beat some pesky hormones right out of his system.

He looked out over the field where the obstacles were set up and cracked his neck, which had a crick in it from sleeping on the sofa, if you could call what he did last night sleeping. More like trying to pretend five-feet-two inches of a certain soft, sexy woman wasn't sleeping a couple feet away. Ignoring every soft sigh and little movement she made as she slept—or didn't sleep, because based on all the fidgeting she did, she was having the same exact problem he was.

But, thank God, it was morning at last, and his favorite event was about to begin.

Ben saw Meg's gaze flicker over the course, first eyeballing the climbing wall, then the logs set up to zigzag around, then the mountain of rocks that had to be scaled up and down. He saw the instant her eyes lit on the rope that swung over the giant puddle they referred to as The Moat. Instinctively, she gasped.

"Oh, no, you don't," he said, grabbing the back of her hoodie as she started easing away. "No backing out now."

"I was happy making blankets," she said darkly, referring to their first activity this morning where they'd tied long lengths of fleece together to make colorful throws with the kids.

Four little girls stood behind her. Knock-kneed, gap-toothed, pony-tailed girls with expectant looks. "I'm only doing this for the kids," Meg said, "since you've gone and gotten them all riled up."

In response, he grinned. "Let's hear it, Team Girl." He loved talking smack to the kids. He went around fist pumping and high-fiving the kids and getting them to fake-taunt the other team, four boys led by Jax and Cynthia. The obstacle course made the kids forget about having diabetes and just rough and tumble it out like any normal kids.

A little girl named Rebecca with lopsided braids pulled on Meg's shirt. "I know you," she said. "You had a date with my daddy."

Ben watched Meg's cheeks turn crimson. "My daddy is Cole Hanson," the little girl continued. "He's a vet'narian."

"Oh, Dr. Hanson," Meg said. "I did have dinner with your daddy. How did you know that?"

"'Cause I heard him talk to you on the phone one night. He said you're a good kisser."

Wait a minute. She'd *kissed* this guy? Ben only knew him in passing. A nice guy, and good-looking enough. Played tennis at the park. Hell, he couldn't even criticize his job, because it was harder to get into vet school than med school.

Meg's face went from pink to deep magenta, but she smiled and tugged the girl's braid. "Your dad is very nice. And he takes good care of my cats." She turned to the other girls. "Are you all ready to rally as a team?"

Rebecca tugged on her shirt again. "I'm feeling low," she said.

Meg squatted down to eye level. "Oh, no, sweetie. Don't get depressed. We're going to whup those boys' butts."

Ben burst into laughter. "She means her blood sugar feels low. C'mon over here, Becca, and get some juice. Didn't you eat any breakfast?"

She shook her head solemnly. Her eyes were big and round and a little frightened looking. "My tummy was hurting."

Ben put a hand on the little girl's shoulder. He asked Meg, "Do you mind rallying the troops while I help her?"

"Of course not. But what should I do?"

"I don't know. Play a game or something."

"Like Duck Duck Goose?"

"They're not five. Just find some way to rowdy them up." He drew close to whisper in her ear. "You know, so they aren't scared."

She swallowed hard.

"Unless you're a little scared yourself?"

"A little bit of mud doesn't scare me." She stuck out her chin and he couldn't resist chucking it. Outrage flashed from her eyes and made him smile.

Just as he steered Becca away, he turned and winked. "Be back in ten, sweetheart."

⊱⋅⊰⋅○⋅⊱⋅⊰

When he returned with Becca, Meg was French braiding one of the girls' hair. All of the girls, including Meg, had on red bandanas tied like do-rags, and her hair was braided, too. Slashes of mud lined their cheeks. They were chanting "We're gonna whup their butts" as Meg handed him a red bandana of his own.

He tied it motorcycle-dude style on his head, knotting it in the back, and pulled Meg to the side. "You know that little girl's really had it tough."

"I know she lost her mom and developed diabetes all in the same year."

She probably would know that if she'd dated her dad. "We may have to help her a little though the course. You know, to build her confidence."

Meg gave him a bright smile and a thumbs-up. "No problem. I just hope you don't end up having to help me, too."

His gaze slid over her body, from her fresh-faced smile to her simple camp T-shirt and cargo shorts down to her bare tanned legs and her tennies. "Honey, any time you need help, I'm your man." He imagined cradling her fabulous ass as she scaled the wall, or zigzagging with her around the logs before he pulled her down into the sweet, warm grass and helped her with something completely different.

They did an all-hands-in cheer with the kids and took their places at the starting line.

One of the counselors shot off a popgun. Ben ran with the first little girl, standing guard at the cargo net wall, but she scaled it with no problem. Meg ran with Becca, who paused fearfully at the ropes.

"We'll do this together, okay? I'll be right behind you," Meg said.

"And I'll be right behind you," Ben echoed, grinning when Meg caught him looking at her ass. "Just in case."

"She's gonna make us lose," a little red-haired girl said, pointing to Becca.

"She's a scaredy-cat," a tall girl said. "And the boys are gonna beat us." Sure enough, the boys were hurling over the top of their wall as easily as a team of Navy Seals.

"Hey, Team Girl, what about working together?" Ben said. "How about that team cheer again?"

"Don't listen to those girls, Beck," Meg said, surrounding the little girl with her own body on the wall. "You can't fall. I've got you."

"Too scared," Becca managed.

"I have an idea," Ben said to Meg. "Why don't you let me cover her from down here while you climb up to the top to help her over?"

He coached Becca basically by telling her exactly where to put her hands and feet as she inched her way up the cargo ropes, while he scaled the ropes behind her.

Meg clawed her way around Becca and scaled up the ropes in an awkward but determined manner. The view of her from below floored him, those long miles of leg and that sweet, sweet ass. "Holy Mother of Pearl," he said under his breath.

She straddled the top of the wall, stretched out with her arm extended toward Becca, and looked down at him. "If you make one crack about the size of my . . ." She used her brows to pointedly convey the rest without words.

So maybe that wasn't as under his breath as he thought. Her rear end was fine, firm and rounded, and he just couldn't help himself. As he followed Becca to the top of the wall, he whispered in Meg's ear, "You—have a tattoo."

A tiny, little peek of one, just over her right hip. It took the willpower of a saint not to inch down the waistband of her shorts and look. He wanted to touch it. Trace it. And possibly lick it.

She stared down at him, her cheek against the wall, fingers clutching the rope, arms braced to help the little girl. "Lots of people do."

Yeah, but her? But then, during every interaction they'd had, she'd continually surprised him. He swallowed hard. "What is it?"

"None of your business."

He skimmed his hand under her shirt and rubbed the spot where he'd seen the tiny peek of ink.

"A flower? A heart? A butterfly?"

"You'll never know." She lowered her voice. "And please keep your hands to yourself."

He threw up his hands in defense. "Hey, just trying to help."

When Becca managed to haul her legs over the top of the wall, her look was one of triumph. Meg watched her crawl down the rope on the other side all by herself. Ben put his hand up toward Meg in a high-five, and when she extended her own to reach his, he intertwined their fingers.

"Nice job."

She smiled. Probably her first smile of the day without sarcasm, and it was brilliant, even through the mud streaks and the badass do-rag. Something inside his chest flipped over like a pancake and he quickly dropped his hand.

"A bird, then." He paused. "I've got it! My initials."

"Keep dreaming, buddy," Meg said with a grin.

After she dropped down the other side of the cargo rope, she zigzagged along the scattered logs with the kids, laughing and encouraging them and cheering them on as they ran up and down the gravel mountain. Even with her natural reserve, she had a bighearted personality that was way too appealing.

The last challenge was to swing over a muddy moat with a rope. The other kids had no trouble using the rope to get over the mud bath, but Rebecca's eyes went wide. "I can't do it."

Meg bent down until she was eye level with the little girl. "This is our last challenge. We can't quit now."

Her lower lip quivered.

"She can walk around the mud course," Ben offered.

One of the other little girls who'd already made it over to the other side called out to him, complaining that she'd twisted her ankle.

"You okay here?" he asked Meg.

"I can handle it," she said, and he ran around the mud pit to investigate.

A minute later, as he was checking out the girl's ankle, another little girl tapped him on the shoulder. "Meg's swinging over with Becca."

He stood up immediately. A muffled *don't!* stuck in his throat, too late to do any good.

Becca clung onto Meg, who basically had to support her weight and Becca's across the moat. Meg pushed them off weakly, their combined weights too much for her petite frame. Becca made it to dry land. Meg did not.

She landed hard in the mud on her ass. All the kids raced to the edge of the moat, laughing and tittering. Even Becca, that little traitor, doubled over in laughter. Meg did her best to smile, even teasingly scolding a kid who'd taken out his phone by saying, "That better not end up on Facebook, Eric!" But Ben recognized by the wateriness in her eyes and the clench of her jaw that she was in pain.

He ran down a few steps of the bank and extended his hand.

"When you smile, your teeth are so white against all that muck," he said. "You all right?"

"I know I have some great padding on my ass, but it hurts like hell," she said in a low voice so the kids couldn't hear. "Is it possible to break your butt bone?"

"You may have bruised your coccyx," he said. "Can you stand up?"

"I don't think so," she said.

When he reached down to pull her up, she resisted. A saucy grin lit up her face as she used all her weight to try to pull him down with her.

"You're evil," he said, easily resisting her ploy to get him muddy. The kids began cheering on the sidelines.

She tugged. Pulled. Used both hands and heaved.

He laughed. "Done yet?"

She ignored him, turning instead to the enraptured crowd.

"I'm sorry, kids. It was wrong of me to try and get Dr. Rushford all muddy . . . unless you all help me!"

Kids tumbled down the incline, working together to push Ben farther into the thick, cool ooze. But he got them all back by slinging mud, and soon they were all covered up to their necks, whooping and yelling and letting all hell break loose.

"Okay," he said once things calmed down a little. "Time to hose off before dinner."

"Hose off?" Meg looked horrified.

"We can't let the kids go back to their cabins like this."

Ben used a hose that ran from a nearby horse barn. One by one, he washed off the screaming kids, who finally left with their counselors to take real showers.

Ben stood with the hose in his hand, tapping it cautiously in his palm. "Your turn, sweetheart," he said.

"You can stop gloating now," she groused from under a tree, where she sat leaning up against its trunk, trying not to put weight on her butt.

"Bet your tailbone smarts something awful after that stunt," he sympathized.

"Bet you got high marks in your empathy classes in med school, didn't you? You're relishing your victory way too much."

"Let's just say there's a time to empathize and a time for payback."

He turned the hose on her, getting close enough to spray most of the mud off as she cried out from the cold. Then just to torment her, he trained the spray up her shirt. She grabbed the hose and turned it on him.

"I've had enough power washing, thanks," she said, pushing back her streaming wet hair. "Your turn."

She gave it all she had, but he came forward through the spray as easily as if it were a squirt gun stream.

"Bet it hurts like hell to walk, huh?" he asked.

She nodded. His lucky day. He scooped her up and carried her across the field, trying not to think of her skin, wet and smooth beneath his fingertips, water drops glistening in the bright sunshine. Or her dark hair, sleeked down with water, and her washed-off face, scrubbed free of mud and makeup. Or the prickling awareness he felt as she quietly assessed him, her hands gently gathered around his neck for balance.

"Seems like you might be a little too much into the caveman thing, Rushford."

"Just because I'm big and strong and can practically lift you with one hand?" He looked at her. A mistake. Her lovely eyes contained iridescent shades of hazel and gold, and a lighter green he'd never noticed before. If he kept staring like this he was going to fumble over his own feet and pitch them both face-first into the grass. He prayed he could keep it together until he could drop her off in their room.

It was difficult not to smile, when on second glance he saw a giant blob of mud still stuck in her hair, and a streak of mud running down her cheek. She was a mess.

An adorable, cute mess that was making his pants tight.

He carried her through the lodge doors, up the elevator, and into their room, where he left her in the doorway before going into the bathroom and cranking on the shower.

"Let me check your back." He steered her in front of the bathroom sink.

"Um, not a good idea." She bit her lower lip with worry. "It's sort of not my back. It's my butt."

"Then I'm *more* than happy to check that out for you," he said, choking back a laugh.

She gave him a *no-way* stare in the mirror.

"Through your clothes. Nothing sexual."

Which was a lie. Everything about her stirred him, from the smartassed go-to-hell look in her eye, to her mud-streaked legs, to her wet T-shirt that outlined her taut, perky nipples.

She didn't fight him when he palpated her back, one vertebrae at a time, while she leaned over, gripping the granite counter with her hands. Because she was cold and wet and covered with goose bumps, his mind kept roaming to ways he could warm both of them up quick. He trailed his fingers down the graceful arc of her spine all the way down to her tailbone, pleased when she shivered under his hands. He was doing so well, keeping his libido in harsh rein, until he reached the inviting curve of her perfectly rounded ass. What he wouldn't do to get his hands on that fine backside, squeeze it gently as she wrapped her legs around him and he thrust into her against the steamy shower stall.

"So what have I got?" she asked.

An amazing body and I've got one huge hard-on.

"Probably just a bruise," he said out loud, but his heart was banging against his rib cage like he was in the throes of a heart attack and he could no longer produce a single useful thought. He'd reached his limit. To hell with all the reasons he knew he should stay away from her. He couldn't remember them anyway, because his entire body was overcome with need for her.

He turned her toward him in one swift motion and covered her mouth with his. And kissed her with slow, languid, all-consuming strokes, taking full advantage of her surprise. He capitalized by plunging his tongue into her mouth and pulling her flush against his body. No more fooling around. No more guilt. Just the heady pleasure of her sweet, yielding body.

She whimpered, a sound that satisfied him immensely.

To his everlasting relief, her tongue met his, sliding against it and meeting his stroke for stroke, wanting him as much as he wanted her. She pushed her wet body up against his until they were touching everywhere. He couldn't hide the arousal that pressed thick and hard between them.

She gave a moan and cupped *his* ass and he nearly died from the pleasure of it all. A low, guttural sound pushed out of his throat. Before he could think, he opened the shower curtain and pulled her with him into the steamy shower.

She winced a little from the movement. *He* was an ass, doing this without regard for her injury, but she made him feel better when she pulled off her shirt and tossed it onto the bathtub ledge, and tugged on his so he could do the same. Water and steam cascaded everywhere, washing off the leftover mud, warming his muscles, and enveloping them in their own little world.

His heart ached at the raw pull of her beauty. With her hair pushed back from her face, her green eyes looked huge and vulnerable. Her dark hair lay wet against her pale shoulders. Rivulets of water traced over them and around the soft curves of her breasts, hidden beneath the lace of her bra, though he could see her nipples were taut with desire.

He had to have more of her. Running his hands under the waistband of her shorts, he traced the satiny softness of her wet skin. He curled his index fingers around the belt loops and tugged her close. Then he smoothed a wet strand of hair back from her flushed face and forced himself to look at her. "Meg, I—"

I *what?* I can't, I shouldn't? He couldn't bring himself to say the words. Because he didn't believe them, couldn't *feel* them.

He feared what he would find in her eyes, but all he saw was a surprising assuredness. A flicker of fun. Could it be possible that she'd wanted him as much as he wanted her right now? His disbelief made him hesitate for one second, until she smiled and cupped his cheek with her hand. That one simple movement made his chest crack open, and for the first time in—hell, he couldn't remember how long—he felt free. Like shackles around his feet had burst open. Like his heart had erupted. It was just the two of them in this steamy little haven and nothing else could enter—no doubt, no pain, no heartache.

She motioned to her back. "My bra—will you get it?"

She turned around, bracing her hands against the tile wall. His fingers itched to soap her up and run his hands along her sleek curves. He didn't hesitate going straight for the hook, which he felt confident he could undo blindfolded and with one hand tied behind his back. It was then that he saw it. The tattoo that had peeked out from over her waistband was in full view without her shirt to obscure it.

It was a four-leaf clover. With a "P" in the middle.

A memorial to her brother.

Ben's hand froze on the clasp. A shiver ripped through him, even though the water was pleasantly warm.

For a few moments, he'd forgotten. But fate, that fickle bitch, had reminded him at the most inopportune of times.

"What is it?" She turned around too quickly and winced in pain. "Ben, what's wrong?"

He shook his head.

There it was in his face, taunting him, the one shame he couldn't forget. How had he ever thought he could have her, this sweet, beautiful woman who made his limping soul sing? He'd deceived himself. Let his passions rule his sense.

"I—forgot."

"Forgot what?" she asked.

"I-I've got to report to the clinic."

"You—you're on call again tonight?"

"Y-yes. Tonight. Now."

For just a second, puzzlement and hurt flickered in her eyes. He would have done anything to kiss those feelings away, tell her how sorry he was, but how could he? Hell, he didn't have the words.

Suddenly it was all too much. The sound of the shower beating down like rain. The steamy air growing clammy and fogging the mirrors and making him sweat. And the pleading look in her eyes that said *Stay. Talk to me. What's wrong?*

"You—you can shower first. When you're done, I'll get in." He couldn't meet her eyes. He left her there, wrapped a towel around himself, and let himself out the door.

><>—O—<><

Meg stared at the foggy mirror. She dragged the backside of her fist over it in circles until a small area cleared and stared at her reflection. Saw her pale, makeup-less face, her straight wet hair, her too-innocent eyes that looked shocked and hurt.

She wasn't like those other women that he preferred. She didn't wear a ton of makeup, or have a hairstyle that required a gallon of hairspray and an hour in front of the mirror every morning. The only reason she wasn't wearing cut-off shorts and T-shirts or her usual flowery skirts and flats was because Alex had insisted on dressing her. She wasn't naturally confident or sophisticated. And she had real curves and ate more than leaves and twigs for lunch.

Hold up a minute. She was always so quick to berate herself. *My fault, my fault,* those damn voices taunted. But this time, she pushed them out of her head. Because he'd preferred her just fine up until the time she turned around. On instinct, her hand flew to the spot over her hip that held her tattoo. It seemed to burn in incrimination. Then she snatched a towel from the shelf, wrapped it around herself, and ran out of the bathroom.

Ben had already dressed in a T-shirt and clean shorts and was headed to the door, his hair still damp. She threw herself in front of it, clutching the towel to her chest.

"Meg, I have to go," he said, not looking at her. "Please don't do this."

She didn't budge. His dark brows were turned up in an anguished curve, and his mouth drew into a thin line of worry. She saw his pain, and her impulse to comfort him was strong. But she knew he would never let her.

She reached out a hand and touched him on the arm until he looked at her. Pure agony simmered in his eyes.

"I know it's something about my brother. If we could just talk—"

He opened his mouth to talk but no words came. He shook his head in frustration and released a sigh. "It reminded me of him, of your brother. Of Patrick."

Hearing her brother's name spoken out loud sounded as startling as an unexpected clap. Her eyes instantly filled with tears as they always did at any mention of him, which was always so rare and tentative, like whoever spoke his name was walking on eggs and praying they wouldn't crack.

"It's like he didn't exist. Like there's shame associated with his death and we can't ever share any memories of him, can't acknowledge how much we loved him."

"I did love him," Ben said in a hoarse whisper. "You'll never know how sorry I am that he died."

"It was a horrible accident. I can't imagine how you ever coped with it, being so young and all by yourself."

"I don't deserve your pity," he said staunchly. "I'm still alive."

She clasped him by the arms then. Tried to meet his gaze, but he refused to look at her. Tears were falling down her face and rolling onto his arms. His eyes were wet, too. "You didn't abandon him. No matter how terrifying it was, you kept searching for him until you found him. You were a true friend to the end."

Ben snorted. He pinched his nose to stop the tears. He put his hands on hers and pried them off his arms. "I need to go. I can't be late."

She'd never seen him like this, looking like a caged and caught animal, desperate for escape. Common sense told her she needed to back off. But she pushed ahead blindly in a last attempt to break through.

"No one in my family ever mentions his name, or remembers the good times, or his sense of humor, or the pranks he pulled. I want us to talk about him, Ben. I don't want there to be anything between us. I want us to have a real relationship."

It was true. She knew it now. There was no use pretending otherwise.

His stance became rigid. The lines of his face hardened, and he did look at her then, but his eyes were impermeable as granite. "I don't do relationships. I never have, and I never can. Not with you, not with anybody. I'm sorry, Meg. It's the way I am. Anything between us is—impossible."

His chilly words took her breath away. She tried to suck air in, but her lungs suddenly forgot how. She opened her mouth to speak but it was too late. He was already headed toward the door.

Impossible. He couldn't have spelled it out for her with any more certainty. Couldn't have pushed her away any more vehemently. A full-out, no-holds-barred rejection.

His hand was on the doorknob, but she stopped him from leaving with her words. "Okay, Ben, if that's the way you want it. But I can't wait for you anymore. For years I've mooned over you like a lost puppy begging for attention, and I can't do it anymore. I need more, and you know what? I deserve more."

He stood still, his knuckles white against the knob. *Please turn around. Please say something,* she silently begged.

But he opened the door. For a moment, the darkness of his shadow loomed against the stark white of the door. Then he was gone.

Pain ripped through her like tiny pieces of shrapnel pricking and burning everywhere. What more could she do or say to make him stay? To save him from his inner ghosts?

Because one thing had become crystal clear. There was another casualty of that accident besides her brother.

CHAPTER 13

Meg was ironing her second wedding gown of the day when Samantha walked into the bridal shop early Monday morning. "How was your weekend?" she asked Meg in a cheery tone, setting down her laptop and a can of bright green paint. Meg pressed the steam button, but the big, satisfying *whoosh* did nothing to soothe her tattered nerves. Gloria, who sat nearby at an old Queen Anne desk, was immersed in something on the computer that was almost certainly not work-related, and looked up at the sound.

"Great," Meg lied, plastering her best smile on her face. Maybe Sam and her grandmother would be too busy to notice that anything was off. She was counting on it, because she Did. Not. Want. To. Talk.

About anything, but especially not about the weekend.

She'd been here since 6:00 a.m., unable to sleep. She'd had to forego her daily run because it still hurt to walk, so she'd come into the shop early, drunk three cups of coffee, two of which she'd shed tears into, ironed two new dresses, and steamed two veils that had just come in. She'd organized callbacks for later, when the rest of the world was actually awake, done e-mail follow-ups about potential dress sales, and checked the books. Then she'd kicked off her heels and was ironing barefoot, an activity that was more physical than mental, but none of her activities failed to distract her from thinking about *him*.

Cole Hanson had called her last night to thank her for helping Becca at camp and he'd asked her out. And she was thinking about saying *yes*.

Why not? He was handsome and nice and she adored his little girl. It was time to realize that sometimes you just couldn't change people. Especially when they tell you flat out they aren't interested in a relationship. *Ouch.*

Another vigorous puff of steam wasn't enough to push away *that* hurt.

"You sound about as enthusiastic as my brother," Sam said. Meg must have looked puzzled because Sam continued, "He's been in a mood. Barely ate any dinner last night, then went off huffing and puffing back to Hartford. You two must have had a great time at camp."

Somehow Meg had survived the rest of the godawful weekend. Thank heaven the last day was crammed full of kid activities, leaving no time for her to be alone with Ben. When they did speak it was through a thin veneer of politeness stretched so tight it practically cracked. She'd managed to get a ride home with the Donaldsons while Ben stayed behind to help pack up clinic supplies.

Meg took the opportunity to gloat a little that Ben might be suffering, too. "Camp was fun, except my butt still hurts like hell from falling into the mud pit. I hope your weekend was better?"

"Harris came up and picnicked with us. Tom and Brad love him. And he bought me this new dress."

"He bought you a dress?" Gloria wretched her eyes from Candy Crunch Saga to take a gander through her beaded bifocals.

"It's Lily Pulitzer," Sam said. "What do you think? Of course, I may need to work out a little more for it to look really nice. Harris says that to get in really great shape, you need to break a good sweat at least five days a week. He wants me to take up running."

"Why, dear, you have a lovely shape just as you are," Gloria said.

Sam had always dressed in lots of black, some leather, funky scarves, and interesting, handcrafted earrings she usually bought from vendors who sold products from women starting up their own businesses from around the world. She had an edgy, artsy style that was as far from Lily Pulitzer as Mirror Lake was from New York City.

"It's a nice look," Meg said cautiously. "What do you think, Gran?"

"Very cheery, dear. The Queen always wears bright colors. I must say, I enjoy them, too."

"Harris said he got it for me so I can have something nice to wear when I meet his family next weekend," Sam said.

More red was flashing before Meg's eyes than at Chinese New Year. "He told you what to wear when you meet his family?" she asked, taking the dress she'd just ironed over to a manikin in the window and gesturing for Sam to come help.

"Oh, it wasn't like that," Sam said. "Just a suggestion."

"Speaking of bright colors," Gloria asked, "what's the bright green paint for?"

"It's leftover from an art class. I was wondering if I could paint this wall." She pointed to a half wall in the middle of the store, where a few dresses hung on racks jutting out from it. "I know you're planning a full remodel, but I thought a vibrant color would really perk things up. And I thought I could do a purple stencil on it."

"Sure," Meg said. "Go for it. It sounds fun." Frankly, today she didn't care if Sam painted the wall orange with purple spots on it.

"By the way, how's Spike doing, dear?" Gran always pried in the kindest way. But if it kept Meg's mind—and everyone else's—off her problems and kept her from crying in her coffee, so be it. With Sam's help, Meg pushed the bell-shaped, Italian satin dress over the manikin.

"Back to causing trouble as usual," Sam said. "I was out with Harris Saturday night and we ran into him. It wasn't very pleasant."

"If he's out and about," Gran said, "then he must have recovered from the accident."

"He's not back to work yet because of the concussion and his arm cast. But Alex and Tom's new housekeeper is Greek and she kind of adopted him. She's been bringing him food since he got home from the hospital."

Gran suddenly gasped. "Oh, my lord." She was looking out the window onto Main Street. "Here comes Maurice Manning."

Meg stopped fluffing the skirt to eye her flustered grandmother. "Gran, are you *blushing*?"

"I'm far too old for that. No, of course not." Gloria craned her neck to see down the street and made shooing movements with her hands. "Send him away."

"I don't send anyone away who comes bearing coffee," Meg said, opening the door. She needed more caffeine to fight against a strong and desperate desire to crawl back into bed and stay there for the morning. Or the day. Or month. "Hi, Maurice," she said as she opened the door.

"Top of the morning to you, my dear. I brought you ladies some coffee to start the day."

Meg took the coffee gratefully. "What a pleasant surprise." He walked over to Gloria, who was focusing so intently on the computer screen she could've been filing her taxes.

Maurice set down a bag on the desk, which made Gloria startle. Her spectacles dropped.

"Brought you something," he said with a smile.

Gloria peeked into the bag, her blush becoming even more furious. "Chocolate croissants. How did you—"

"Ted told me you liked them. Well, I've got to be going. Have a good day, ladies." A mischievous look filled his blue eyes, even though he nodded solemnly as he backed away and left the shop.

Meg examined the bag. "Can I have one?" Caffeine and chocolate, two legal drugs to fight her sorrows.

"Have both," Gloria said. "I won't touch them."

"Gran! Why not? He's sweet on you."

"Bite your tongue! I've had one dog and one man, and I'll never change."

Meg bit into the chocolaty croissant and washed it down with a swig of perfect coffee. Suddenly, her day was looking a little brighter. Or at least survivable.

"Oh, come on, Gran, he's nice and maybe he just wants to be friends."

"I don't care how old men are, they never want to be just friends. I'm too old for that nonsense."

"What nonsense?" she teased.

"Hanky-panky," she said throwing up her arms in frustration.

"How is it you could give me the sex talk without batting an eyelash but you get flustered when a gentleman caller brings you pastries?"

"I loved your grandfather."

Oh. "Of course you did, Gran." Meg put a hand in her grandmother's and squeezed. "We all did."

"I have wonderful memories. I—don't want to sully those by getting involved with someone else, if that makes any sense."

"It's like you'd feel unfaithful to Gramps?"

"Oh, I really don't want to talk about this anymore."

Meg smiled. "You'd much rather spend your time tormenting me about my love life."

"Since you look like hell today, we can give you a break and tease Samantha about hers, can't we, dear?" Gloria said.

"Oh, no," Sam said. "There's nothing to tease me about. I'm just minding my business under this dummy's skirts, staying away from trouble."

"Speaking of trouble, here he comes now," Gloria said.

Meg followed her grandmother's gaze. A tall man with longish black hair, dressed in a black T-shirt, jeans, and motorcycle boots, was striding purposefully across the square. Even from a distance, he cut a dramatic figure.

"Lukas Spikonos," Gran said.

"How do you know him, Gran?" Meg asked.

"Oh, everyone knows about the Spikonos brothers. Had a hard time of it, they did. Both parents were alcoholics, and all four boys ended up in different foster homes."

"That's a shame," Meg said. "Is he engaged?"

Samantha snorted. "Why on earth would you ask that?"

"Because I'm trying to figure out another reason why he'd be headed to a bridal shop."

Sam popped her head up from pinning the gown to stare as Spike skirted the rest of the distance across the grassy square and crossed the street, keeping the shop in his sights. As he approached, Meg noticed that even the cast on his arm was black. Before Meg could say *Johnny Depp*, he was opening the door to the shop, its telltale bell tinkling as he entered.

His gaze honed in immediately on Sam, who had bent back down and was pretending to be hard at work. He gave a cursory nod to Meg. "Ma'am." Then he turned all his testosterone onto Sam, who had suddenly found fitting the gown to the manikin fascinating. "I need to talk to you."

A head poked out from underneath the dress. "I'm working now, Spike."

Spike turned to Meg. "Ma'am, would it be okay if Sam took a break for ten minutes?"

Sam spoke up preemptively. "No, Meg, that's really not nec—"

"It's fine with me," Meg told him, "but it's up to Samantha whether or not she wants to talk with you."

Spike eyed Meg patiently, as if she were just one more obstacle he had to surmount before he could get what he wanted. And it was clear what he wanted, because he looked at Sam with a gaze that seemed like it could burn a hole in one of the old plaster walls. "Please, Sam," he pleaded in a voice that sounded deep and Jack Daniels smooth. "Just a few minutes."

Suddenly, Meg understood why the Rushford brothers were so worried. He had large brown eyes, almost doe-like, set into a fine oval face with olive-colored skin. Thickset brows and the shadow of stubble completed his lady-killer look. Heavily inked tattoos peeked out from under his cast and all along his uninjured arm. Every pore of this guy's body oozed heartbreak with a capital H.

"C'mon, Gran, we've got boxes in the back to sort." Gran was gawking, but Meg managed to steer her firmly to the storeroom. "Nice to see you again, Lukas. Glad you're out of the hospital."

Spike gave a brief nod in response. Meg and Gran weren't more than four feet away when he said to Sam, "You let that preppy son of a bitch take you parking."

Meg dragged herself and Gran into the back room, but they could still hear the conversation. And there was no way they were missing this. She and Gran huddled near the door, barely catching a glimpse in between racks of dresses.

"It's not your business," Sam hissed right back.

"What do you see in him? He's not good enough for you, Sam."

"No. I'm not doing this. You pushed me away with both hands last summer. You crashed your bike into a *chicken* truck. It's none of your damn business who I'm dating."

Spike trawled his hands through his hair. "For the record, the chicken truck braked suddenly and I avoided it—and all the other traffic—by swerving. It wasn't my fault."

"Whatever. You almost died."

"So you *do* care about me."

"I care like one-human-being-to-another cares. That's it."

"You don't even look like yourself anymore."

"How dare you. Just because I'm not wearing ratty old jeans doesn't mean anything."

"You've changed the way you dress, the way you wear your hair. You've lost sight of who you are. You're turning into his puppet."

"Why do you care?" she asked.

"God knows I shouldn't." A heavy sigh. Another long pause. "When are you going to realize you're like an angel and . . . and he's clipped your wings."

Silence. A *lot* of silence. Meg peeked around the curtain that separated the back room from the shop. Gloria pushed on her shoulders from behind, struggling to see.

A movie kiss moment was taking place, right in her own store. Powerful, possessive, testosterone flying everywhere. Spike cupped Sam's delicate neck in his long-fingered hand, which tangled in her hair. They were flush up against one another, making Meg feel like a bad chaperone at a school dance. She slunk back into the storeroom, stifling a sneeze.

One vote for Spike. She had to hand it to the kid, he had quite a presence. Lots of passion. And a hot bod to boot.

Finally, the bell over the door tinkled, signaling Spike's exit. Meg made sure she and Gran got busy sorting boxes.

"He's a hottie," Gran said. "He might just be more of a bad boy than Prince Harry."

"Gran, shhhh," Meg said.

"I'm going to work on the computer," Gran said. "Maybe you two can have girl talk while I'm gone."

Talk? Meg had to admit she was impressed by Spike's on-the-nose assessment. She'd long suspected Sam was trying hard to please her family in the wake of her brother's death, as she'd done herself. And still tended to do. But her own love life was a mess and she had little to offer in the way of advice. Especially about a boy the family was convinced was the devil's spawn.

Samantha walked into the back room and flopped down on an antique settee near the shop's old runway, where many past brides had walked down a pink carpeted runway to a large three-way mirror to view themselves in their dresses.

From the corner of her eye, Meg saw Sam sitting curl-into-a-ball style, her arms wrapped tightly around her knees. "You know," Meg said, "if you ever want to talk, I'm happy to listen."

"Thanks, but I'm okay."

"He seems like a nice young man," Meg said. "Very polite."

"Well, you'd be the only one around here who thinks that. Spike's not nice. He's a tatted-up auto mechanic who eats virgins for breakfast and any smart girl would stay away. Not to mention the fact that my brothers would kill him and me if I ever took up with him again." She looked at her cell phone. "It's still early but would you mind if I took a lunch break?"

"We'll review the vendors' list for the show this afternoon, okay?"

"I've already done that." She paused. "You don't need to be nice to me because you want to date my brother."

Oh, hell, was that what she thought? "I'm not being nice to you because of Ben. I'm being nice to you because I *like* you. This may be none of my business, but I know what it's like to want someone who no one else who loves you thinks you should want. It has to be your choice, Sam. Not someone else's choice for you." She'd spoken boldly, on gut instinct, but she could be reading it all wrong. She didn't know Spike and she wasn't even family.

"I meant what I said about talking to someone. Because if you can't talk to your family about this and you want a neutral ear, I'm here." Her speech met with stunned silence. "And you can leave now."

Samantha mumbled a quick thanks and bolted.

Meg looked around the silent storeroom and sat down hard on the settee, leaning back and staring up at the ancient wood-beam ceiling.

She'd just been forceful and direct, things that tended to scare the shit out of her. Why did she do it? Because she felt she had something to offer Samantha, something that probably no one in her family could see.

Ben and his brothers had characterized the kid as a no-good deadbeat from the wrong side of town, and they'd been desperate to keep their sister away from him.

But she wasn't so sure. At least, judgment was out for now. Spike had called Sam out on something that maybe she'd needed to hear. He also seemed to be trying, albeit unsuccessfully, to stay away from her.

Meg couldn't help but wonder if it was the same way with Ben. Confident, easygoing Ben, who clearly had another side.

He had wanted her, yes he had, before he was reminded of Patrick. Maybe he had wanted her for years. But she couldn't change the past. Couldn't go back to that one moment in time when she could've told her troubled brother to stop taking daredevil risks, especially the foolish one that had cost him his life. She didn't fully understand the trauma and guilt that Ben felt. He didn't make Patrick do what he did. He wasn't even there when it happened.

All she knew was that when you loved someone, you worked through problems, didn't run away from them. Didn't say, *sorry, I don't do relationships*, and use that as a blanket excuse for not facing the past.

This whole thing was just too large. Too insurmountable. And frankly, she'd had enough heartache. She pulled out her phone and tossed it lightly from hand to hand.

There was only one thing left to do—prove she could go on with her life. She called up Cole Hanson's number on the screen to text him *yes* for Friday night.

CHAPTER 14

MacNamara's Pub was crowded with happy people on a rainy Friday evening. Even the songs sung by Spike and his band, who were set up in a tiny corner, were mellow and surprisingly upbeat. Meg enjoyed the music, sipped a glass of wine, and read a book on her phone while she waited in a booth for her date, who had texted her he was running late. She could do this. Take her first real step in moving on from Ben. Because pretending to be happy was the first step in getting happy, right?

Cole Hanson walked in, shook out his umbrella, and left it near the door. Judging from how wet he was, the rain was really coming down. As he walked confidently through the central aisle toward her, she couldn't help comparing him to Ben. *Not quite as handsome, not quite as tall.* She hated herself for being so shallow.

"I wish I could've picked you up tonight," he said, "but one of my old dogs passed away and I did a house call." He pecked her on the cheek and sat down.

What a nice man. Visiting old dogs and helping them pass on. He'd even sent her a bouquet of flowers to thank her for helping his daughter. And what a nice, pleasant peck. Like Gran's.

Oh, shame. Stop analyzing every kiss and just have fun.

He ordered a beer and she ordered a second glass of wine. Because she was going to get over Ben Rushford once and for all, no matter how many glasses it took.

Wasn't she glad she'd told Alex and Olivia she'd had a date tonight? The word was sure to flow through the Rushford pipeline to get back to Ben. Great. Because she wanted him to know she wasn't sitting around pining for him.

Wasn't she glad she'd finally decided that whole crazy thing with him was toxic, and wasn't she *really* glad she'd finally figured all that out before she'd gone and slept with him?

"I'm sorry, what did you say?" she asked Cole. Dogs. It was something about dogs, and being part of his patients' families. See? He was a nice, nice man. If Cole asked her to sleep with him, what would she say?

She'd do it, that's what. Anything to drive Ben out of her mind once and for all. She was ready for the next step with a man who could offer her the things she wanted from life. He was handsome and ambitious and kind to her animals. What wasn't to like?

Just the fact that he's not Ben, that damnable voice in her head said. She shut it up with another sip of wine.

Cole reached a hand across the table and grasped hers. "You look amazing."

She smiled "Thanks." She'd curled her hair, put on a sparkly purple minidress, and took extra care with her makeup. And she hadn't even consulted Alex.

Brownie points for trying her hardest.

When he gave her hand a little shake, she realized her mind had been wandering again. "You seem worried about something," he said.

"Nah," she said, giving her hand a carefree flap. "Work's just been a little crazy lately. I'm actually happy to be out tonight—with you." She smiled again in what she hoped was a sincere way and looked straight into his deep blue eyes. He sort of looked like a blond Bradley Cooper, if she squinted a bit. Another glass of wine, and he would for sure.

You don't like blond guys. Even hot ones. Another voice joined the torment.

It's hard to give up when you were so close, whispered the third voice, which she recognized as her deepest most innermost self, and it made her heart break a little more. *But the dream has to die.*

She was embarrassed to find that her vision was blurred by a sudden spring of tears that she quickly blinked away. If she wasn't careful, she was going to ruin this for herself. She was twenty-six years old, not old, but thirty was right around the corner. She had to make compromises. Stop dreaming of fairy tales. Stop acting like a high school girl with a stalker crush that kept resurrecting again and again like a creature from a bad horror movie. Nice, good-looking guys she might actually have something in common with were rare enough in Mirror Lake, and those who were as interested in her as Cole was, even rarer.

"Thanks for the flowers," she said. "You didn't have to do that."

"Did you like them?"

He'd sent two-dozen red roses. "Roses are my favorite." Not true, she preferred something less formal, picked from the garden, like daisies.

"I can't thank you enough for what you did for Becca," Cole said. "She—I don't know, Meg, she seems more like her old self again, something I haven't seen in a long time. After the last few years we've had, that's a miracle. And she can't stop talking about camp."

"She's a very sweet little girl."

"I don't want you to think the flowers are just for helping her. I've been wanting to ask you out again for quite a while. Now that she's doing so much better, I—" He tangled their fingers together.

This is what you wanted, the voices all said in chorus. She waited for the tingle. The zap. The shooting stars.

Nothing. That sexy look in his eyes wasn't turning her on, nor was his touch, which was warm and gentle. His voice was a little on the high side, not that it was effeminate or anything, but none of it was Ben's, damn that dimpled devil anyway.

Cole looked eager and intent. "Say, listen, Meg, The Palace is showing the sequel to some road trip comedy. Would you be interested in seeing it with me this weekend?"

Before she could answer, his beeper went off. He took it out of his pocket and squinted at it. "I'm not on call tonight, but sometimes the animal hospital calls me if one of my patients is admitted. Would you excuse me a moment?"

"Sure. I'll look over the menu while you're gone." She didn't need to look at it, because she'd grown up in this bar and knew the entire thing by heart. In college her standard order was nachos and beer, with girlfriends it was margaritas and quesadillas, and for date night it was a Reuben and fries. She snuck her phone out in front of the menu and kept reading her book. The rugged Navy SEAL alpha hero was just getting ready to grovel to the heroine after being an ass when Meg heard her phone suddenly ping with a text. She glanced down at the screen.

Sequels suck. From Ben.

She sucked in a breath. Perused the bar, but other than the usual patrons, she saw no one.

Another text. *Never as good as the original. Besides, you're busy.*

"Meg."

Her heart gave a ridiculous knock against her rib cage. Every cell in her body went on alert at the sound of that voice calling her name.

No. She willed her overactive neurons to stop firing. Willed the adrenaline to stop pumping. Because she was done with him. He was what he was, and she was not going to forgive him after one mere glimpse of his killer smile.

She looked up to see Ben, dripping wet, in a navy T-shirt and shorts, standing beside the booth.

She played it casual. "Hi." It sounded diminutive, like a squeak. Not the calm, cool, mildly annoyed *hi* she was aiming for.

She steeled herself against him. Hardened her resolve. He was so tall, she had to tip her head back to see him. Despite his being wet and rumpled and looking genuinely distressed, her stupid heart jolted again.

He sat down urgently across from her and seized her hands.

It felt nothing like Cole's grasp. This one seared her straight through to her soul, made her tremble as if no guy had ever held her hand before.

His dark gaze took no prisoners. "I have to talk to you."

Wait a minute. He'd had *days* to talk. She wasn't about to drop everything for him even if the mere touch of his thumbs smoothing the back of her hand was setting her panties on fire. She pulled her hands away. "I'm on a date," she said.

"Forget your date. This is more important."

Oh, the arrogance! She was not caving in. Letting him off the hook. Or interrupting her date for him. "Call me tomorrow and I'll schedule you in."

"Tonight. Now."

She rolled her eyes. "You're forgiven for not wanting me. I've moved on. No hard feelings."

"Please—give me a chance."

He looked a little desperate. "Okay," she said, relenting a little. "You have one minute before Cole comes back."

"Come with me and let's talk."

"If you think I would up and abandon my date right this second for you, then you are the most egotistical . . . jerk I've ever met." She paused. It was now or never. She had to take a stand. "I-I have to ask you to leave before he gets back."

"Fine. I'll leave. But only if you promise to meet me afterward."

"Ben, I don't know what I'm doing afterward."

"What . . . do you mean?" he asked cautiously. His eyes opened wide as realization set in. He reached over and seized her shoulders. "Meggie, no. Don't sleep with him."

"Why shouldn't I?" She sounded a little petulant as she shrugged out of his reach. But his desperate tone intrigued her. Made her curious. Made her *hope, dammit.*

There she went again, so easily swayed from her purpose. She was here with Cole. She was not looking for another excuse to go back to wanting Ben.

"Because he's not right for you." He shifted in his seat. Trawled a hand through his wet hair.

"Since when do you get to evaluate my dates? Last I looked, you weren't my chaperone." She leaned over the table. He looked seriously affronted and she was strangely pleased she was getting to him.

"Why are you really here?" she asked. "Do you just feel bad you hurt my feelings? Well, guess what? I'm over it. I can accept I'm not the kind of woman you want, so you can leave with a clear conscience." She sat back. "Please go now."

"Don't sleep with him until you hear me out."

"Not your business, and I've heard plenty. You'd better go." At the front of the bar, she watched as Cole stepped back in from the restroom corridor and was now chatting up the bartender.

Meg waited until she saw Ben walk out the door before she rummaged in her purse for a Kleenex. She blotted her eyes and downed the rest of her wine in one gulp. Then she put on more lipstick. She was shaken up, but she wasn't faltering. Ben was a dead end. He would suck her back into his force field with his good looks and his charm, and she'd be in menopause before she'd finally be over his spell.

She already lived alone with three cats, so she needed to do everything in her power to fight the stereotype.

"Was Ben Rushford harassing you?" Scott MacNamara, the owner, asked teasingly on a pass by.

"No more than usual," she said darkly.

Cole sat down. "That's odd, my seat's wet," he said, brushing off the wet leather of the booth.

"Must have been from my raincoat," Meg said with a shrug, looking up at the hook where her coat rested. "Shall we order?"

"Sure." He grinned widely. "I just want to tell you it's great to be here with you. I—think very highly of you, Meg. You're not only beautiful, you're a class act, and I want to get to know you a lot better."

"Oh, Cole, that's so sweet." Before The Elevator Incident, she would have done a happy dance in public to hear those words. As she smiled pleasantly, she tried desperately to summon the thrill, but it refused to overtake her.

"Excuse me, Dr. Hanson," someone said.

Startled, Meg looked up to find Ben standing beside their booth—dripping wet again—and holding a black cat.

A black cat?

Apparently Meg wasn't the only one fighting Ben's company. Because the struggling, clawing, pissed-off animal clearly wished he or she were anywhere else but in MacNamara's Bar.

Out of spite, Meg hoped it was a she. It would be great to find solidarity with another woman who couldn't stand him.

"I think my cat's been hit by a car," Ben said.

Meg gasped. Cole immediately rose, but Meg held out her hand to stop him. Looking at Ben, she said, "You don't have a cat."

"I do now," he said. "See?" Ben did everything possible to hold onto the writhing animal. Scratch-mark graffiti edged down his arms. Some of the scratches were bleeding.

"What happened?" Cole asked, assessing the cat.

"I found her at the side of the road, not moving. Can you check her out?"

She was certainly on the move now, twisting and squirming and freaking out, desperate to be free.

"Are you certain that's your cat?" Cole asked.

"Yeah. Of course. Its name is"—Ben glanced around the bar—

"Claddaugh. It's okay, Claddaugh, settle down. This nice man is going to help you."

Meg rolled her eyes. *Unbelievable.*

"Because there's no collar or tag," Cole said, his critical gaze sweeping over the very active cat.

"I took them off to give her a bath today."

Cole's eyes narrowed. He opened his mouth to speak just as the cat tore out of Ben's arms and raced for the bar. At that moment, Meg wished she could go with it, because she seriously needed another drink.

Ben moved to chase after the cat but Cole stopped him. "You're a doc, right?" Cole asked.

Ben nodded slowly. He stared down at Cole's hand on his upper arm like it was a fungus.

"Then you should know better than to bring a feral cat in here."

Busted. Ben closed his eyes for a moment, to admit defeat or regroup, Meg wasn't sure. "Can I talk to you—alone? Man to man?"

"Oh, no, you don't." Meg grabbed Cole's arm and pulled him toward her. "Anything you have to say, you can say in front of me, too."

"Okay, fine," Ben said, his brows knit into a menacing vee. "Don't date him."

Meg tapped a finger on her cheek. "Um, not your call, is it?"

"We"—Ben looked at Cole and pointed at himself and Meg—"have unfinished business. She can't date you."

"Don't listen to him," she said to Cole, hooking her arm through his elbow. To Ben, she said, "We're leaving."

Cole stood between Meg and Ben. "You heard her, buddy," he said. "Back off."

Meg gathered her purse and her jacket and walked down the aisle with Cole toward the door.

Ben's voice reached her halfway down the aisle. "I know I don't deserve another chance. But at least give me an opportunity to try."

Meg froze in her tracks. Nearly tripped on her black platform open-toe shoes with bows that she'd worn just for this date. She willed herself to move, but her body didn't catch the signal. She didn't know whether to laugh or cry, but within seconds, the tears threatened to win. Every single time she tried to move on from this man, he somehow managed to pull her back in.

"Don't let him harass you," Cole said, his grip around her arm tightening.

Meg bit back a sudden sting of tears and turned to face Ben, steeling herself with every muscle. His hair was wet and disheveled, his shoes muddied. Strain drew his mouth into a tight line. Gray circles rimmed his eyes, making her wonder if he'd just gotten off a long hard shift.

For a moment, she weakened. Yes, she wanted desperately to hear what he had to say. She wanted to understand him.

But a sudden exhaustion overcame her. She was tired of the endless cycle of hoping and then being let down. Besides, she was on a date with a great guy. A man who let her know in no uncertain terms how much he liked her.

Maybe Ben was jealous of Cole, or protective of her as he'd been in the past, but that wasn't her problem. It was *his*.

"It's too late for that," she said, "and I-I've got to go. Goodbye, Ben."

She walked out of the bar with Cole and forced herself not to look back.

CHAPTER 15

How long did it take for people to have sex? From his vantage point in his car overlooking Cole Hanson's house, Ben Googled the question on his phone, and learned the range fell anywhere between eight minutes and two hours. He checked his watch for the hundredth time. Meg had been in Cole's house for a grand total of ten minutes. Cole didn't strike him as the eight-minute type, but he wasn't taking any chances.

He felt pretty sure she didn't have a thing for the vet.

She had one for *him*. Or she used to until he'd gone and messed everything up.

He glanced down at his scratched arms, a reminder of what desperate lengths he'd gone to in order to get her to listen to him. He had to find a way to tell her how sorry he was for running out on her, for messing everything up last weekend. He'd been afraid. Of telling her about the night that Patrick had died, of his ineptitude. His utter helplessness. How would she look at him after he'd told her?

Even though he didn't deserve her, he couldn't bear to hand her over to another man. Ben looked at his hands, fingers balled into frustrated fists. The jig was up. He had to come clean. The consequences of confessing his shame about the night her brother died were too terrible to bear, but not as terrible as losing her for good. He wanted her like he'd never wanted any other woman, and for the millionth time, he'd have given his right arm to change the past. To come to her as someone worthy.

But he was what he was. And the thought of Cole's hands—instead of his—sliding over her satiny skin fueled a bonfire of outrage in him that superseded every other thought.

He slammed the car door shut and was halfway up the walkway when Meg walked out of the front door. Looking as put together as ever, in a sleeveless purple dress that stopped mid-thigh and heels. No mussed hair, no swollen lips. He untensed just a little.

What guy allows a gorgeous woman to leave his place after ten minutes? If he himself had taken on the fine task of making love to her, he wouldn't have let her out of his sight until Wednesday at least.

Make that the *next* Wednesday.

Seeing her made his heart trip all over itself like he was sixteen again. He'd kissed her once, long ago, and if life would have given him a chance, he would have kissed her thousands of times.

He prayed that maybe she would give him that chance now.

"Can I give you a ride?" he asked, shoving his hands in his pockets. The rain had stopped, and a light breeze caught the silky strands of her hair and blew them about her face as she looked up and saw him. It took everything he had to restrain himself from gathering her up in his arms, but her expression was a mix between bewilderment and annoyance, and he knew he had to try something with her he hadn't dared to before.

Honesty.

And it might cost him everything.

She hiked her hands up to her sweet hips. "What are you doing here?"

"I—um—don't want you to walk home alone. What kind of guy lets his date walk home alone?" *He* would never have let her do that. But then, by now he would have given her a million reasons not to want to leave his place. Starting with kisses and caresses and soft touches. What was wrong with that guy, anyway?

In response, she pulled off her heels and walked away from him barefoot. "First of all, I'm not walking home. I'm walking to Olivia and Brad's, because I'm house-sitting while they're at the beach with Annabelle overnight. Second, it's a beautiful night for a walk. And third, Rebecca was asleep. He couldn't leave."

"So nothing happened?" He was completely out of line and he knew it down to his bones. But again, he could not stop himself. He'd never felt such desperation.

She halted on the sidewalk. Did a slow turn toward him and canted her head like she didn't hear him right. "Excuse me?"

"Did you make love with him?" The tension in his jaw was so tight, it could crack a walnut. Every muscle was wound up, tight and tense and ready to spring.

"That is absolutely none of your business."

He got in her face. "Yes, it is." *Because you belong with me, not him.*

She threw up her hands in a gesture of exasperation. "You've made it clear on more than one occasion that you aren't interested in me. Why on earth do you care if I slept with Cole Hanson?"

A dog barked. A porch light flicked on. Ben steered her down the sidewalk, a little toward his car. "Do you remember your prom night?"

"You know damn well I don't want to remember my prom night. My date got drunk and left without me." She stopped on the sidewalk. "Why are you bringing this up now?"

He grasped both her arms and turned her so they were face to face. So she could hear every word. So she could see he meant them. "Listen to me, Meggie. For one second. That night, I found you walking home alone and picked you up. Then do you remember what we did?"

"You bought me a hot fudge sundae. But high school was a long time ago and I am so over it."

"Do you remember what I told you?"

She rolled her eyes. "I honestly don't remember." But he thought he saw a flicker of hesitation in her eyes.

"I told you that you deserve better. Someone who understands you. Who appreciates you."

"And that was great advice. Now let go of me so I can go take it."

"What I really meant was that *I* wanted to be that guy, Meg. I've wanted you ever since. Every blessed time I've seen you laughing with your friends, at picnics, and generally when you're paying attention to any other guy but me. Up to and including the time you got your shoe stuck in that elevator."

Incredulity clouded her eyes. "If that's true, then why haven't you done something about it?"

"Because I—" *Because of Patrick. Because of what happened.* Sweat trickled down his neck, but he felt cold all over. The words froze in his throat.

Meg's patience was up. "Okay. Well, I'm going home and you can go chase after someone who has much lower expectations, because I'm sure there are plenty of women who might actually want to date you."

"I'm pretty sure you want to date me."

"What makes you think that?"

"Because if you didn't, you wouldn't have spent less than ten minutes with that other guy. At least, I'm praying that was the reason." *Please, God, it had to be.*

She shook her head. "I'm tired of games, Ben. I've played them for too many years. I'm going home."

She took off barefoot down the sidewalk, lit by the bluish-white glow of streetlights.

"Megan, please." He stood in the middle of the sidewalk, pleading. "Get in the car and let me explain."

He saw the moment her body reacted to the sound of her name, her *real* name. Her shoulders stiffened, her pace slowed. She slowly turned to face him.

"You called me Megan." Under the old-fashioned lamppost, her silky dark hair looked luminous. The maple leaves shimmered in silvery bunches and the green Cherry Street sign glowed. "Not Margaret, Maggie, Peggy?"

He'd finally gotten her attention. "I'm done joking around. Please get in." He took advantage of her semi-stunned state by leading her the rest of the way to his car, opening the passenger door, and helping her in before she could put up a fight.

"Ten minutes, Rushford."

"How about a half hour? I want to take you somewhere."

"I've already been on a date, remember?"

"This is different."

And to prove it, he revved the engine and took off down the street.

><+>-0-<+><

As the Mustang let loose on the country road that led out of town, Meg inhaled the fresh scents of woods and summer night air. The cricket song seemed constant and magnified as they sped along with the top down. She remembered the reckless sense of freedom she felt as a kid on these moonlit rides, on the rare occasions Ben and her brother chose to include her, when she'd abandoned all her cares and worries to the soft night breeze that blew all around them.

She was more cautious now. Every nerve hummed with the sensation, hopeful and terrible at once, that something was different, about him, about *them*. She felt as if she were standing on a precipice, her old life behind her, and something unknown and dangerous ahead that she couldn't quite see.

The car slowed, and Ben took a sharp left onto a narrow service road on the backside of the airport acreage. Gravel crunched and spit from beneath the car wheels. "This is a back road to Dove's Point. I thought it would be a quiet place to sit and talk."

"It might be full of teenagers making out. It is Friday night, you know."

"No one knows this place. It's super secret."

"Super scary if you ask me," Meg said, looking around at the dense brush that practically scraped the car. "And I think all the kids know about this place. In fact, in recent years the cops have cleared it out. Too much trouble going on deep in the woods."

The car rolled to a stop. Ben opened his door and walked around for her. "Let's go sit over here."

They were about a quarter mile from Dove's Point, the fan-shaped ripple of rock that had reminded someone long ago of a dove's tail. He led her through some brush to a clearing with a bench that overlooked the lake.

"What is this place? Your private make-out spot?"

"I took girls to the Point but I came here by myself. To think. It's along one of the old trailheads. Out of the way. Private."

They stood against an iron rail and admired the view of the water. The lake spread itself wide and dark in the distance, a few lights from town twinkling like little diamonds at its periphery, its middle regions pure black velvet.

"I've always wanted to live on the lake," he said.

"Why's that?"

"It's an instant de-stress, looking out on something so peaceful and quiet. Sort of makes you forget your own troubles, you know?"

He'd always been trouble. From the thickly shorn layers of his hair that had always made her yearn to tug her fingers through it, to the sharp-angled profile of his face that stood out against the dimly lit lake behind him, to the hard set of his shoulders as he leaned against the rail. Even now, when she was wary and angry and uncertain, his physical presence impacted her and she supposed it always would.

"Who was that guy you were with up at the point that one time?"

"You scared him off. I was so embarrassed."

"He was out for one thing."

"I could've handled him myself."

"Well, I wasn't taking any chances."

"You did play big brother to me after Patrick died."

He turned abruptly and grabbed her by the upper arms, his eyes drilling into hers. "I wasn't being brotherly," he said. "I was being *jealous*."

She searched those eyes, dark and mysterious as the night but with a strange flare of brightness. An uneasy feeling fluttered around her insides like moths circling light. He'd been jealous? Ridiculous. No. *Impossible.*

"I let you think I was looking out for you." His grip on her was relentless, his voice filled with passion.

"You—why?"

He released her suddenly and turned toward the lake, leaning his elbows on the railing. For a long time he didn't say anything. She saw his Adam's apple working. He seemed lost in a world of his own.

Or a hell of his own.

At last he spoke, so quietly she had to strain to hear. "Do you blame me for your brother's death?"

"Of course not." An easy question. She never had. Unlike her mother, Meg knew that Patrick wasn't a saint. He'd engaged in dangerous behaviors, but unlike most teenagers, wasn't lucky enough to survive them.

"Your mother does."

"My mother's never been able to accept that Patrick sometimes did foolish, risky things." She stood a little behind Ben, uncertain what this was leading up to. He stared over the quiet water, stock-still, an explosion of raw emotions threatening to break loose, held in check only by years of keeping them behind locked doors.

She saw the price it had cost him. His shoulders were steeled as if he were in combat against some imaginary foe, his posture rigid, his chin set. Suddenly all the anger she'd felt earlier in the night dissipated like a handful of glitter a child tossed into the wind.

She curled her hand around his arm, feeling its hard, solid strength. "Seeing you will always be a reminder to her of the son she lost."

Silence stretched long and wide as the clear, calm lake. Crickets and bullfrogs sang background, and somewhere in the woods, an owl hooted.

He turned. "I want to talk to you about that night."

Her grip on his arm froze. Part of her wanted to run. She didn't want to stir the terror that still managed to chase her, usually in the depths of night when she relived it all in her dreams. Every day she felt a void, a sadness that never quite went away, and it was a feeling she chose to avoid at any cost, like touching a sore. What kept her planted was one thing—Ben needed to talk, and he'd chosen her to listen.

They'd finally broached the one topic they'd managed to dance around for years. It had become an invisible wall that had kept them apart. And no matter how painful, she wanted to claw away at every blessed block.

"Tell me," she said quietly.

"I was a wreck that summer. Acting out after my parents died, feeling sorry for myself and angry at the whole damn world. I drank, smoked weed, even tried blow. Thank God my grandfather intervened or who knows where I would have ended up. I was so pissed when he told me one Friday night to report to his office at 8:00 a.m. the next morning. I got in his face and said *make me, old man*. That night when I was asleep he snuck into my room and took my wallet and car keys. Woke me up at seven the next morning and told me I wouldn't get them back until I reported for duty."

He absently plucked off a leaf from an overhanging oak and fingered it. "I spent that whole first day greeting patients, signing them in, taking their pulses and blood pressures. I saw things. Heard things. Understood that I wasn't the only one on the planet with problems. A long time later, I learned that my grandfather's nurse had quit and he was short in the office." He laughed. "He saved me from myself. He saved my life. I owe him everything."

Meg stood quietly beside him, leaning on the railing, although she longed to surround him with all of her warmth and strength, wrap herself around him until he would know beyond all doubt that she would be there for him, for the traumatized boy he was and for the tortured man he was now.

"A few weeks after I'd started working for my grandfather, Patrick asked me to party with him one night at the quarry. I was tempted, but we'd just found out my Grandma Rushford's cancer had recurred and I'd gone to visit her in the hospital. She was hooked up to oxygen and monitors and IV's. My grandfather was at her side, holding her hand, stroking her fingers, singing some old-fashioned song. He looked stricken, like if he lost her, he wasn't certain he'd be able to go on.

"It shook me to see my grandfather like that. I never thought he could be vulnerable to the same things I was. He saw me looking at him and he said, *This is what you hold on for. What you become a good man for, a man worthy of being loved.*

"I cancelled on your brother. I thought he was meeting another buddy of ours, but the guy never showed. I ate dinner with my grandfather in the hospital cafeteria, and on the way home I ran into that kid. He said Patrick was upset about something. Really upset."

"My parents had had a huge fight," Meg said. "We overheard them talking about divorce. I knew he was upset—we both were, but I had to work and he told me he was meeting friends. Besides, I was wrapped up in my own troubles. I never thought twice about leaving him."

"When I found out he'd gone alone, I went to the quarry. But when I got there, it was too late." His voice cracked.

She moved to hold him, but he held her at arm's length. "You have to hear what I have to say. And you're not going to like it. It may make you hate me."

She looked into his eyes, so serious, so burdened. "I could never hate you," she whispered.

"I called for him so loudly and so long I got hoarse. Finally I jumped into the water and swam to this island, this mound of gravel in the middle where we used to hang out and sun ourselves. There was a bunch of beer cans scattered around, and his shirt and wallet.

"I had no phone. I didn't know what to do. I was so scared, the kind of scared you get when you know—you just *know*—that something terrible has happened."

Meg shook her head and squeezed her eyes shut. She didn't want him to go on. But she knew he had to, for both their sakes.

"How did you find him?" she asked.

"I dove in a handful of times before I did. Somehow I managed to pull him up."

His gaze was focused on some faraway place, deep in the past. She reached up and cupped his cheek with her hand, pulled his face toward her until he saw her. "It's enough. You did all you could. Don't relive it again."

"You don't understand."

He heaved a heavy sigh and sat on the bench. "I shook him. I screamed his name. I tried to blow breaths into him but I had no idea how to do CPR. Basically I floundered for ten minutes while I tried to figure out what the hell I was going to do without any way to call for help. Fortunately for me, a sheriff's deputy was doing his rounds and found me. By then it was way too late. If I would have known what I was doing he might have had a chance. Funny thing was, I blew off CPR class in health. I was cocky and arrogant. And that cost my best friend his life."

"Ben, how do you know he wasn't gone when you pulled him out?"

"I'll never know. I was panicked, I didn't try for a pulse, I didn't listen for breaths. I tried to breathe for him but I just . . . fumbled."

"Nothing you could have done would have been enough. But you didn't abandon him. How many people would be brave enough to do what you did? Your actions were brave, not cowardly. And you were just a boy."

Ben shook his head adamantly. "I should never have let him go alone. I've never felt so helpless in my entire life. I vowed never to feel that way again."

Grief strained around his eyes and mouth. She suddenly saw a man who had spent his entire life from that defining moment trying to make amends for circumstances he couldn't have prevented. The reasons he became a doctor suddenly became abundantly clear.

Tears were rolling down her face. She touched his cheek, spoke in a choked whisper. "There's nothing you could have done. You're—you're a good man. A kind, good man."

"Your mother doesn't believe that." Her mother, in her grief, had not been kind to him. She'd lashed out at him at the funeral, saying it was his bad influence that had driven Patrick over the edge.

Her own family had perpetuated his guilt, and his mind had magnified it. An image suddenly came to her of her brother, laughing as he usually was when she thought of him. On his eighteenth birthday, he and Ben had lit sparklers and were dancing around their backyard with them. There was a photo of the two of them, arms around each other's shoulders, holding the sparklers and grinning like they were little kids.

That was how Patrick would have wanted to be remembered. Happy. He never would have wanted the friend he loved to carry this burden all his life.

"Ben, I—"

He held up a warning hand. "There's nothing you can say. But I wanted you to know what really happened. I wanted you to know how sorry I am."

"I'm sorry, too. For my brother's bad choices. For my mother's anger. For the wasted years you and I could have had."

He looked at her then. "Every time I look at you, I feel the pain of what I could have done for him. What I *should* have done."

"Every single one of us feels that, Ben. My mother feels upset that she fought with my father. If I had known how upset Patrick was, I never would have gone to work. Maybe I could have stopped him. Sometimes I'm still so angry at him for a stupid, stupid choice that cost us everything. But all this pain has to end. Patrick wouldn't have wanted it. It's torn apart my family and none of us have been able to heal."

The wound had been stripped open again. She could tell from his face he was unconvinced of anything she'd tried to tell him.

"Let me take you home," he said. He pushed his tall frame off from the rail. Without waiting, he made his way back to the car, and she had no choice but to follow after him.

She wanted to utter some magic words that would absolve him, absolve them all, but she knew there weren't any, at least not from her. So she got into the car and closed the door.

CHAPTER 16

"Hi, Prince Albert," Ben said the second he walked into Brad and Olivia's darkened house and was suddenly attacked by a giant hairy creature with hair in his eyes and a predilection for sniffing Ben's crotch.

As he bent to pet the Saint Bernard that Meg was dog sitting, the animal didn't hesitate to give him a big slurpy lick all along the side of his face.

"Albie needs his nightly gallop around the square," Meg said as she turned on lights that illuminated the back hall, a brand-new kitchen, and a family room with a large fireplace and two cushy couches. The corner was littered with a pink push-scooter with wheels, several baby dolls, and enough large pink plastic toys to supply a full yard sale. The old Victorian had been under constant renovation for the past year, a headache Ben vowed he'd never undertake when it came time for him to own a home.

The dog parked his rump on top of Ben's feet, basking in being petted and rubbing up against his legs. There was never any problem getting affection from Albie. But after all the emotional baggage Ben had just spilled, he'd pretty much guaranteed there was no possibility of that from the one who really counted.

He should feel some sense of relief from their conversation but he was more riled up than ever. He could tell that dredging up the past had upset Meg, and she kept sending him sympathetic looks. But he couldn't bear to have her pity him. A jog around the square with the animal was just what he needed. "I'd be happy to take him," he told Meg and headed out the door.

The summer night was hot and humid after the earlier rain. Tourists strolled along the lit pathways of the square and queued up in a long line outside the Dairy Flip for homemade gourmet ice cream that was always worth the wait.

Ben jogged around the square three times with the dog, who would've dared him to go a fourth, then took a breather on a park bench. Families strolled over to the marina, a short walk away. Long tendrils of vines spilled over moss-covered baskets that hung from old-fashioned lampposts, and bright-colored flowers displayed their full blooms. Happy couples meandered by holding hands, their little tinkles of secretly shared laughter making him irritable.

Meg was right. It was time for the pain to end and for healing, but how? She said she didn't blame him, but how could he believe her when he still blamed himself?

He felt caught in a tangled web of anguish and need, a conundrum of wanting and not having. Restless, he raced the dog into the quiet neighborhood off the square—Albie bounding gleefully, happily keeping pace. Except when he took time out for his usual nightly romp through a neighbor's lawn sprinklers.

Meg's words swirled around Ben's fatigued brain. *You didn't abandon him. How many people would've been brave enough to do what you did?* She'd put her hands on his face and looked at him so tenderly he thought he might die. Not from the bittersweet war with himself he'd fought all these years, but from the absolute mercy she showed. *Not your fault. You're a good man.* Words he drank in like a man dying of thirst. Words he wanted to wash over him and absolve him forever, to wipe away the ugliness that still clung to his skin and his soul like dirt that never washed off.

Anger rose up inside him. At himself, because she made him hope. Her kindness and her genuine belief in him—her soothing touch—had tricked him into believing for just a brief blaze of a second that he could overcome this, that this scar could heal. He wanted it to heal. He wanted a chance with her, but all the pain they had dredged up had made it seem impossible.

Even if Meg understood and didn't hold it against him, there was still the problem of her mother, who over all these years had barely thrown him a glance. Nothing he could do would ever fix that, and he would never force Meg to choose between her mother and him.

He needed to leave. He vowed to say a quick good-bye to her and hightail it back to his apartment in Hartford where he could drink beer and watch movies all night, ones with lots of shooting and cussing and where the good guys always closed the deal.

A good twenty minutes later, he entered the back door of the house and let himself into the old slate-floored hallway. The dog bounded in before Ben could remove his leash, eagerly lapping water from his bowl and making a slobbery mess. Ben liked animals but this guy needed some serious table-manner training.

"Don't forget to wipe off his paws," Meg called from the great room, clearly aware of Albie's sprinkler addiction.

Ben went to seize the dog by the collar, but at the sound of Meg's voice, Albie bounded down the hallway, leaving a trail of black finger-paint paw prints. Ben grabbed an old towel off the row of coat hooks hanging in the hallway and ran after him.

The family room was dark, except for a dozen candles flickering on the coffee table. The soothing aroma of vanilla cupcakes reminded him vaguely of the times his grandmother would bake a batch of his favorite treat to take to class on his birthday.

Ben's vision adjusted to the darkness in time to see the dog go on a seek-and-find mission, bounding over to Meg where she stood against the wall nearest the kitchen wearing a pink robe. As she reached down to grab the dog's leash, Albie dodged and dove, yanking it and Meg a little way across the slippery floor.

"Ow," she said, dropping the leash and holding her flank.

"Damn dog," Ben mumbled, grabbing the leash as the dog flew past and dragging him into the back hall. "Are you okay?" he called as he wiped Albie's muddy paws.

"Twisted my back," she said, her voice guarded with pain. She limped gingerly to the couch and sat down. "Before you go, would you mind having a quick look at it?"

He went and sat beside her. A plastic toy person's arms poked him in the butt. He pulled it out from between the couch cushions and set it on the table.

Meg was barefoot and had on a light cotton robe. At first glance, he'd simply written it off as her settling in for the night. But the candles made him wonder if she was up to something.

"I know you're anxious to get back, and I don't want to keep you," she said.

He instantly felt guilty for thinking something was up. Of course nothing would be. Meg was as transparent as sea glass. An open book. The ability to connive simply wasn't in her DNA.

"Let me see," he said as professionally as possible. Except there was no way he was going to open that Pandora's box of a robe. He could not touch her bare skin. Or look at it. Or it would be hormone Armageddon.

He was certain she'd pulled a muscle, maybe needed a little assurance that nothing else was wrong. He'd peruse it quickly and bring this murderous night to a quick end.

Meg stared at him with wide, serious eyes. Her grip tightened on the belt.

"What's wrong?" he asked.

"It's just that it—it really hurts. I must've done something bad to it. Especially after hurting it last weekend at camp."

"Well, here, let's have a look." Dammit. He'd have to lay eyes on her. She couldn't be naked under that robe, could she? Not her style, but then, she hadn't been wearing underwear when her dress tore, either.

He took the belt from her and unworked the knot. The garment flapped open, revealing a silky lilac—*thing*—that clung to her amazing curves from the tip of its lacy bodice to its hem, which barely crossed her satiny midthighs.

He let out an I-can't-fight-this-anymore groan of helplessness and lust and despair. He'd fought so hard and so long to do the right thing. And now it was all going to shit.

He must have hesitated, sitting there trying to tear his eyes away from her. It was she who took his hand and placed it carefully over her hip. The warmth of her skin permeated the thin fabric as he slid his hand over it.

He ventured a panicked look into her eyes, which in contrast were tranquil and assured. "Right here," she said in a seductive tone, rubbing his hand over the area, her gaze unwavering.

"I thought you said it was your back," he said.

"Yes, my back. And my side."

He swallowed hard. He thought he saw triumph in those wide-eyed, innocent green orbs. Or perhaps it was the victory of a predator when its prey was finally cornered.

"Meg, I—this a bad idea. You know it is."

She rotated his hand in a little circle. "I think it's a very good idea, actually, Benjamin. A little lower, please. That's it. Ooh, yes. Feels *much* better."

He ripped his hand away like he'd just touched a hot pan, but that didn't stop her. She fisted his wet T-shirt and tugged. "The past is gone. Let it go."

Somehow she'd snaked off his shirt and tossed it backwards over her shoulder and somehow, he'd let her.

"I'm sweaty from running with the dog," he said.

"You're going to get even more sweaty."

"I'm wet, too."

"So am I." She let that settle. "I'll lick the water drops off you with my tongue."

"Geez, Meggie!" He looked around helplessly, desperate for some other thought to enter his head that wasn't related to ripping that silky thing off her and pinning her to the couch. As if she could read his mind, she lay back, propped up on her elbows, and let the robe drop open. She arched her back a little so he could catch the perfect view of her beautiful breasts hidden behind violet lace.

He was holding onto reality by nothing more than a thin silk string. "I-I think I forgot to lock my car."

"I'm going to make you forget about everything that's ever bothered you. Even possibly your name."

That made him laugh. Suddenly he became aware that he was still resting his hand on her hip. The satin thing was warm, but the soft flesh underneath seemed scalding. He slid his hand down the silky garment and hitched it up until the skin of her hip and thigh was exposed.

That's when he spotted the thin film of her lacy pink panties.

Call it lack of restraint or self-control, or just plain surrender, but he tossed up the flag.

"Better. Keep going." She closed her eyes, like she was relishing every movement of his hands, memorizing every move he made.

He slid the nightie up another few inches. Ran his fingers over her flat stomach, along her midriff, and down the sides of her abdomen, luxuriating in the softness of her skin and the way her muscles flexed lightly under his touch. She shifted a little and let out a soft sigh. "How's that feel?" he asked.

"I feel a little hot," she said, sitting forward and yanking off the nightie.

Then, lord have mercy, she was lying in front of him naked except for that tiny scrap of panty. The candlelight played off her curves and angles, emphasized the fine contours of her breasts. He skimmed his hands over them like he was touching something reverent. "God, you're beautiful."

She reached for him, brushing her hand over his chest, tracing the lines of his muscles with her fingertips. Every touch seemed electrified, sending a jolt of arousal straight to his groin.

He placed a knee between her thighs, and gently lowered himself down, burying his hands in the luxuriousness of her silky hair. As he lowered his mouth to her neck, she angled her chin upward to give him better access. He bit down gently on the soft skin between her neck and shoulder until a gasp escaped her. Pleased, he kissed the sensitive skin, inhaled her soft clean fragrance, and reveled in how responsive she was to just this, the very beginnings of their touching.

At last, he worked his way to her mouth. Lowering his lips until they almost touched hers, he felt her tremble as his words brushed softly against her mouth. "I don't want to hurt you. But God help me, I can't stay away."

Her fingers tangled in his hair, scraped against his scalp as she cradled his head firmly in her hands. She looked lovingly into his eyes. "I don't want you to," she said, and pulled his head down to hers.

Their kiss was perfect. Long and slow, like they had the rest of their lives to get it exactly right. The kind of kiss a man waits a lifetime for, that he feared he'd never experience, the kind that tastes of forgiveness and hope and a pureness way too good for his sorry ass. One that makes every kiss he'd ever had before seem pale in comparison.

Ben suddenly felt something cold nudge his back. Startled, he turned to find the dog standing near the couch, his wet nose nuzzling him.

"He's lonesome," Meg said, reaching over to pet Albie. "Either that or he thinks you're smothering me. You know how Saint Bernards were bred for rescue."

"Sorry, buddy," Ben said, giving the dog a gentle push, "but the only one who's going to drool over her is me."

As Ben's lips teased her soft, pink ones, he had the sense that something had cut loose from around his neck. He wasn't sure, but he thought it might have been that albatross that had been strangling him for years.

Meg hoped that someday Olivia would forgive her. For bringing Ben back to her house. For raiding her drawers for a racy nightgown and getting her hands on all the candles she could find. And the worst thing of all, rummaging around her medicine cabinet for condoms, no easy task in a pregnant friend's house. But after a lifetime of waiting, she was taking no chances in giving this night every chance to work out.

She stretched out under Ben in languid supplication, enjoying the weight of him, the tickle of coarse-soft chest hair against her bare skin, and the wicked tug of his lips as he teased and stroked and explored. He smelled like summer night and an essence that was uniquely his, which she couldn't get enough of. Now he was exploring her breasts, taking up a nipple in his mouth and teasing it with his tongue. Each time his lips pressed against her skin, she shivered with anticipation, as if she were a long-awaited birthday present left for last and he was unwrapping her bit by bit.

"Ben," she said as her body arched uncontrollably under his licks and teases. Her hands drifted along the solid muscle of his torso, and came to rest on his belt. She gave it a serious tug.

"Yes, Megan," he said, tracing her cheek with his thumb.

"I didn't—seduce you or anything, did I? I mean, you're doing this of your own free will and accord, right?"

He laughed, a rowdy, raucous laugh that sounded snorty and funny and made her laugh, too. "If you mean are you making me do something I haven't wanted to do for years, the answer is no. There isn't anything I want more than to make love to you. But we may have to do some other fun stuff tonight. I didn't bring any protection." He grazed a finger lightly over the edge of her panties.

For a second, her chest strained against his as she reached under the couch and pulled out a box. A ribbon of condoms unfolded like a fan.

"Wow," he said. "All this in twenty-some minutes. You're good."

"Don't get too excited. They're Brad's."

"You stole my brother's condoms?"

"He won't be needing them for about seven months anyway. We'll replace the one we use."

"Ones, *plural*," he said, shaking the box.

"Optimist," she said.

"Realist," he countered, still smiling. A smile that reached his eyes, that for once didn't appear to carry a trace of worry or concern.

"And here I always thought I was the one who was optimistic about our relationship."

"I'm very, very optimistic . . . that we will use this entire box."

His grin faded and his magical lips pressed against hers, kissing her in soft, slow strokes. He undertook a slow, careful exploration of her body, every lick and touch drawn out and thorough.

"Ben, I'm so ready." She tugged on his belt until it slid free, then at last slid her fingers under his shorts. "Take these off." She wanted to feel him, all of him, naked and warm on top of her.

He traced the lace of her panties again, nudging a finger gently under the edge and running it teasingly along her lower abdomen. Lord, she felt fragile as a sheet of glass, ready to shatter into a thousand desperate shards. "*Please,*" she added.

"Patience, sweetheart. We've waited years for this. Let me work my magic. I am the anatomy expert, after all."

"Well, my anatomy's going to explode right now and we're not even completely naked yet."

He stood up. "Well, first thing is, we're going to start with a real bed." He scooped her up into his strong arms as if she weighed as much as a couch pillow. "One where there's not a hundred-fifty-pound dog drooling all over us."

She reached out her arm toward the couch. "Don't forget the box." He leaned forward until she was able to snatch it up. "Got it. All set, Mr. Optimist."

Meg felt as light and as carefree as dandelion fluff as Ben walked with her down the back hallway and into the spare room, which was lit by a small bedside lamp. She kissed his neck, nibbled his ear, and ran her hands up and down the smooth, taut lengths of his arm muscles, unable to get enough of touching him. She wanted to kiss every blessed part of him, wrap herself around him, touch every part of him with every part of her. Everything she'd imagined for so long was now real, hers for the taking, and if she had her way she was going to savor him for hours on end. *At last.*

He tossed her lightly onto the bed and quickly shed his shorts and boxer briefs. The sheer beauty of his naked body made tears prick her eyes. He saw them before she could blink them away.

"Why are you crying?" He sat on the bed and gently swiped the tear track with his thumb.

"Happy," she managed.

He nodded solemnly. "Me, too."

She didn't want him to think she was melancholy, so she tugged on his arm and smiled. "Really happy."

"Well, hold that thought because we're only just getting started, sweetheart." With that, he grasped the sides of her panties and rolled them off of her in one practiced movement.

He came to her, stretching out his long lean body. His skin was so much darker and more tan than hers, and the contrast between bold and fair fascinated her. "Let me make you come," he whispered in her ear, making all thoughts flee as he traced his fingers along the inside of her thigh, slowly slipping into her slick heat.

"No," she said, sighing a little as she struggled to speak over the rapidly building pleasure. "Together the first time."

She wrapped her hands around the perfect hills and valleys of his back, vastly aware of his pure male strength as she tugged him over her.

He paused to roll on a condom and lowered his weight down until he was on top of her, propped up by his arms. His warmth engulfed her. She luxuriated in his masculine heat and the surprising softness of his skin against hers as their bodies poised to join. He brushed back her hair, stroked her face with his fine long fingers. "I always want to remember how you look right now," he said as he kissed her forehead, her cheeks, her nose. "So beautiful."

His gaze was intent, and she matched it, unable to take her eyes off of him, either. "I've waited a long time for you, Ben Rushford."

"And I promise you, Megan, you won't regret it," he said, dipping his head to place full, languid kisses on her lips.

She lowered a hand to guide him into her body.

He entered her slow and heavy, taking his time, allowing her body to adjust to his long length, and filled her completely, each inch rife with heart-stopping pleasure.

"Together the first time," he said, kissing her deeply as he began a rhythm of relentless strokes that she met and matched with her own, until she threw back her head and cried out his name, and he let out his own guttural cry.

><+>-0-<+>-<

Meg had never known such—joy. She'd never made such desperate, greedy love, where she shuddered and trembled and collapsed exhausted, only to want him again moments later.

It was the *only* upside of wanting him and not having him for so many years.

At three in the morning, they raided the refrigerator. Ate cold pizza by candlelight. Suddenly, Ben tugged her up by the elbow.

"What are you doing?" she asked, giggling, but she went with him willingly. She'd go to Botswana and back if he asked.

He took up one of her hands in his big, competent ones, and rested the other on her waist. They'd just made love three times, but her body was getting ready for him again. "Giving you a dance lesson. Dancing can be an expression of intimacy."

She stopped for a minute to roll up the too-long sleeves of her robe. "We've already been intimate."

He twirled her around. "Not like this."

He tugged her close and held her tighter. "Close your eyes," he said, and started to hum. The low, sensuous tones wafted around her.

She did close her eyes, and leaned her head tentatively against his bare chest, reveling in the barest brush of his hair against her cheek, the hard planes of muscle, and his enveloping warmth.

She began to recognize the melody to a love song, sweet and slow, that she heard through the vibrations resonating between their bodies as much as through her ears. They swayed together, and she got lost in his confident guidance and the soft notes of the music.

"Why don't you like to dance?" he asked.

"Because at prom, Ryan Miller—who happened to be my bio lab partner—told me I was as asexual as an amoeba. That I had no rhythm and I was embarrassing him."

"Douche bag. He was just saying that because you wouldn't sleep with him."

"Well, I believed it. After that I—I just couldn't risk ever being seen like that again."

He unthreaded their hands and brought his to her cheek. "Darlin', you're the cutest little amoeba I ever did see. And trust me, I've seen a lot of amoebas."

She gave a little shrug and looked into his sinfully dark eyes. "Who am I to argue with a medical expert?"

She settled back against his chest, and he began singing some country love song she'd never heard before, low and sweet and kind of off tune. "By the way," he said, "I can dance but I sure can't sing, but that doesn't stop me."

"Well, that's the difference between you and me."

"What's that?"

"I actually suffer embarrassment for doing things badly."

"You can't do anything badly in front of me."

She'd never felt so accepted for exactly who she was. And powerful, as Ben responded enthusiastically to her every touch. During their lovemaking, he'd told her over and over how beautiful and exquisite she was, something no other man had ever done.

After a long while, he pulled back and looked down at her. He was so tall, her neck strained to look up at him. "You like?" he asked with a lazy grin.

She smiled right back. "I *love*."

Happiness radiated through her. This was not the dreamy haze she used to feel anytime she was near him, the one that clouded her brain and made her mouth work as creakily as the Tin Man's before Dorothy oiled his joints.

It was deeper, more real, and all encompassing, and she knew exactly what it was.

Love. And she would never, ever say it, because he would run away fast and furiously.

She loved him.

She gripped him hard, held him so tightly he backed up a little and looked at her strangely.

"You okay?" he asked in a low, concerned voice.

"Never been better," she said.

"I'll take that as a challenge," he said. He kissed her temple, her earlobe, then her neck just under her jaw. The last one made her shiver.

"I want to take you back to bed," he said, scooping her up in his big arms and carrying her to the table where he held her as she leaned over and blew out the candles.

She wrapped her arms around his neck. "You knew all along dancing was foreplay," she said a little indignantly.

"Precisely, my little amoeba. Precisely."

CHAPTER 17

As Meg approached her shop early the next morning, she found Spike lazing against the glass door in his black leather jacket, jeans, and a plain white T-shirt, drinking some fancy coffee drink and texting on his phone.

It was one of those dewy summer mornings, angled sunlight kissing the tops of the old buildings and making the town look fairytalish in its quaintness. Early-bird tourists lined up at Mona's for their coffee hits, and a few runners and bikers putzed around the square with its tall oaks and wide walkways, the row of old Victorian houses staunchly standing guard.

Nothing could stop the hum of contentment that radiated all though her body, the feeling that for once, everything in her life, at least the important stuff, was headed in an upward direction. She had never felt such a ridiculous rush—it was something for other people to experience, not her. Yet in her own life, a kind of miracle had happened, and she basked in it like it was sunshine on the beach.

"Hi, Lukas," she said cheerily.

He arched one raven brow and looked her over with a mistrustful glare.

"That is your name, isn't it?" Meg asked.

His answer was a squinting of his dark-as-coal eyes. "Ma'am, I'd like to know when Sam's coming in today."

He moved to the side as she unlocked the door. "I'll tell you if you wouldn't mind helping me move some dress boxes upstairs." She didn't really need help from an exotic and interesting loner whom everyone had pegged as bad news, but what could she say, she'd always had a soft spot for wounded animals. "Come in," she said as she opened the door and held it for him.

He pushed off carelessly from his slouchy position and walked into the shop. Out of the corner of her eye, she noticed Maurice, coffee cup in hand, headed out of Mona's and steering himself in her direction. She locked the door behind her and made sure the Closed sign was still facing outward because she could only triage one problem at a time. She placed a bakery bag on the counter and gestured to Spike to check it out while she went around flicking on lights.

"No, thanks," he said. That same hungry look inhabited his eyes as always, except this time, since Sam wasn't around, it might just be from wanting food. Meg pushed the bag under his nose. "You're helping me, remember? That means you get paid in cinnamon rolls. Take one."

He reached for it tentatively. Every finger wore a ring of hammered silver, each with exotic engravings that looked to her like Egyptian hieroglyphs.

"What do the symbols mean?" she asked, grabbing a roll from the bag.

"They're African symbols of peace and tranquility."

"You made them yourself?"

He looked surprised she'd asked.

"Sam showed me the work you put on Etsy. You're quite a talented artist."

Maybe an emo artist, but she was going to give the guy a chance.

"Look, I'm not here for small talk. I just want to know——"

"Why don't you fight for her?" She had no time for bullshit. Maurice was strolling back and forth, peeking in the windows, and she had a full day booked ahead.

Spike flinched just the slightest bit. Crossed his arms so his muscles flexed and his tattoos became prominent. His diamond studs glistened. Everything about him looked intimidating except for a flash in his eyes—of doubt, or hurt, or something she couldn't quite get a handle on. "I'm not for Sam," he said.

"And that other guy is?"

"What's it to you, anyway?" His eyes narrowed. "You mean to tell me you'd rather see her with a guy like me than with him?"

"I want to see her with whoever makes her happy. And I don't see Harris Buckhorn, the third, doing that."

"I don't see me doing that, either." He started to walk toward the door.

She should have let it go. Let *him* go. Maybe she was too sleep deprived to care. Maybe she was so sexually sated that she'd temporarily lost every single one of her inhibitions. For whatever reason, she went after him.

"Then get yourself in shape. Don't be a quitter. *Make* yourself worthy of her."

He spun around. "Excuse me?"

"Do whatever it takes. Look, I don't know you very well except that you've managed to keep my old Malibu running far past its expiration date. But I overheard you talking to Sam the other day. You know who she is. You *see* her."

"I'm not from her world."

"So what?"

He smacked his hand against his head in frustration. "Man, you don't understand at all. You live in a fairy tale. I have nothing to give her. I would only drag her down."

Meg tossed her arms up in the air. "You have a job, don't you? You make her laugh. What else do you need?"

For years she'd accepted that same doctrine. *I'm not good enough* kept her from doing a lot. Like talking to Ben, being honest with him, getting to know him. Fear of failure was a bitch.

"The family hates me."

Oh, and then there was that. But today, no problem seemed too impossible not to fight for. She shook him by the shoulders. He shot her a *don't-touch-me-you-crazy-woman* glare.

"The family doesn't know you. Hell, I don't know you, but I tend to think the best of people. What you told Sam was the truth. She needed to hear it, because no one else has dared to tell it to her."

He looked stunned. Maybe she'd finally gotten to him. Or maybe he was just thinking he'd better do his business on the other side of the street. "Besides,"—she poked him in the chest with her finger— "whining is so unbecoming for a badass like you." His expression turned murderous but Meg did her best to ignore it. "Sam's coming in at ten," she said. "Now, would you mind carrying up those boxes?"

He sighed. "Where do you want them?"

"Up the stairs, first room on the right."

As soon as he got busy hauling, she opened the front door. "Maurice, get in here. I have hot buns."

He looked her up and down in a flustered sort of way and blushed. "Indeed."

"From Mona's," she said to clarify. "Gran doesn't come in until eleven, but I'm glad you're here. I need to ask you a professional question."

She waited until Spike left, which for him couldn't be fast enough, and Maurice had eaten his fill of rolls. Then she sat him down in one of the big cushy chairs, took the other for herself, and leaned over to speak.

"This is—" She took a breath. Craziness gave her courage. "This is about my brother."

He looked down his spectacles at her. "Your deceased brother. The one who died years ago from an accident at the quarry."

"Yes. Patrick." Her voice cracked a little when she said his name. But it was about time somebody had finally said his name out loud without cringing or apologizing. *Oh, Patrick*, she prayed. *Please give me the strength I need to ask this one question. Because if there was any chance to change things, you would want me to ask it.* "It's about how he died."

Maurice set his coffee down as carefully as if it were a glass figurine. He folded his arms and set his face in a serious but attentive expression that reminded her for the first time that he used to be a physician. "Go on," he said.

"When Ben Rushford pulled Patrick out of the water that night, he said he panicked. He attempted to do CPR but he didn't know what he was doing. He feels that if he would have done it right, Patrick might have had a chance.

"I was wondering if—if that's completely true? I thought you might know how I could find the autopsy report. Maybe you know who was coroner at the time, or where records for these kinds of things are kept? I just wondered if there was medical evidence that suggested my brother might have been dead a long time before Ben got there, or something—"

"You mean your Ben has felt guilt for all these years because he couldn't save his friend?"

"Yes."

"That's quite a trauma for an eighteen-year-old to sustain. Finding his friend in such a state, trying to save him, and then losing him. Or for a grown man to carry. Especially if he's in love with his friend's sister."

Meg couldn't think about the *love* part. She just knew that for Ben and her to truly have a chance, she had to help him release this burden. For their sakes and for her family's, too. The old man reached over and took up Meg's trembling hands. His grasp was firm, his voice steady and sure. Meg, on the other hand, felt like some critical thread holding her body together had snapped and she was coming unraveled at the seams.

"CPR in this case would not have made one bit of difference," Maurice said. "Your brother hit his head on the bottom of the quarry and surely died instantly."

Meg looked into the old Irishman's bright, intelligent eyes. "H-how do you know that?"

"Because I was working in the ER that night when they brought him in."

Meg was shaking so hard she had to sit down before her knees gave way. "I knew about a head injury but—"

"A very serious one. Nothing your Ben would have done would have made a difference. When your brother dove into the quarry, he severed his spinal cord." Maurice placed a hand on her shoulder. "I'm so sorry, dear."

Meg put a hand over her mouth and sobbed. For her brother, for his sudden, sad, unnecessary death. For the aching loss of him over all these years. For her family, still so broken. And for Ben, who'd carried this burden for years in silence.

Maurice drew a real handkerchief out of his pocket and handed it to her, and she took it gratefully, blowing her nose long and hard. "How is it no one spoke to Ben about this?" he asked.

Meg took a deep breath. "The whole thing was horrible for him. My mother always thought he was a bad influence on Patrick and hasn't spoken to him since the accident. I'm not sure Ben has really discussed it with anyone."

"Shame is a perilous thing. It makes people not talk about things. Not ask questions. Maybe no one realized how he suffered over it. With all the trauma of what he went through that night, it's a miracle he's come to achieve what he has."

"He loves being a doctor and he's good at what he does."

He patted her hand. "And you love him."

She managed a small smile. *With all my heart.* "I'm glad you gave me information for his sake. Maybe I can somehow use it to fix this for my family."

"And for the sake of you both as a couple. May I ask how your grandmother feels about Ben?"

Meg waved her hand. "Oh, you know Gloria. She never met a soul she didn't like."

"Except for me," he said.

"Speaking of Gran, there she is now." Out the big plate glass window, they saw Gloria walking down the sidewalk, arms laden with shopping bags. Today's color was vivid purple, which she wore on everything from her rimmed feathered hat to her skirt and jacket, to her massive satchel and all the way down to her cute kitten heels. Maurice watched her with an expression of undisguised longing.

Meg hugged the elderly doctor. "Thank you, Maurice."

He switched his gaze from outside to Meg. "I'm truly sorry about your brother."

"I know you are," she said, giving his hand a pat. "And I appreciate the handkerchief. I'll make sure to wash it for you."

He made a dismissive motion, like that wasn't at all necessary.

As she wadded up the handkerchief and stuck it into her skirt pocket, she said, "You know, my grandmother's not that tough an egg to crack. You just need to know the secret."

CHAPTER 18

"You're here," Ben said with a feeling of disbelief, standing up from the collapsing front stoop of what was once his grandparents' graceful red brick home and brushing off the butt of his dress pants. Meg walked up the cracked cement walkway, not wearing anything out of the ordinary, just a patterned skirt and a yellow blouse, with her hair pulled back in a ponytail. The way his heart was crashing into his rib cage, he felt like one of his patients who just might need a high-joule shock to straighten it out. He had to stop himself from dropping to his knees in gratefulness for being the lucky bastard to have spent an entire night with her.

She smiled widely as she approached, and he flashed her back what was probably the same stupid grin he'd been wearing the whole damn day. Everything he saw and felt seemed magnified a hundred times over. The gummy smile the cute baby with the runny nose gave him this morning, the pat on the back from the old nurse when she handed him a very-needed cup of coffee. Hell, he'd even shrugged off the fact that he'd had to wait an hour for some results because one of the lab machines had broken down.

He kissed Meg on the lips and smoothed back a strand of her raven-dark hair that had come undone from her ponytail. Her green eyes seemed to dance with happiness, the same giddy feeling that coursed through his veins now, making him feel more alive than he had in years.

"Hi," he said dumbly.

"Hi." She giggled. They stared at each other for a few moments, basking in each other's presence. He ran a hand up and down her soft arm, inhaled her pretty lemony scent, kissed her again on her lips, and tasted the unique essence that was her and only her.

"We're in public," she said, pulling away a little.

"So what?" he asked, pulling her closer.

"You don't do PDA," she reminded him.

He chuckled. "I do now," he said, just before planting his most mind-blowing kiss on her, teasing her mouth open, kissing her slow and softly, then stroking her tongue with his until she gave a little moan. A couple of car horns beeped and they both pulled apart.

"Guess I got carried away," he said, touching her blushing cheek. More like *blown* away by a petite, five-foot-two hurricane who made him want to skip work—which he never, ever did—and spend the rest of the day naked in her bed.

"I have something to tell you," she said, taking up his hand.

He could tell from the way her eyes shone that it was good news. "You got the loan?"

"Nope. Something bigger."

"Pippa Middleton really is coming with an entourage to check out your shop?"

"Nothing to do with the shop." She pulled him over to the crumbly front stoop and sat him down.

"If I have to sit down, maybe I should be getting nervous."

"Ben, I . . . did something on your behalf. At least, I was asking a question on your behalf and I accidentally got an answer right away. But I'm worried you're going to think I was meddling."

"Is it about the ER job?"

"No, of course not. I would never interfere with that. However you take this, I want you to know I did it to help not just you, but us together. Both of us."

He could tell from the deep knit of her brows that she was worried. He gathered up her hands, used his thumbs to stroke her soft skin. "Whatever it is, we'll deal with it. Tell me."

"I asked Dr. Manning who the coroner was when Patrick died."

Instinctively, Ben withdrew his hands. "Meggie, no. Not that."

"Please hear me out. I kept thinking, what if there was some evidence Patrick was already dead—some concrete proof, so you'd stop tormenting yourself over it."

"It's done, Meggie. He drowned. No one can say exactly when. He probably was gone by the time I got to him. We'll never know for sure."

"Dr. Manning was working in the ER that night. He said Patrick hit his head when he dove in and severed his spine. By the time you got to him, it was already too late. The worst thing you did was be in the wrong place at the wrong time, to have been the one to find him like that."

Ben stared at the ground. He happened to spy an anthill with dozens of ants in a line busily doing the mundane chore of carrying particles of sand to add to the hill. It took a little while for her words to register. He felt like he was someone else, not himself, who could somehow make his body move.

"Please don't be angry with me," Meg said.

Instinct made him reach for her and pull her in close. She was warm and real and tangible and such a contrast to the paling ghosts from the past who finally had a reason to release their grip. They sat like that for what must have been a while, because she finally drew away enough to look at him. "Say something. Please."

"The doctor in me understood for a long time that your brother was probably dead. But I could never stop asking myself the question, what if he wasn't?" She'd given him evidence, despite the emotional price she'd paid to get it. He pulled her to him again almost violently and kissed the top of her head. "Thank you for what you've done."

He couldn't find words. No one had ever put themselves so unselfishly on the line for him. She brought out feelings in him he'd never felt for anyone else. "Meg, I—" The words choked in his throat. Worse, he discovered he was crying, making him swipe quickly at his eyes with his fist. He wanted to say he loved her. But he didn't want it to be about Patrick, about her helping him to heal his past. When he said it, he wanted it to be about her. About them. About the future.

He didn't have to worry about what to say, because she kissed him gently on the lips and stood up, wiping away her own tears.

"So, your grandparents' old home is zoned for business?" She stood in the walkway and looked up, shielding her eyes from the hot sun. He stood with her, relieved to change subjects and get to the reason he'd asked her to meet him here in the first place. She took in the peeling paint on the white trim, a dangling disconnected gutter, and patches on the roof where the old slate had been replaced by cheaper roof tiles. Not to mention the marquee-like sign planted in the middle of the front yard that read *Hometown Insurance, Goddard Optical, Leonard Portraits*, and *Jones, Day, and Coleman Law Offices*.

"Actually, the businesses all left and the city's about to tear it down. Jeannie Marshall gave me the key and told me I could take all the time I wanted to go through it."

"Oh. The teardown's a shame," she said. "It has majestic bones."

He had to agree. It was majestic in its traditional boxy way, with a massive oak in the front yard that used to hold a tire swing. To the right stood another century home that was now a funeral home and to the left was a little park that connected to wooded bike trails he'd explored many a time in his childhood. It saddened him to see the house at the end of its lifespan.

"I thought we could look around, maybe take a few pictures. My grandfather's office was on the left." He pointed to a side addition. On the opposite side of the building a closed-in sunroom reflected the classic Georgian symmetry of the house. "What time do you have to be back?" he asked.

She shrugged. "I left Gran and Sam in charge. I'm good for, I don't know, an hour?"

"You say that like you don't take a lunch hour very often."

"Actually, almost never. But maybe I should do it more."

"And maybe we should have arranged to do something else besides look at a dusty old house." He kissed her to make sure she knew what. Then he took her hand and squeezed it a little. "I'm glad you came. This place is really special to me."

If she felt any skepticism about why the hell he would ever want to tour such a rundown place, she didn't show it. He unlocked the sun-faded front door and led them into a dark foyer.

Meg examined a transom with lead work shaped like a spider web that graced the top of the door. "So far I like it," she said.

"This was the living room," Ben said, looking in a large room to their right. About all he could recognize was the big fireplace, which used to be bright and crackling at Christmastime, to accompany the big fat tree that always towered in the corner. Now the room, which had been converted into a waiting room for the optical business, was covered with cheap laminate paneling with a hole cut out for a reception window. No faded but beautiful oriental rug, no gleaming wood floor, no candy dish his Grandma Rushford always kept full of M&M's for his siblings' many after-school visits.

With a sense of sadness and an intense need to stop looking at the ruined room, Ben steered Meg to the left, past a grand staircase covered with brothel-red carpet that curved upward above their heads.

"Are you okay being here?" Meg asked, gently touching his arm.

"Sure. Why do you ask?" He felt especially raw after her news, but he suddenly realized, *yeah*, he was okay being here. More than okay. As long as she was here with him.

She held up their joined hands. "Because you have a death grip on my hand. Maybe it's better to remember it as it was."

He shook his head. "I have to see my grandfather's office one last time."

Ben led her through a door beyond the stairs and walked down a dark hallway. He stopped at the first room on the right and opened a heavy paneled door.

"This is it." Still-beautiful walnut bookcases lined an entire wall. The far wall held a large arched window that overlooked the park next door, and under the window stood an ornately carved cover for the steam-heat radiator. "Funny, but this room seemed so much bigger when I was a kid. My grandfather used to sit at his desk and do paperwork, and I'd crawl under it with my cars and trucks. It was a great place to hide out from my brothers. When I was older, I used to look at his Netter medical atlases."

"What are those?" Meg asked.

"Frank Netter was a famous physician-artist who illustrated all the anatomy of the body. There was a big green book for each organ system. That's how I learned about the birds and the bees."

"Through medical illustrations?"

Ben ran his fingers along the dusty wood shelves. "One day, Gramps caught me reading the one about the reproductive system. I was terrified he was going to tell my mom or something. Instead he sat down with me and explained it all. I knew more proper anatomical terms for sex organs than any other kid at school."

"Impressive."

He snorted. "I think he recognized I was fascinated by the body, you know? My brothers thought the pictures were gross." He turned from the window and ran his hand along the once-polished shelves. "Gramps didn't just read medical books. These shelves were filled with everything from classics to Asimov to crime thrillers. And I borrowed it all."

They peeked into the exam rooms, now green-shag carpeted with beat-up white walls, and the reception area at the end of the hall. "Gramps used to let me watch him do things like stitch people up, clean wax out of kids' ears. Once he pulled a couple of raisins out of a kid's nose. They'd swollen to three times their size."

Back in the office, he walked to the window and tried to focus on the park, which was the one thing in sight that was beautiful and well maintained. Suddenly he felt her behind him, curling her body around his back, wrapping her arms around his waist, and for a moment he leaned back into her, staring out at the ugly wooden fence somebody had put up when the city had bought off most of the big backyard for the park.

"Thanks for being here," he said. His voice sounded funny—low and a little cracked.

She could've joked or expressed her distaste about the ugly carpet or the peeling paint or the watermarks on the ceiling. She simply held him, and for a long time they just stood there.

"I'm named after him, you know."

"He would be proud of you, Ben."

"He had the most integrity of anyone I knew. He was hardworking and honest. I could spend my whole life trying to be a small fraction of the man he was."

"That's a good life goal," she said, as he turned around and took her into his arms.

His lips quirked up in a faint smile. "How much time until lunch hour's over?"

"Twenty minutes," she said.

"We can drive through for some food."

She waggled her brows. "Or we can go back to my apartment for a quickie."

"Come to think of it, I'm not so hungry after all."

They left the house to find Dr. Donaldson walking towards them, gingerly stepping around the crumbled cement of the front walkway.

"I saw your car parked out front and couldn't resist stopping," he said. "How'd it look in there?"

"Like it's been through a war or two," Ben said. "But I have a lot of great memories of this place."

"Many a citizen of Mirror Lake visited your grandfather's office back in the day," Donaldson said. "We have him to thank for founding the hospital and recruiting some first-rate docs to town." He stood in the middle of the walkway, looking over the dilapidated facade of the building. "Needs a nice young couple to give it some TLC."

"Doesn't need TLC," Ben mumbled. "More like a total body transplant."

Donaldson laughed. "Well, maybe saving this thing from the wrecking ball is too much of a challenge but there are others. I've seen signs on a few properties on the west side of the lake."

"On Pill Hill?" Ben asked. That was the chichi section of town, mockingly christened with that moniker due to the number of docs who had bought houses there. Big-assed McMansions with million-dollar lake views. He couldn't ever imagine kids running around the pristine golf-course-quality yards getting dirty or racing through the designer-decorated rooms.

Dr. Donaldson put a fatherly arm around Ben's shoulder. "You know, Benjamin, the committee meets for the final time today. Over the years, I've seen candidates come and go because they didn't have ties to our community. It's so refreshing to see a young couple house hunting." He dropped his voice. "I hate to interfere, but on behalf of the committee, I feel I must ask, are you two . . . moving in together? Without the benefit of marriage, that is."

"No, of course not," Meg said adamantly. "We would never do that without being married."

Ben looked at Meg's face, sincere and determined. She was still sticking up for him, still working it to get him that job, as she'd done from day one. But something poked at his gut. It was none of Dr. Donaldson's business what he chose to do or with whom he chose to do it. "Shacking up" or not, it was their decision to make, not a hospital committee's that had been dangling this carrot of a job in front of his nose for months.

Dr. Donaldson sported a wide grin as he patted Ben on the back. "So I take it there's happy news in the air? I'd love to report that to the committee, Benjamin. Because you *are* our number one candidate. Of course, several of the committee have expressed their reservations about your . . . er . . . active social life. "

Sweat pooled at the back of Ben's neck and under his arms, and it wasn't from the noonday August sun beating down mercilessly on their heads. *Number one candidate* resonated through his mind. He couldn't blow this now, not after all this.

Because what Dr. Donaldson was talking about wasn't just his job, it was his *life*. He could not imagine himself anywhere else. For the sake of his grandfather's legacy, for his family—and dammit, for *himself*— he wanted to be here, in Mirror Lake, as tightly knit into the community where he was born and bred as the thread on his best winter socks.

And nothing or nobody would keep him from that dream.

All he had to do was go with it. He'd set up the lie himself, and so far it had worked to his advantage. He simply had to acknowledge Dr. Donaldson's one simple statement.

Meg would understand, just as she'd understood everything so far. She'd accept that all the anticipation and anxiety had made him just a touch on the crazy side. The consequences would only be temporary. Just for today, until the committee met and made their final decision.

Dr. Donaldson waited expectantly. "Any news on your part would certainly sway the few vocal naysayers we have left."

Panic rumbled through Ben like a volcanic eruption and he blurted, "Actually, we may have only been dating a short while but we *are* getting married." He wrapped an arm around Meg's shoulder and shot her a syrupy smile before turning back to Dr. Donaldson. "So of course you can share the news."

⊰⋆⊱

Meg really should have gotten more sleep last night. Because she couldn't possibly have heard that right. Ben couldn't have just crossed the line from a fake date to a fake *marriage*, could he?

Meg endured the congratulations with the widest, most jaw-aching smile she could plaster onto her face. Somehow she made it last until Dr. Donaldson climbed back into his black Caddy and drove away down Forest Glen Avenue back to the hospital.

Then she turned to Ben, who at least retained enough conscience to wear a sheepish look on his face. "We're getting *what?*" she hissed, hands on hips.

She'd rarely seen his face color before, but it was heating up now as he shifted his weight from foot to foot. "You know why I said that. I didn't have a choice."

"No, you *thought* you didn't have a choice. The last time I checked, getting married is an issue of mutual consent. You can't pretend-decide we're getting married by *yourself.*"

His brown eyes, which she'd thought were so open and expressive, looked a bit calculating now. "I couldn't ruin my chances. Not when I'm *this close* to getting that job." He gestured a miniscule distance between his index finger and thumb. "Not after all this work we've done. I'm sorry, Meg. I'll make it up to you. In a few weeks, we can break it off and it won't matter."

"Ben, you ass, it does matter!" She snapped her own fingers in front of his face. "I understood the dating thing. But this is *marriage.* Word is spreading now as we speak, and by the time we get back, the entire town will know. That is a *super* lie."

"It's just temporary. Until I sign the contract." His voice sounded weak, as if what he'd done was finally beginning to sink in.

"People will be happy for me," she continued. "They'll congratulate me about one of the most important events in a person's life. My gran will cry. This is *not* okay, Ben. I'm not going to lie about this for you."

"You don't have to worry, because none of our families will believe it."

Outrage shot through her. "Why not?" She crossed her arms and tapped her foot so hard that stones scattered under her sandals.

"Because they know me. I'm not the marrying kind." He looked at her with a worried expression. "You weren't hoping that was real, were you?"

Meg's head was whirling. To think she'd thought everything about last night had been special. A beautiful night she had hoped would lead to all kinds of wonderful things, maybe even a real marriage proposal one day. Instead it had led to this.

"You just don't get it, do you? I'm not disappointed that you didn't really ask me to *marry* you, you idiot. I'm upset that you *lied* about such an important thing. You threw me under the bus for your job."

She searched her purse for her car key, finally finding it tucked into her skirt pocket, and took off toward the street.

"Meg, wait. Please." He started to follow her but she spun around.

"And by the way," she said, poking him in the chest with the key, "we haven't been dating. Last night was *not* a date. That was a little drive and sex. And camp and dinner—just to be clear, those also were *not* dates. I'm done being your cheap date, Ben. I'm done covering for you, and most of all, I'm done lying. See you around."

She stalked off down the crumbling walkway, then down a flight of crooked stairs built into a grassy hill, to her car. He trailed right behind and leaned his hands on the window ledge of the car as she started the ignition.

"Don't do this," he said. "We have something . . . special."

"Something special can't be built on a lie. Something special has the potential for a future, which you don't believe in, because you're not the marrying kind." It was so difficult to look at him, but she was determined to hold it together for the few more seconds it would take before she drove away. "I really do hope you can stop tormenting yourself about my brother's accident. It's time to forgive yourself. Free yourself from the past. And now that includes me, too."

Meg drove away, leaving behind the train wreck of a house and the man who had used her to secure the job of his dreams.

CHAPTER 19

The car clock told Meg she had ten minutes to get it together before her one o'clock appointment. Sweat trickled down her back and beaded on her lip, and her idling car was starting to feel like a sauna. She couldn't stay in the Bridal Aisle parking lot in the ninety-degree heat with the windows up bawling her eyes out. Well, technically she could, but she'd already had to duck her head twice so the mailman and the UPS woman wouldn't recognize her. Plus, she had no Kleenex or sleeves on her blouse, and she'd taken Dr. Manning's handkerchief out of her pocket at her shop. She'd already wiped her nose on her arm once and that had been disgusting.

Finally, she got up the courage to leave the car and duck into the service entrance of Mona's, because she just couldn't face going into Bridal Aisle like this. A comforting warm-dough smell coming from the oven hit her instantly and drew her through the rows of boxes in the bakery storeroom to the kitchen area, with its industrial-sized ovens that included a built-in brick pizza oven, and a couple of baking racks that were full of giant-sized chocolate chip cookies, still soft and melty.

She wiped her nose with a piece of parchment paper she found on one of the racks. She was on her second cookie when Teddy walked in and screamed.

He held a hand over his heart. "Holy shit, I thought you were a hungry homeless person. You scared the sam-hell out of me." He walked closer. Recognition dawned that this was not an ordinary day. "You look like Helena Bonham Carter in *Sweeney Todd*."

She swallowed the final bite, which went down hard because her throat was dry, leaned her head against the bakery rack, and released a sob. "This is why I never leave the shop for lunch. One time I leave, and look what happens. A life crisis!"

"Okay, this requires an intervention." He pulled her away from the rack, probably so she wouldn't cry all over his perfect cookies. "But I need to know what I'm dealing with. Is it family, love life, or job?"

"B-Ben," she squeezed out. Saying his name made her chest hurt, which made her cry even harder.

"Mmm-hmm. Thought so. Sit down here, away from the sugar." He led her to an old bar stool propped against the marble island. "Do you promise you'll be right here when I get back?"

She must've nodded. As she smoothed her hand over the cool surface of the island, which used to be a fudge-making station for the candy shop that at one time inhabited this space, she heard him announce to his customers, "Okay, people, we've just had a water main break and the shop is closed. Y'all come back in a half hour, okay?"

"It's going to be repaired in that short a time?" a woman exclaimed.

"But your sign says hot cookies at 1:00 p.m. That's five minutes from now."

"The plumbing crew is very talented. And the cookies have been delayed until further notice."

After he'd chased off his customers, Teddy pulled Meg up from the chair and steered her into the main part of the bakery, sat her down at a table, and flipped the sign on the door to Closed. Then he poured her a large black coffee and handed her a box of Kleenex. "How about a sandwich?" he asked. "Veggie and red pepper hummus on ciabatta, your fave."

"Th-thanks, Teddy," she said with a hiccup, "but I have to be back in the shop in a few minutes."

He pulled out his cell. "Hi, Grandma G. This is Ted. Meg's over here helping me with my budget. Is it okay if she's just a smidgen late for her one o'clock?" He put down the phone and pushed the coffee and a bunch of napkins toward her. "You're covered. Drink. And tell me what happened."

She obeyed, enjoying the slight scald of the hot coffee as she swallowed it down, mainly because it took her mind off her greater pain for a few seconds. "We had a magical night. And today he wanted me to come see his grandfather's old house before it got torn down. But Dr. Donaldson stopped by and got the impression we were a couple house hunting. He implied that if Ben and I were engaged, that would push Ben's chances over the top to get the job."

"So Ben actually told him you were engaged? That rat."

"I—thought we had something special. But he used me to get that job."

There was a sudden pounding on the door. The faces of a gaggle of senior citizens appeared in the plate glass window.

"Damn that bus," Ted said. "Leaves them off from Assisted Living every blessed afternoon. They want the cookies."

Ted opened the door, told the water main break story again, and shut the blinds.

"It's Labor Day weekend and I'm making you lose business," Meg said.

"Honey, these folks are retired. They can shoot the shit with each other until I let them in. Now, what did your man have to say for himself?"

"*Don't worry. In a couple weeks we can break it off.* Like breaking off an engagement is as easy as pie. And—like he didn't *ever* want to be engaged to me. He said he wasn't even thinking about marriage at this point in his life. He's enjoying his freedom, and he's not the marrying kind. Hell, he's not even the *relationship* kind."

"Oh, honey. That skunk. That swine. That lousy excuse for a man." Ted violently pulled out one Kleenex after another and handed them all over.

Good thing, because she needed every single one. Plus now she was shaky from all the coffee she just drank. Mascara rolled off her face in inky wet streaks. As she wiped her chin, melted chocolate came off. How was she going to get it together enough to go to work?

"Go home, Meg," Ted said. "Take the afternoon off."

"I can't. The bridal show is *tonight*."

"You've taken on too much already. You're stressed to the max. Don't go in when you feel like this. It will only lead to more disaster."

"The bank president and her husband have front-row seats for the show. They're about to decide on our loan and after all this work, I have to prove that my shop is a worthy investment. I *have* to." Not just because of the loan, either. Her shop was the one part of her life that felt alive and intact. The rest was the equivalent of plague, pestilence, and nuclear disaster combined.

"Okay," Teddy coached, "just take deep breaths. If you take a couple hours to regroup, it might help you in the long run."

"I cannot take off. I have three appointments this afternoon plus Sam's been working on all the final details for the show and we have to go over them one last time." She swallowed down the rest of coffee. "I can do this."

Teddy made her go and wash her face in the bathroom, and when she came out, he dabbed at her puffy face with her compact. "You got lipstick? Put some on then you're set."

She reached for her lipstick and her compact mirror but when she examined her reflection, she winced and tossed the compact back in her purse.

"It's all right," Teddy said. "You'll look better in a few hours."

After giving him a good glare, she gripped his hand tight and kissed his cheek. "Thank you for helping me." She would survive this. For years, she'd looked at Ben from afar, dreamed and fantasized about him. She knew now that not one of those fantasies would ever equal the reality of the past twenty-four hours. Maybe someday she'd be grateful for that Cinderella moment but for now it was past midnight and her shop was going to turn into a smashed pumpkin if she didn't get going.

"The whole town probably knows about the engagement by now," she said. "Please don't say anything. I need time to figure out how to handle this."

"Honey, you're not alone. Just say the word, and we've all got your back."

"Thank you." Then she left out the front door, making sure to flip the sign back to Open.

▷┼◁▷•○•◁▷┼◁

After fighting her way through the senior citizen cookie line, Meg walked into Bridal Aisle to find Priscilla Kline and her mother talking heatedly with Gloria, who was inspecting Priscilla's wedding dress through her bifocals as it was laid out on the countertop in all its ballgown grandeur.

"It's too plain on top," Priscilla said. "It's just a little . . . I don't know . . . boring." The elaborate decoration on the bodice with handsewn beads and pearl sequins could be called many things, but boring wasn't at the top of Meg's list. "I think it's beautiful," Meg said. "All the handiwork is exquisite." *Gaudy* to normal people. Besides, it was a week before her wedding. It was too late to change.

"I know," Priscilla said, "but my neck and shoulders will be bare. Maybe the problem is I need something around my neck to sparkle and shine."

Meg bit down hard on her lower lip. She'd like to put something around Priscilla's neck, all right, but that might just be her hands—to wring it. "Didn't you say you were going to wear a diamond pendant of your great-grandmother's?" she asked.

"Evan says it's too old-fashioned looking. It doesn't go with the dress."

"Pearls never go out of style," Gloria suggested. "The Queen wore a double strand at her wedding." She walked around the glass display cases that contained all of their accessories. "You're welcome to look around, dear. But a large necklace might detract from all that beautiful beading."

"Oooh, how about this one?" Priscilla pointed to an elaborate statement necklace, with rows of different sizes of pearls twisted together with a winding rhinestone chain and topped off with a big, sparkling brooch. It had just come in this morning. Meg had unwrapped it just before lunch to check it before she called the bride and told her it was in.

"This was a custom order," Gloria said, "done by an artist in New York. The bride's picking it up today."

"Can I order one?" Priscilla asked.

"There's not enough time," Meg said. "Custom orders take six to eight weeks with our designers."

"Call the bride," Priscilla said. "I'll pay double whatever she paid."

"Before I do that," Meg said politely, "I think you should try it on with your dress to be sure you like it. We also have other necklaces that aren't custom."

Meg didn't feel comfortable having Priscilla try on someone else's necklace. But she did let her, praying she wouldn't like it.

"I love it," she said as soon as it was around her neck. "I've got to have it."

They put in calls to the bride, which made Meg cringe, and to the artist, but those only confirmed what Meg already knew.

Priscilla was tapping her nails nervously on the top of the glass case. Meg had handled a lot of stressed-out brides. She felt confident that she could handle Priscilla, even with a throbbing head and a caffeinated, broken heart. "You know, the last week before the wedding is very anxiety-provoking. It gets very stressful near the end and—"

"Everything is perfect," Priscilla snapped. "And if I could only deal with people who knew what they were doing in this stupid small town, my look would be perfect, too."

Meg ignored the insult. "You're putting so much pressure on yourself. Maybe if you just—"

Priscilla slapped both of her hands against the case. "I am marrying into a political dynasty. Dignitaries from all over the east coast will be there. It's . . . it's like uniting the Kennedys and the Roosevelts. And I'm going to have a great life. I really am."

Priscilla's eyes grew watery. *Don't say anything*, Meg warned herself. *It's not your business.*

Mrs. Kline said, "There's got to be a local seamstress who can give us an assessment. Maybe add a bit more beading to the dress."

"You don't understand," Meg said, forcing herself to speak calmly. "Those beads were ordered from India. Even if they're in stock, they have to clear customs and ship to the U.S. It can't be done in time."

"Then we'll order a new dress," Priscilla said.

Now Meg bit down on the insides of her cheeks to keep from saying something she'd regret.

"What is that look on your face?' Priscilla snapped. "I said I want a new dress. Mother, tell her I need a new dress."

"Well, I suppose it wouldn't hurt to look, dear," Mrs. Kline said.

So this was to be the culmination of a year and a half of putting up with every whim, every ridiculous request. Bending over backwards and over the moon to please people who were simply unpleaseable.

Just then, something inside Meg snapped. She was so done kissing ass. "You don't need a new dress," she blurted. "You need a new *personality*."

The air stood still. The silence was funny, like the kind that comes from walking outside a noisy bar after listening to a rock band for a few hours.

"A new *what*?" Priscilla said.

"You heard me," Meg said. "I wish your fiancé all the best in trying to please you, because we sure can't."

Mrs. Kline bristled. "So you've insulted us and you won't find us someone who can help us."

"No one in this country—no, on the *planet*—is going to touch this dress again a week before the wedding," Meg said. "I'm sorry."

"You'll never be a destination shop if you can't stand behind the products you sell," Mrs. Kline said.

Meg ignored her. "Priscilla, you'll never be happy if you keep focusing on *things* instead of what's really the problem. And maybe the problem is you're not sure you really want to marry this guy."

Priscilla started to get that blotchy look again, like she did back in the hotel room a few weeks ago. Meg absently wondered where she could get a paper bag on short notice.

"Think about it," Meg said. "I mean, do you love him? Does he make your heart sing just looking at him? Do you see him and picture the beautiful children you'll have, that maybe they'll have his big brown eyes and long lashes and maybe his wavy hair? Do you picture long nights making love by the fire and talking about everything and anything under the sun, and do you have the feeling that of anyone in the world, he just *gets* you? Like no other person in the world ever can?"

Now Meg was crying. She'd gone and lost it at work, in front of her most difficult but most influential clients. Priscilla and her mother stood there, open-mouthed, shocked at the spectacle. Her grandmother sent her a concerned look.

"That's enough," Gloria said, grabbing Meg by the arm. "My granddaughter is right. We've done everything possible to accommodate all your needs and wants. We're going to insist that you take any further business elsewhere." She strode over to the door and held it open.

Mrs. Kline huffed to the door, Priscilla in tow. Then Mrs. Kline got in Gran's face. "I'll make certain the loan committee knows just how accommodating you are to one of your most important clients."

"Every client of ours is important, Irene," Gloria said. "But not all of them are—are bloody *plonkers*."

Meg gasped. The Queen never cursed and her gran sure as hell never did. But that was the closest Meg had ever seen her come.

Gran closed the door firmly and turned to Meg, who was just shocked as the Klines had been. "If you've ruined your chance at the bank loan, then I went ahead and ruined it right along with you."

"Oh, Gran." She ran to her grandmother's arms and cried like she was six again. Her blurry gaze lit on Samantha's newly painted bright green wall with the unfinished purple cursive stencil that so far spelled out only the word *Beautiful*. Her mind filled that in with *Disaster*.

And she wondered just how the hell her entire life could implode so spectacularly in a mere handful of hours.

CHAPTER 20

"Mom, you shouldn't be doing that," Meg said when she found her mother kneeling in the garden pulling out weeds. Guilt washed through her as she thought of the craziness of the past few weeks and the neglected task she never completed. She'd left her shop for just a little while to try and calm down and get her head clear before she had to go back for the big show. She couldn't afford to fall apart, despite feeling like she was on the verge. To be honest, she desperately wanted her mother's comfort but she knew her mother would never be sympathetic to any story involving Ben Rushford.

Her mom sat back on her garden stool, trowel in hand, and managed a weary smile. "I was just tired of looking at this eyesore and thought I might give it a go." Her gaze zipped up and down her daughter's form and she frowned a little, no doubt taking in the fact that her daughter looked worse than the thistles she'd just yanked out and left to languish in their wilted state over the side of a plastic garbage bag.

"This is my fault," Meg said. "I should have done this weeks ago."

Her mom stopped pulling. "Stop treating me like I'm helpless. Do you think I like seeing you work yourself to the bone to get my chores done?"

"I'm not working myself to the bone."

"Yes, you are, and it's high time we put a stop to it."

Meg dropped down next to her mom and started pulling. "Let me worry about what's too much work for me."

They worked in aggravated silence for a few minutes. Finally, her mother's bright blue eye searched hers. "Is it true?"

"Is what true?" Oh, no. She couldn't have heard. Not already.

"That you're engaged to Ben Rushford."

"No! Of course not! Never!" But even as she said it, she broke down with a sob. All the strain of the last weeks and all the bad shit that had gone down today seemed to heap on her like this enormous expanse of dirt that was now blanketed with weeds.

Her mom ignored Meg's tears for the moment. "That's not what Brenda at the Curli-Q told me. She did Lillian Donaldson's hair this afternoon and she said Ben Rushford is about to get offered the ER job . . . and that he and his fiancée were house hunting. How could you, Megan?"

"How could I what, Mom? Love the guy who was best friends with Patrick? Because we all know *that* could never happen."

The sun was hot. Her head was pounding, her blouse was sticking to her armpits, and she didn't have any sunglasses. No surprises there, on the most miserable effing day of her life.

"I'm just shocked I had to hear such a horrific thing at the *beauty shop* instead of from the mouth of my own daughter."

Meg supposed she could go on denying it. But this was her mother, for God's sakes. And she'd spent the last ten years smoothing things over, sugarcoating her own problems, and appeasing everyone so her mom could have a better life.

But not anymore.

"Ben wasn't with Patrick when he died. I know you think he was. I know you've held it against him all these years, but he wasn't lying, Mom. He didn't want to get drunk with Patrick that night. He said *no*."

Her mother had gone pale as the white roses behind her. "It would be just like him to say that just to save his own skin. Ben Rushford was a hellion. He bought liquor for Patrick. He was a troublemaker."

"He may have done some bad things but he didn't talk Patrick into drinking, or fail to save him, or do anything other than be a friend to him. A *best* friend, who refused to abandon him, and it cost him everything. He dove into that water over and over to find him and he pulled him out by himself. Can you even imagine how traumatic something like that must have been? Yet for years he felt guilty because he didn't know CPR and thought that if he did, he could've done something. But it wouldn't have mattered. Ben doesn't deserve your anger. And this has to stop."

Meg doubled over and leaned her throbbing head on her knees. She was hot and thirsty and miserable and exhausted. And tired of pretending that everything was fine, just fine, for everyone else's sakes. Because she *was not fine*. At all.

Suddenly she felt her mother's hand on her sweaty head. She combed Meg's hair back gently with her fingers. "I never blamed Ben for not being able to save Patrick."

Meg pulled herself up and faced her mother. "He blamed *himself*. Maybe if you would've spoken to him just once in all these years you would've known how much sorrow and regret he carries. You've never forgiven him and he's never been able to forgive himself."

"He was a wild boy. I blamed him for leading Patrick astray."

"Patrick was already astray, Mom. His grades were bad and he was angry."

"Patrick was a good boy. He never drank or got into any kind of trouble before he started going around with Ben."

Meg shook her head. "How can you not remember? He got a ton of detentions and had incomplete assignments, and he got suspended that time for starting a fire in the boys' restroom."

"He was always so sensitive. He took it hard when your father and I weren't getting along. I tried to talk to him, discipline him, but your father was no help. Then he took up with that—woman—and that's what started everything that night. We'd argued and he left to be with her. Trust me, Megan, Ben is not the only one who carries a burden of guilt for what happened that night."

Meg supposed they had all second-guessed themselves. "Patrick asked me to watch a movie with him, but I went to work. I had no idea he was that upset."

"You couldn't have known," her mother said, shaking her head sadly. "None of us could have known."

"Just once, I wish we could talk about the happy times. All those photos he was always sneaking up on us to take. The drawings he loved to make. I miss saying his name, sharing how sad I am when it's his birthday or Christmas, or when it's soccer season and I see all the boys at the high school practicing like he did. All this anger and silence—it's torn us all apart."

Her mother sighed. "I have been angry. It's a bitter, devastating thing to come to grips with, losing a child so—senselessly." She was still a long time, staring out over the garden, before she turned back to Meg. "As for Ben, I suppose a lot of it was just that—that my boy was gone and he wasn't." Her mother broke up then, her face contorting in pain. The garden trowel fell to the ground.

Meg hugged her mom. They were both crying. "I'm sorry, Mom. I'm sorry we lost him. But he's gone and we're still here. We've got to make peace with the past and move on."

After a while her mother asked, "Are you in love with him?"

"At first we pretended to date to help him get hired at the hospital, but then it turned—real. But he's not interested in a relationship."

"Sounds like he was out to serve himself all along."

"He's not like that. He wants to be a doctor to help everyone like his grandfather did. He's kindhearted and good with kids and loves his family and . . ." Oh, God. She'd jumped to his defense without even thinking. The scary thing was, she believed what she'd said, despite what had happened between them.

"You love him," her mother said.

She nodded . . . and proceeded to cry a big, snotty cry.

Because she *did* love him, and not from afar, not with the moony dreaminess she'd used as a crutch for so many years, but with a deep, aching tenderness she felt might just kill her.

Her mother paused and wiped a tear that had trailed down Meg's cheek. "I'm so proud of you, Megan. You're everything a daughter should be and more. If Ben doesn't see that, then he doesn't deserve you."

Meg cracked a smile through the veil of tears. "I love you, Mom."

"The hell with the garden," her mother said. "Let's go order pizza."

>—●—<

Ben had walked four blocks from his grandfather's neighborhood before he realized he'd left his car parked in front of the old house and had no time to get it if he was going to be back at the hospital by one. But his legs weren't walking him to the hospital, they were walking to the lake-front. Then he did something he'd never done before. He called Jax, who was working, and asked if he'd cover for him for another hour, promising he'd make it up to him next time their shifts overlapped. His legs led him straight to Reflections, his brother's restaurant on the lake.

Brad was in the kitchen, bent over a saucepan with his head chef, Phillipe.

Ben gave a nod to the chef but honed in on his brother. "I have to talk to you."

Brad held out a spoon. "You're just in time to try the *beurre blanc*."

"The burr-what?"

"It's a sauce made of white wine and butter. Except we used champagne and it's to die for."

Ben paced a little. "Look, Brad, I've got to get back to work. I just wanted to talk with you for just a few—" Ben broke off. His big brother was assessing him with a look he hadn't seen since one awful Saturday night when Ben was seventeen and had come home drunk or high or both. Brad had cleaned up his puke and put him to bed and the next morning, Ben had awakened to find that his Mustang had vanished. And he didn't get it back for six months.

"Phillipe, this is excellent," Brad said. "Let's serve it with the lobster tonight." Then he walked his brother back through the kitchen to his office, which overlooked the pier, stopping to grab a couple of wrapped sandwiches out of the fridge. They walked through a door and sat outside on a little deck with an overhang. "What's going on? You look like hell."

"The thing with Meg sort of went from fake to real."

Brad sat down, propped his feet on the wooden deck rail, and tossed his brother a sandwich. "We sort of surmised that when Annabelle handed us an empty box of condoms this morning."

"Shit." Ben set the sandwich down and trolled his hands through his hair, making it stick up in seven different directions. "I thought I took care of that."

"On my couch, though? Really?"

"Just for the record, it was *not* on the couch," Ben said. It was mostly in the bedroom. And once on the kitchen island, but he wasn't about to admit that. "That's all I'm saying."

"Thank God. Please continue," Brad said.

"I asked her to come and look at Gramps's house with me today."

Brad paused before he bit into his sandwich. "I ran into Mike Garcia, who's done a lot of work on our place. He said they're demoing it next week."

Ben nodded. "The whole reason I got into this mess was because I knew Donaldson was looking for a family-oriented candidate. Someone sure to stay here. So I faked a girlfriend. Only today, I turned her into a fiancée. Without her approval."

Brad set down his sandwich and sat forward. "You didn't."

Ben nodded, his lips pressed tight. "I told him we were engaged."

"And Meg let you have it."

"Yep."

"You're a real a-hole, you know that, little bro?" Brad slapped him on the back—hard. "Just saying."

"It gets worse."

"You're giving me indigestion."

"I told her it was only temporary, that we'd break it off in a couple of weeks. She basically told me to go fuck off."

"I knew I liked that girl." Brad set his plate on the floor and dusted off his hands. "So now what?"

Ben squinted out across the water, at the lake he loved. A few sailboats slid effortlessly across the horizon. Motorboats puttered back and forth, cutting paths through the water. Seabirds swooped and dove and squawked. But everything that used to calm him made him feel ragged as an old knife's edge.

"She talked to old Doc Manning about her brother's autopsy report—for me. Turns out hitting his head on the quarry bottom is what killed him. For so long, I'd believed it was my incompetence, that after I pulled him out, I had no clue what to do, how to breathe for him or do chest compressions. I felt . . . helpless, that if I would have known what the hell I was doing, there might have been a different outcome."

"You never told me that."

He shrugged. "It wouldn't have changed anything. And I was too ashamed."

Brad put an arm on his shoulder. "So you never told me that, but you told her."

"She found out the truth. For *me.*"

"I'm sure that was tough on her."

Ben drummed his fingers on the wooden railing. "I just keep thinking about Gramps. He knew exactly what to say to make people laugh, to make them feel better. He cared, you know? And he had the most integrity of anyone I've ever known."

"Gramps was a kind man," Brad said. "Hardworking and . . . you're right. He really cared about people."

"I just feel like I'm made for that job. I want to make him proud. I want to step into his shoes and try to be all he was for this town." Ben rubbed the back of his neck. "That committee is meeting this afternoon. I'm *this close* to getting that job. I don't know what the hell to do."

"Gramps would be proud of you, Ben. You've come a long way."

"He wouldn't be proud of me today."

Brad put an arm around Ben's shoulders, for comfort, but then he squeezed a little hard, for emphasis. "I think you may have just answered your own question."

Ben thought about that for a long minute before he stood up. How could he have done so much damage when he'd started out with the best intentions? "I've got to get back to work. Thanks for listening."

"Anytime. But there is one thing I have to ask from you in return."

"What is it?"

"Please don't have sex in my house ever again. It gives me the creeps."

>—•◦—○—◦•—◦

Jax was a little ticked off when Ben finally showed up in the ER at two o'clock.

"That was a mighty long lunch hour. Considering I've been here since midnight and I want to get the hell home."

Ben pulled an electronic tablet out of Jax's hands. "I wasn't fooling around if that's what you're implying. And I really appreciate what you did. I'll come in two hours early for you next time."

"Well, when Stacy has the babies I may be calling on you to take a shift."

"Happy to help out."

Jax signed off on a couple of loose odds and ends, and Ben was relieved that for once the ER was fairly quiet.

"Jax," Ben said before Jax took off, "can I ask you a question?"

"Sure. What is it?"

"Do you want this job?"

Jax paused long and hard. "Yeah, I do. We love the community, and it's a short distance from Stacy's family. And I like the staff here. But this place isn't perfect. There are things that need to be done to make it excel."

"Well, Donaldson said the committee's meeting for the final time today. I just wanted to wish you good luck." Ben held out his hand.

Jax shook it. "Thanks. Good luck to you, too. Although I think you're the man."

"You never know."

A nurse walked up to Ben. "There's a non-urgent patient we just put in room seven."

Ben headed there and snaked back the familiar yellow curtain.

Meg's mother sat on the gurney, looking like she'd rather be getting a colonoscopy than sitting there fully clothed.

"Mrs. Halloran," he said.

She nodded. "Benjamin."

He leaned against the counter and crossed his arms, trying to look like he looked every day—competent and casual. But the hair on his arms had raised up and a bad sensation in his stomach told him his shitty day was about to get even worse.

"I'm not really sick," she said, clutching her handbag a little nervously. "I told Gina I needed to talk with you."

"I gathered that." He'd have to talk to Gina about letting half the town back here to see him at will. He glanced at the chart. "Your chart says 'Feels sad about something.'"

"That's why I'm here. To say I'm sorry."

Whoa. She looked nervous. Uptight. Maybe even a little scared. Humor always served him well in situations like this. "I could have made a house call for that," he said with a slight grin.

"No. I needed to come right away." He should be shocked, or surprised. Instead, his first thought was to wonder if Meg had put her up to this.

He rolled a stool closer to the gurney and sat down. Maybe she was sorry that her daughter had the misfortune to get involved with him and she was here to give him hell.

And if that was so, he deserved it.

"I'm sorry I've given you the cold shoulder for so long. I know what happened to my son wasn't your fault. And . . . I'm sorry if the way I've treated you has caused you pain."

The words registered, sort of. But all he could think was that this was Meg's doing. She'd talked to her mother about him, despite being furious with him. How could she have done such a generous thing, even after what he'd done to her? "Look, you don't have to . . ."

"Yes, I do. That night, his father and I—we'd been arguing. I had no idea Patrick had heard us until I heard the door slam and his car start, and I knew he was upset. My daughter told me today how you went looking for him. You were all by yourself. I always thought you'd said that to protect yourself, that you'd been there drinking with him the whole time."

"Maybe I should have been. Maybe if I had been there I could've stopped what happened."

She shook her head. "I can't imagine what that was like for you to find him like that. You were just a boy. I was too wrapped up in my own misery to understand. I didn't understand the guilt you felt."

Ben shrugged. "I was just a kid. It was traumatic, and I was ashamed."

"I hope you can forgive me."

"I think it's time for both of us to put our regrets to rest."

Ben could only see a blurry image before him. He reached over and hugged Meg's mother. She was crying, and oh, hell, they were both crying. But some of the tears were filled with relief. At last, he was free to mourn his friend. And to start to leave the past behind where it belonged. "I loved Patrick as if he were my own brother," he said. "I can't tell you how much I still miss him."

Almost as much as he missed her daughter.

Oh, God. He was such a dumbass. He'd used her and hurt her, all for the sake of a job he didn't deserve to get. He'd lost the woman he loved and thrown his integrity overboard in the process. But instead of feeling lighter, he felt like he was sinking without her. How could he have ever thought a job could be more important than she was?

He glanced at his watch. "I love your daughter, Mrs. Halloran. I did something wrong that I've got to fix. But I swear, I will fix it." He kissed her on the cheek. "I've got to go."

⋄

Jax wasn't happy when Ben paged him in the parking lot and begged him to cover him even longer. But for what Ben was about to do, he figured one day Jax might even thank him. The conference room in the administrative wing of the hospital was full of a dozen women and men in suits sitting around a big table drinking coffee and shuffling paperwork, some of it with his photo on it. Ben knocked but then entered without waiting for permission.

Dr. Donaldson, who was seated at the head of a long, shiny table, rose in surprise. "Why, Ben. We were just discussing—"

"I don't want the job, Dr. Donaldson, Committee," he said, looking at the faces staring at him in shock. "Because I lied. Something my grandfather never would have done. I wasn't really dating Meg Halloran. She agreed to help me because she wanted me to have the same shot at the job as everyone else. I let my desire for the job cloud my judgment, and I've hurt people in the process. I'm not the person you want."

He could have told them they were crazy to impose their restrictions on the job. That he could take them to court if he wanted to because what they were doing was discriminatory. But he'd blown it. And worse, he'd chosen the job over the one woman he'd ever really cared about in his life.

"You're saying you made up a relationship to impress us?" the director of cardiology asked.

"That's correct."

Dr. Donaldson spoke. "But I saw you together earlier at your grandfather's house—kissing, holding hands. Was that fake, too?"

"No, but I haven't asked her to marry me yet."

Yet. Holy shit. An idea had come to him, a big idea that made his knees quiver and his hands tremble from the scope of it. "Although I want her to be my wife, because I love her. More than I've ever loved anyone."

"I'm not understanding," the hospital CFO said. "This whole thing started out fake, but now it's real?"

"It was real, until today when she dumped me after I lied. I'm sorry, I have to go."

"This is most unusual, Dr. Rushford," Dr. Donaldson said. But Ben barely heard. He'd made his peace, and he no longer cared about the job. He had to find a way to show Meg he loved her, more than this job, more than anything. Because there was no way he was going to lose her for good.

CHAPTER 21

"What do you *mean* the band's a no-show and we're missing three people for the bridal show?" Meg asked late that afternoon as she sewed and safety-pinned one of Sam's college girlfriends into a plum-colored bridesmaid's dress. She was busy directing and dressing everyone who was involved in the bridal show that was to begin at 5:00 p.m. at the marina. And almost too busy to feel the skewering stabs of pain that pierced her gut every time she thought about Ben. Which was at least once every twenty seconds or so.

Gloria, Effie, Olivia, and Meg's sister Sheri had all come to help prepare for the big show. Sam was helping a gaggle of women, dressed in any of a wild rainbow of bridesmaids' gowns, with their makeup. Regardless of her heartache, Meg was determined to see this through to the end. She refused to fall apart until then. Her shop and everyone who worked so hard to help this show get off the ground meant too much.

"My friends' car broke down on the way from Providence," Sam said. "And I don't know what exactly happened to the band."

Meg glanced at her watch. "We've still got a half hour. Are your friends close? Maybe we can send someone to get them."

"No, they're . . . like an hour away," Sam said.

Meg frowned. "And you're just telling me this *now*?"

"Um, their cell phones died. They're . . . not going to make it. Sorry."

"The idea is to make this part of the show look like real weddings, with bridesmaids and a bride. How can I do that if I'm missing one bride and two bridesmaids?"

This show was *the* representation of her shop. They had sold tickets and the waterfront was filled with chairs. Vendors were set up— bakers and photographers, wedding planners and limo companies. They'd invited a bunch of last year's brides to model their own wedding dresses. And everyone was expecting a fashion show, which would be done as a series of mock weddings where the bridal party would march down the dock and the designated bride would follow.

"Take a deep breath," Olivia said, placing her hands on Meg's arms. "Sheri and I will go into the crowd and recruit a few more women. It'll be okay."

"I'll go right now," Sheri said, being surprisingly helpful for once. She'd even come from Greenwich for Meg's big show today. There hadn't been time to have more than a brief discussion with her and their mom, but Meg felt that at last their family would have a chance to come together again.

"Sam, do you have any local friends we can call?" Meg asked.

But Sam was barely listening.

A sleek black Jaguar had pulled up to the shop. A dark-haired man with a white polo shirt got out, lifted his sunglasses to the top of his head, and knocked on the window.

"Meg, I'll be back in a sec, okay?" Sam said as she ran out the door and began talking heatedly with the man. A few minutes later, she opened the door and yelled in for one of her friends to please hand her purse to her. A minute after that, she came back in without the purse, carrying an armload of junk—a wallet, a brush, a sample bottle of hair spray.

Everyone looked up when she closed the door behind her. "Harris said I shouldn't be in the bridal show," she said. Friends and family stopped dressing, sewing, and pinning to listen. "That it would be putting myself on display. That one day, I could potentially be a politician's wife, and anything I did would be heavily scrutinized."

"It's a bridal show, not a striptease!" her friend Jess said.

"That boy has far too many rules to follow," Gloria said.

"And I'm done following them," Sam said, dumping her stuff on the nearby desk and dusting her hands clean. "I told him to stuff the Dooney & Bourke purse he just bought me right up his entitled, from-the-Mayflower—"

Just then, a very noisy muffler scraped the road in front of the shop, so hard that sparks flew. A vintage Camaro with rust spots and mismatched tires pulled up and a man walked in. With a black cast and a shit-ton of attitude. "I wanted to let you know I'm leaving," Spike said, mostly to Sam, but there was a good chance the twenty other women or so in the shop might have heard, too.

Sam looked at him. "For the weekend?"

"No, I'm leaving *for good*."

Meg stopped pinning the dress, and gestured to the girl wearing it that she was done. Everyone pretended to be busy, but it was impossible not to attend to what was going on in front of them. Sam blinked furiously, and her voice went up an octave. "But—your arm is still in the cast. You're still getting therapy. Y-you can't leave yet."

"I've got a singing gig in New York. This could be my big break."

"But your job is here."

Spike shrugged. "If I stay in Mirror Lake, I'll be stuck at Clinker's my whole life."

"There's nothing wrong with that," Sam said.

"There is to me." They were standing close together in front of the window, unaware that, once again, everyone around them had stopped running around the shop in a flurry.

"I broke up with Harris," she said softly.

His mouth quirked up the tiniest bit. "I'm glad." Then he curled his hand around the back of her neck and kissed her. Hard.

Women gasped. One whistled. And a few exclaimed.

Spike pulled back, leaving Sam standing stock-still, looking like she'd just won the Powerball.

"Oh, I almost forgot," Spike said, pulling an envelope out of his back pocket and placing it in Sam's limp hands. "This is for you. Open it later."

And then he was gone.

But not quite. Meg dashed after him, pins in her mouth, and grabbed his arm before he could step through the door. "Wait. You can't go yet."

Spike looked at her like she needed a softly padded room and a big shot of Haldol.

Meg loosed her grip—a little. "My band cancelled and I know you're in one. Can you play a gig right now? For my bridal show?"

He frowned. "What kind of music?"

"Anything you want. Happy music. Joyful. Stuff that makes people think of love and weddings." She grabbed his other arm, too. "Please, Lukas. This show means everything to me and despite months of preparation, it's turning to dog poo in front of my eyes." Like everything else in her life.

"Okay, relax," Spike said, prying her fingers off his skin. "I'll do it."

No sooner had she given Spike a few instructions and showed him out so he could go prepare for his gig than Olivia came up to her holding out a bell-shaped wedding gown. *Priscilla's.* "You're going to have to put this on."

"No way. Find someone else." It had nothing to do with the fact that it was Priscilla's abandoned dress. Well, okay, it did. But mostly, she just couldn't do it. The last thing she wanted to do in her current state of mind was to parade down the dock dressed as a bride. Her dream of love had died and that would be the cruelest reminder she could imagine.

"Look," Olivia said. "You've got to set your personal feelings aside and get through this next hour." Meg must have looked about to lose it because Olivia grabbed her by the shoulders and shook hard. "Just one hour, Meg. After a lifetime of hard work, this is what it's going to take to save your shop."

Meg blew out a breath. "Right. Save the shop," she repeated dully.

Even if today weren't the worst day of her life, the thing she hated above all others was to be the center of attention. Just the thought of all those eyeballs on her as she walked out in this fancy dress made her want to run screaming for the hills. As she stood there semi-panicking, Samantha came over and began doing her makeup.

"Are you sure no one could find some sweet young girl who's dying to model a wedding gown?" Meg asked out loud.

"No bride yet," Sheri said, dragging Stacy, Jax's pregnant wife, into the shop, "but I did find us another bridesmaid."

"You all must be pretty desperate if you need someone like me to do this shit," Stacy said.

"Stacy!" Meg said, gave her a big hug, and looked her over. "We have a plus-size gown that would fit you, but it's not plum."

Sam continued to work on Meg's eye shadow, lipstick, mascara. "I know the gown you're talking about. Pale pink is close enough it won't clash," she said.

"I know exactly where it is," Olivia said, then took Stacy in the back room to dress.

"What else can possibly go wrong?" Meg went behind the dressing screen they'd set up earlier to help with all the changes for the show. She eyed the gown, which she knew she'd have to squeeze into and do something to fill up the bust. On impulse, she tossed the dress over the screen and ran upstairs. She yanked the alencon lace gown she loved off its hanger. If she was going to have to parade in front of the entire town, she was going to do it *her* way. And look damn good doing it.

While Meg dressed, Gloria peeked her head over the side of the screen. She was channeling Jackie Kennedy in a bright pink tweed suit and a tiny matching pillbox hat covered with pink netting. "Hello, dear," she said, her voice unusually quiet. "Turn around and I'll zip you up."

Gran zipped the side zipper and fastened the hook-and-eye closure. But then suddenly Meg felt something slide over her eyes—something white and silky, a sash. She felt a sharp tug behind her head as a knot was tied tight. "Gran, what the hell!"

"It's for your own good, dear," Gran said in a strangely calm voice.

Someone grabbed her hand and gave her a quick squeeze. "Just go with it, sweetie!" Olivia whispered.

"Come in," Gloria called. "Let's go, ladies, and give them privacy."

Feet shuffled. "Wait! Don't go! We're twenty minutes to show time!" Meg wasn't sure if everyone had really left or was hovering on the sidelines, but the entire shop went dead silent. The panic that had seized her for the past hour rose to fever pitch levels, her heart beating crazily out of her rib cage. Why the hell would these crazy ladies leave her like this?

"Meg," a familiar voice said.

"Ben?" She stopped tugging at the knot, which, considering it was tied by an old lady, was surprisingly tight. "No, I can't talk to you now. The show—"

"Can wait. I have something to say to you."

"I'm taking off this stupid—"

"I'm afraid you can't do that just yet, dear," Gran said in that same low, calm voice. "It's bad luck."

"It's bad luck to have someone kill you, too, Gran," Meg said. "And I thought you were giving us privacy."

"With all the people in here," Gran said, "if you want privacy, you may have to take him to the bathroom."

A loud crash sounded. "What the hell," Ben said.

"What happened?" Meg asked.

"No one told me there was some—thing in the middle of the floor."

"It's probably the dressing screen," Meg said.

"Thanks, my knee just discovered that."

"W-what are you doing here?"

"I came to talk to you. Only those batty old ladies blindfolded me, too."

"You came to talk to me?" Meg asked. Maybe being blindfolded had enhanced her sense of smell. Because she could tell from the familiar scent of soap and August sunshine that he was close by. Her misguided heart quivered with a buoyant sense of hope despite her warning it not to.

The calm tones of his voice soothed her frazzled nerves. "I was wrong to do what I did in front of Donaldson. I'm sorry."

There had been a time when an apology would have been enough to send her over the moon without demanding more discussion. When she would have tiptoed around the truth just to have his attention. But she'd finally left that crush thing in the dirt. This was real, and she was going for full disclosure or nothing. "You picked the job over me. You told me you didn't do relationships. And I do. I want the whole shebang. Love, family, a fixer-upper that drains the budget, and a big, slobbery dog."

"The whole shebang, huh?" he asked. He sounded a little wary. Like maybe he just couldn't do it. Like he simply wasn't capable of having a real relationship.

Well, all right then. No matter what the outcome, she was going to get everything off her mind. She took a big breath and kept going. "I understand how badly you want that job," she said. "I just wish you'd wanted me as much."

She heard him shuffle a step forward. He was so close now that she could feel his breath on her cheek. "Well, see, that's where you've got me wrong because I do want you," he said in a quiet, even voice. "Even more than that job. I spoke to Donaldson and the committee. I took myself out of the running. Told them the truth."

"Oh, God, no." Meg's muscles froze in dread as what he'd just said sunk in. He was giving up the job he'd loved for her? "I don't want to be responsible for you giving up your dream."

"It's only a job, and there are other jobs in Connecticut. The worst thing is that I blew the best thing that's ever happened to me. Do you want to know what that is?"

She might have nodded, who knew. Because her heart was squeezing so painfully it hurt, and she couldn't breathe, and of course she couldn't see. And she might have been crying, too.

A hand grazed over her hip. Patted her skirt, then finally found her hand. At last he gathered up both her hands in his big warm ones and she gripped them for all she was worth.

"You, Megan. Losing that job is nothing compared to the thought of living my life without you." His voice rolled over her, soft as spring rain. "I want to show you I'm a better man because of you. For the first time since Patrick died, I want to take the risk of loving someone. I want to take that risk with you because I—love you." He smoothed her fingers, rubbing them between his own, and the firm, reassuring pressure of his touch felt so damn good she almost forgot there were hundreds of people waiting to see a put-together, elegant bridal show instead of a three-ring circus. Then his grip on her hands shifted. She heard something hit the ground. Maybe his knee.

"Wait." In a panic, she tugged at the godforsaken sash that Gran must have tied with a sailor knot. "I need to see you." She'd just heard the audio she'd been yearning to hear him speak for half her life and she was missing the visual feed. She needed to look into his deep brown eyes and see what his heart was saying.

"The grannies told me it's bad luck to see the bride before the wedding," Ben said.

"Before the—what?" Her blood froze cold. *It's just a bridal show.*

"If you say yes, we can walk down the aisle right now."

"I don't—get it." Had someone spiked her tea? Or had stress simply sent her careening over the edge?

"The real bridal show will go on after we're done. But I've got everyone lined up out there. All our friends and family. A priest, a minister, a rabbi, and a judge. And a license that's waiting for your signature. So, Megan Louise Halloran, will you marry me?"

Everything was trembling. Her hands, her knees. Dimly, she wondered if she was hallucinating. That the stress of the past few days had simply thrown her over the edge.

"Ben, this is crazy." It *was* crazy. Because she thought she'd just heard the man of her dreams tell her he loved her.

"Not so crazy. I've always loved you. I just never thought I deserved you. But you fought for me. You gave me back a peace of mind I lost at an old quarry long ago. I'm all in here, sweetheart."

Could she take this crazy risk? She'd wanted to live a bold life. To fight for what she wanted. And dammit, she wanted *him*. "I've always wanted you. But I'd sort of invented a dream version of you. These past weeks have shown me you're *better* than my dreams."

She felt her way up his arms, up his tuxedo jacket, up his starched collar and his bow tie, through the silky-coarse layers of his hair, until she was kneeling beside him and touching every part of his face like a blind person trying to use only their sense of touch to imagine their beloved. Maybe she did it to reassure herself it was really him. Same beard. Same stubborn chin. And at last, the same beautiful mouth, which she targeted with her own lips. The kiss was long and lush and maybe it was even better blindfolded because in the darkness, she felt every single passionate stroke straight down to her toes.

His kiss reaffirmed his words. "Yes," she said at last. "I love you, Ben. I've always loved you, and I want to marry you."

"She said yes," he yelled.

Feet shuffled into the room. People cheered. Cries of *finally* and *it's about time* and *glad that's over* filled the air. But when someone finally ripped the sash off her head, he was gone.

Her mom and gran each took an arm. Sam, smiling, ran in front of her to fluff her hair and touch up her makeup.

"Oh, Gran, I wish I had your veil," Meg said, on the verge of tears.

"Brought it," Gran said, and Sam helped secure the comb of a simple fingertip-length veil edged with delicate lace.

"Time to go," Gran said, teary eyed. "You look prettier than Princess Kate."

Meg looked from her grandmother to her mother. "But, Mom—"

"I owed Ben a big apology, and like the good man he is, he took it. I want you to be happy, Megan. And I want us all to heal, starting today. Patrick would have wanted that."

"Oh, Mom." Meg kissed her mom. And Gran. Then she started crying, too.

"You look beautiful," Sheri said, giving her a squeeze. "And Mom's right. We never healed, just covered up the scars. But I think this is a good start."

Olivia peeked outside the door and then returned with a report. "Are we ready? The groomsmen are lined up in front of the gazebo, and looks like all the officiants made it."

"I can't believe you guys did all this," Meg said.

"It was Ben's idea," her mom said.

Meg walked out of her shop, her mother on one arm, her grandmother on the other, following Olivia, Sheri, Stacy, and Sam. They crossed the street that she had crossed practically every day of her life, with all its familiar sights, but today everything looked surreal. The row of brick shops facing Main Street looked postcard perfect, their plate-glass windows shiny, their sidewalks swept clean, every potted geranium the brightest scarlet or the most vivid red. They followed the walkway through the middle of the square, waving to onlookers who were heading to the nearby marina for the show, then down the grassy aisle that someone had lined with two rows of white rose petals. Chairs had been set up in front of the gazebo, which were now occupied by the family and friends Meg loved. Alex blew a kiss from a wheelchair in the front row.

Then she saw Ben for the first time, standing in front of the gazebo next to Brad, Tom, Teddy, and Jax, and for a moment the world stood stock-still. Meg thought of all the times she had had that reaction on first seeing him—the jolt of her heart, the stampeding of her pulse, the warm spread of heat everywhere—and this reaction was like that times a hundred. He looked like a dream in elegant black tux pants, a white jacket, and a black bow tie, his beard trimmed close and the thick layers of his hair cropped and elegantly precise. The look in his eyes promised a lifetime of love, humor, and something dark and sensuously dangerous that both thrilled and strangely soothed her at the same time.

Odd that she'd lost count of all the times she'd looked at him from across a room, and felt such a desperate pining it was almost a physical ache. She thanked God for the crazy, miraculous turn of events that had finally broken down the walls between them for good. This time, when she stared at him, he smiled. A beautiful, wide smile that made her heart ache from all the joy that was overflowing from it.

She smiled right back. Because this time it was for real.

Ben left his place to meet her. He kissed her mother and her grandmother. Then he placed something into her hands—a bouquet of daisies, tied with a bright green ribbon. "Thank you," she whispered. "They're perfect." *Just like you.*

He stood in front of her, gazing long and hard into her eyes. Her full grin must have matched his own, except she was spilling tears of happiness everywhere. "Time to start our journey together, sweetheart," he said, tucking her hand into the crook of his arm. Good thing he was holding her tightly because she went boneless as a blob of Jell-O from the sheer joy of being with him.

But she couldn't start walking yet. Urgently, she tugged him back. "Ben," she whispered. "Are you sure? This is a pretty big show of PDA considering we've technically never gone out on a real date."

Ben turned to face Meg and took up both of her hands. Slowly, he brought their joined hands up to his mouth and kissed every delicate finger in turn. He looked at the strong, determined, beautiful woman before him, radiant in her lacy gown, her green eyes vivid and bright against the stark white of her veil. Honesty and unconditional love beamed from her gaze. "I never thought I'd be free to love you. You gave me that gift. And I don't want to waste another minute apart. I love you, Megan."

Her hands were trembling, but her voice was calm and clear. "You make me feel like I can do or be anything I want to be. And I love you, too."

He looked from Meg to his brothers, standing in a row, their Rushford good looks unmistakable when they were all cleaned up. His sister stood with the bridesmaids, looking more like a woman than a little girl. And his Grandma Effie sat in the front row of chairs beaming. Everyone he loved and who had loved him all his life was here.

For a second Ben thought of his parents. His grandparents. Patrick. All the important people who weren't here. They would have loved Meg. He liked to think that Patrick would have laughed and slapped him on the back and warned him that he was watching, so Ben had better not eff this one up. In his heart he felt their blessing and knew they were here with him in spirit.

The minister cleared his throat.

Ben took a step forward, but someone called out in the crowd. "Excuse me, before the ceremony begins, I'd like to make an announcement." It was Dr. Donaldson, dressed in a suit and tie.

No, not now. He wouldn't tell everyone about his deception, would he? What could he possibly object to now?

"Did we invite him to the wedding?" Meg asked.

"Honey, to be truthful," Ben said, "I don't think we invited anyone."

Dr. Donaldson clapped his hands to bring everyone to attention. "The committee has made a decision regarding the Emergency

Medicine job. We've decided to hire two candidates, Dr. Rushford and Dr. Jenkins. We feel you're both excellent physicians."

Stacy let out a whoop and gave a little wave to Jax.

Ben looked at Meg, wanting to be sure she was okay with it. "What are you waiting for?" she asked. "Say yes!"

"Thanks, Dr. Donaldson," Ben spoke loud enough across the gathering so everyone could hear. "It'll be my pleasure to serve the wonderful citizens of Mirror Lake."

Everyone cheered and clapped, but the applause was cut off when a tall, balding man in a dark suit stood up a few rows behind Dr. Donaldson. Mayor Kline. "While we're delivering good news, I just wanted to say the bank has approved the loan for Bridal Aisle. The town of Mirror Lake is proud to count such a unique business among its many attractions. And Priscilla and my wife send their apologies. Especially since my daughter's wedding has been cancelled."

"I'm sorry to hear that, Mayor Kline," Meg said. "But thank you from the bottom of our hearts." Now it was Meg's turn to whoop. Ben saw her scan the crowd, no doubt looking for Alex. Sure enough, Alex fist pumped and blew kisses from her wheelchair. Ben was just about to turn back around and tell the reverend—or rabbi or priest or judge—to get started when Alex's smile suddenly faded to a look of pain. He'd seen that look many times on women in the ER and it was nothing to mess around with.

"Oh my God," Alex said, clutching her belly. "My water broke and I think I'm having a contraction."

><+>+○+<+><

"Harris has called my phone fifty times and Spike left without saying good-bye," Sam said to Meg a few hours later in the Labor and Delivery waiting room where family and friends had gathered. "How could he?" Sam wore a sweatshirt and jeans, her curly hair tied back in a ponytail, her makeup washed away by the tears she'd been crying. Meg felt an enormous relief at her lack of preppy clothing and accessories.

"What was in the envelope?" Meg asked. Several hours ago, after they'd rushed Alex and Tom to the hospital and learned the births were imminent, Meg had abandoned her wedding gown for ankle jeans and a tailored blue button-down shirt. She and Ben had decided to hold off on the wedding until they could have the peace of mind of knowing the twins were safe and sound. Besides, Meg could never get married without one of her two best friends present, and Ben felt the same way about his brother.

Sam opened her palm. In it sat a set of car keys, attached to a key ring that was a pair of wings crafted from hammered silver.

Meg picked up the wings. "He's a talented artist."

"He left me this, too." Sam pulled out a folded piece of paper. Meg read the artsy cursive writing: *My wish for you is that you spread your wings and learn to truly fly. Lukas.*

"What do you think?" Sam asked, her big blue eyes full of hope.

"Before I answer that, what kind of car do the keys belong to?"

"This 1993 Camaro he was working on. It's a diamond in the rough."

Rough was right. Meg was at a loss for words, but just then Sam started to cry, so she hugged her.

"What does it mean?" Sam asked. "Do you think he'll come back?"

"I don't know. But giving someone a car is quite a gift." *Provided it ran,* she thought silently.

Sam broke into a sob. "I don't want his gift. I want *him.* There's so much I want to say."

"Maybe he wasn't quite ready to talk, you know? I think we're all diamonds in the rough. We come into our own in our own time."

Just then the double doors to the Labor and Delivery area opened, and Ben walked out, wearing a surgical hat, scrubs, and booties on his feet. "It's a girl . . . and a boy. And everybody's doing great." He pulled off his surgical hat and met Meg's gaze across the room. "So, who's still up for a wedding?"

EPILOGUE

"I know getting married in a hospital room at midnight wasn't the most romantic setting for a wedding," Brad said. He raised a glass of champagne to all the family gathered before him in the fenced-in yard on Forest Glen on the quiet mid-October evening. He held his glass in one hand, while holding his rambunctious eighteen-month-old daughter Annabelle in the other, "So it's nice to finally be able to formally celebrate your wedding at your new home."

Meg looked around at the entire Rushford family, her mom and grandmother, Sheri and her husband Pete and their two little girls, and Dr. Manning, and her heart swelled with a happiness that mere weeks ago she doubted she'd ever experience. "I thought the fluorescent above-the-bed lighting was especially romantic," she said. "And the maid-of-honor's gown covered in pregnant teddy bears—stunning."

"Hey, what about the co-maid-of-honor?" Olivia asked. "My yoga pants were expensive—Lululemon."

"You always look stunning, no matter what you're wearing, sweetheart," Brad said, flashing her a grin that proved they were even more in love after a year and a half of marriage.

"Instead of bouquets, you held the babies," Gran said. "So adorable," she added, turning to the twin that Tom held in his arms and chucking the baby under one of his chins.

"Well, you had all the necessary elements," Alex said, "your Something Old and Something Blue was your jeans, and your Something Borrowed—Gloria's string of pearls."

"And Mom's pearl earrings," Sheri added. They'd given her their jewelry so Meg could look a little classy in the pics. Which she thought she did, with a smile so wide she could drop half of Connecticut into it. And she hadn't stopped smiling since.

Then there was her Something New—a tiny kaleidoscope from the hospital gift shop from Ben. For looking forward to their bright new future. Where every day would always be different. Which so far it was. Ben was different, too—lighter, happier, at peace. As was she. They'd both seemed to bring out the best in each other.

"It was nice of the nurses to bring us flowers someone left behind for your bouquet," Meg's mom said.

"Good thing the hospital chaplain was a friend of mine," Ben said, "and didn't mind performing the ceremony just before midnight."

"Or playing Pachelbel's Canon on his iPhone," Brad said.

"For someone who owns a bridal shop, you certainly didn't have a dream wedding with all your favorite brands and designers," Meg's mom said.

Meg patted Ben lightly on his fine muscular thigh. "It was a tradeoff for a life with the man of my dreams." Who was now the man of her *reality*. And real life was so much better than any fantasy she'd ever had.

"When do you get to move into the house?" Tom asked.

"Within a month," Ben said. "I'm happy not to be sharing space with the Royal Family at Meg's apartment for much longer."

"Those kitties are going to love this yard," Gran said.

"And sometime in the next year, we may actually be able to go *inside* the house," Tom said, looking around at the giant dumpster parked in the backyard that was filled with construction debris, including a green toilet seat crowning the top.

"Oh, c'mon Tom," Ben said. "You can always go pee in the woods if you've got to go."

"I want to know how the house went from commercially zoned and on the demo list to this." Brad waved his hand around the yard.

"Mayor Kline felt so bad about all the commotion his wife and daughter caused at Meg's shop that he went to bat for us," Ben said.

"Sip, Daddy, sip!" Annabelle said, reaching with chubby hands for Brad's glass.

Olivia quietly smoothed her daughter's curly dark hair and snuck a sippy cup into her hands while Brad continued his toast. "To my baby brother, who has become a duly employed doctor, a homeowner, and a husband all in a month's time."

"You might want to add *father* to that list," Meg said softly.

"Oops," Alex said, covering her mouth with her hand and smiling. Gasps went up from everyone. "Mary Queen of Scots!" Gloria exclaimed.

Brad shook his head in disbelief. "No way."

"Um, yes?" Meg said.

"Did you skip the family planning lecture in med school?" Tom asked.

Ben ignored his brother and beamed. Every time that man showed his dimples Meg swore her toes curled. "When we make changes in our lives, we go full force ahead," Ben said, sliding an arm around his wife's shoulder and giving her a big kiss.

"Besides, we're making up for lost time," Meg said, kissing him again, this time a little longer. He'd definitely appeared to have gotten over his dislike of kissing in public, because he couldn't seem to stop doing it wherever they went. And she loved every minute of it. As long as he didn't grab her ass in front of her mother.

"No champagne for you," Alex, who was holding a twin in one arm said, then promptly removed the glass from Meg's hand.

"Oh, come on, Alex, just a taste!" Meg said.

"Here you go." Alex traded Meg's glass for a can of sparkling water. "But don't worry, I'll drink this for you so it doesn't go to waste."

"Such a good friend," Meg said.

Effie, Gloria, Sheri, and Meg's mom were crying and exclaiming.

"I wish Sam could be here for the news," Effie said, "but she won't be back from college until Thanksgiving."

"Let's give her a call," Ben said, pulling out his phone and getting ready to dial.

"We're going to have a little prince or princess," Gloria said, clapping her hands together. "Isn't that wonderful, Maurice?"

Maurice laughed and clinked his glass with Ben's. Then kissed Gloria on the cheek. Which made her blush like a teenager.

One of Alex and Tom's twins let out a cry. "Speaking of princes and princesses, I think we should be getting all of ours home soon," Alex called to Rosie and Noah, who were running around the trees in the little park with Sheri's little girls.

"We'll round them up," Pete said, and he and Sheri went to chase after the kids.

Gloria helped corner Alex and Tom's toddler, Jacob. "I'm so glad you managed to name little Grace after royalty, Alex. But I do wish you would have taken my suggestion for Daniel."

"Well," Alex said, "Ranier isn't exactly a popular boy's name, Gloria."

"Maybe next time," Tom said, smiling at Alex.

"For us, more babies are going to happen exactly never," Alex said.

"Say that again like you mean it, honey," Tom said with a big grin.

"Children are wonderful," Maurice said, joining in the hugs. "And Megan, I will feel privileged to take on the role of grandfather, if you'd allow it."

"Maurice, we'd love it," Meg said. Any man who can win Gran's heart deserves the honorary title."

"How did you finally get Gloria to go out with you?" Ben asked Maurice.

"He took me to a tea," she said.

Ben's brows rose. "That's all?"

"It was a very special tea," Maurice said with a wink.

"The Palace—Theater, that is—had an English tea open to the public and set in the period of the 1920s to celebrate the new season of *Downton Abbey*. We ate scones and had clotted cream with our tea. And we dressed in period attire. It was Megan's idea."

Meg gave Maurice a wink. The key to winning her grandmother's heart hadn't been that complicated after all.

"Gloria, the only thing you two are missing is British accents," Tom said.

"I've changed my mind about that a little, dear," Gloria said, patting Maurice's knee. "I'm rather starting to prefer an Irish brogue."

"Grandma and Grandpa Rushford would be proud that you two saved this old place," Brad said, looking around at the ugly fenced-in backyard, the big dumpster, and the stomped-down grass.

"The house has great bones," Meg said, "if we ever get down to them." They'd torn out enough laminate paneling, fake partitions, and office cubbies to supply the town. She couldn't wait to see Ben's face at Christmas when they'd put their tree in the window just like Grandma Rushford did.

Olivia looked over at the funeral home on the other side of the park. "At least you'll have quiet neighbors."

"And we can take a ride or a jog on the bike trails whenever we want," Meg said. It was a trade-off for not having a bigger yard, but they'd been biking almost every evening on the well-maintained trail that snaked through dense woods along tributaries from the lake.

Effie raised her glass. "To a long, happy, and prosperous life."

"Filled with many children," Gloria added.

"You've done it, Benjamin," Brad said. "You've landed the job of your dreams in your hometown with the girl of your dreams."

"I'm going to have to disagree with that a little," Ben whispered to Meg as he pulled her close.

"What do you mean?" Meg asked, gazing into her husband's dark brown eyes, eyes filled with mischief and love that she prayed she'd be lucky enough to look into for a long, long time.

"Because," Ben said, "being your husband is the best job I could ever have."

GRANDMA GLORIA'S BETTER THAN SEX CAKE

1 heaping cup walnuts, finely chopped

1 cup flour

1 stick butter, softened

¾ cup confectioners' sugar

1 8-ounce package cream cheese, softened

1 large container Cool Whip, thawed

1 large box instant chocolate pudding

3 cups milk

Preheat oven to 350°F.

Crust: Mix butter, flour, and most of the nuts together (reserve 2 tablespoons for garnish) and press into a 9 x 13-inch pan. Bake for 20 minutes and cool completely.

First Layer: Beat confectioners' sugar, cream cheese, and 1 cup of Cool Whip with an electric mixer until well blended, and spread carefully over crust.

Second Layer: Beat pudding and milk for 2 minutes with an electric mixer and spread over first layer.

Third Layer: Spread Cool Whip generously over the pudding layer and garnish with remaining nuts. Refrigerate several hours before serving, and then enjoy! (Alternatively, let the pudding set for a few hours before adding Cool Whip Layer (makes Cool Whip easier to spread).

Warning: Aphrodisiac properties well documented. Consume at your own risk!

ACKNOWLEDGMENTS

Thanks so much to my wonderful agent, Jill Marsal, for guiding my career and for being a consummate professional. Thanks also to my editor Maria Gomez, who among the many other things she does, gave me the opportunity to bring Mirror Lake to life, and to the entire team at Montlake (Jessica, Susan, Marlene, and many others) for your enthusiasm and tireless support. And to my developmental editor Charlotte Herscher, who amazes me with her ability to understand imaginary people and bring out their (and my) best.

For your critiques, feedback, and support, thanks to the women of the Sunshine Critique Group (Chris Anna, Mary, Sheri, Vicki, and Wendy), my NEORWA sisters, and my Lucky 13 Sisters, especially Sandra Owens who read an early draft of this book.

I'd like to thank the wonderful women of Something White Bridal Boutique in Cleveland, Ohio, Karin VanCure and Rebecca Somnitz, who welcomed me into their beautiful and unique shop, told me what it was like to be best friends and business owners, and patiently answered my many questions. Any mistakes I've made in portraying the bridal industry are entirely my own.

Thanks to Edward J. Esber, MD, for answering my medical questions.

Special thanks to H.R.H. Cindy Randazzo Witherup, whose love of all things royal was the inspiration for Grandma Gloria. (Of course it had nothing to do with the fact that she is also kind, hilarious, and welcoming.)

And thanks to Charlotte Scott, who introduced me to the joys of pudding dessert (aka Grandma Gloria's Better Than Sex Cake) long before I knew what that was. Since then, I've made it with every type of pudding there is and it's amazing every time (though nothing beats chocolate). But why believe me, you can try it yourself!

Thanks to my husband for his boundless love and support and his smart, snappy sense of humor. And his ability to eat anything for dinner and like it. And my kids, who are growing up to be wonderful people. Keep doing that, I love you!

The character of Ben's grandfather is a tribute to the memory of Dr. Omer C. Hurlburt II, who was everything Ben's grandfather was as a doctor and person and more.

Lastly, thanks to my readers. It's been an honor and a privilege to take you back to Mirror Lake for another visit.

ABOUT THE AUTHOR

While growing up, Miranda Liasson was a willing courier for the romance novels her mother traded with their next-door neighbor, as it gave her a chance to sneak a peek at the contents. Today, Liasson writes award-winning romances herself. She has received the Romance Writers of America's Golden Heart Award for Best Contemporary Series Romance for the story that became the first book in the Mirror Lake series: *This Thing Called Love*. She enjoys writing about courageous but flawed characters who find love despite themselves. She resides in northeast Ohio, where she shares her home with her husband and three children, and her office with Maggie, a yellow Lab, and Posey, a rescued cat with attitude. Visit her online at www.mirandaliasson.com and follow her on Twitter @mirandaliasson.

50012380R00156

Made in the USA
Lexington, KY
25 August 2019